A
Bloody Good
Cruise

by

Diana Rubino

A Bloody Good Cruise

Cover Art by *RJ Morris*

The Wild Rose Press, Inc.
PO Box 708
Adams Basin, NY 14410-0708
Visit us at www.thewildrosepress.com

Publishing History
First Black Rose Edition, 2014
Print ISBN 978-1-62830-316-2
Digital ISBN 978-1-62830-317-9

Published in the United States of America

Mona forced a dose of cheer

through her jangly nerves. Vampire hunters wouldn't attack Fausto and his friends on this ship. Security was tight. "Well, you're here, so does that mean you've been going out, and aren't confined to your house any more?"

Fausto shrugged. "Almost. I couldn't wallow in self-pity forever. And I knew seeing you would make it worthwhile."

She smiled and gave him a genuine Italian cheek pinch. "I'll cheer you up, *faccia bella*, you can count on that. You must feel safe." She gestured at the tacky duds. "I mean, relatively speaking."

"Don't let this scare you, but—" He glanced around over the rims of his shades. *Uh-oh.* Whenever he said, "Don't let this scare you," it sent ripples up her spine. "I got an ominous message at the doctor's office earlier."

"What?" She swallowed a lump. "What kind of ominous message?"

He looked away, shaking his head. "Nothing to get alarmed about. The hunters just want me to know they're here. After the initial jolt wore off, I said, 'Okay, I'm being stalked again.' But I'm used to it. It doesn't make me constantly look over my shoulder like in the old days. My family's murder gave me a reality check. If they want me, they'll get me. I can't let it interfere with my work, or what little leisure time I have here. And you shouldn't either." He gazed at her adoringly and cupped her cheek, warming her entire body. "But you're still scared. All the blood's drained out of your face, and not in a good way."

Dedication

To Chris, my hero

Chapter One:
Are We Being Watched?

The Romanza Sun Deck, Rome, Italy

Mona Rossi gazed at Civitavecchia Harbor glistening in the sunset. The calm water did nothing to soothe her jittery nerves.

"Chill out. Fausto's safe, and so are you. This'll be the best New Year's ever," Mona repeated, trying to steady her voice. "So I look like a nut talking to myself. But it helps. The homicidal stalkers didn't make it on board, and we're gonna have a blast." The possibility of a shipboard murder aside, the cruise ship *Romanza* was a palace of pampering: gourmet meals, massages, partying under the stars...

...Roman orgies...

But nothing *that* wicked ever made the daily Cruise News. She'd have to find one. Or plan one.

When not indulging in any of those decadent delights, chatting with the other pink ink authors, sashaying around the ballroom as Cleopatra, or autographing her novels, she'd be jotting notes for new ideas. By the looks of her last royalty checks, her readers were jumping ship. Her romantic suspense series lost its zing, especially after the hero went monogo and married the heroine. Her dwindling bank account nudged her to start a hot trend.

1

She went to the opposite railing, overlooking the deck below. The band played the Italian classic "Love Me The Way I Love You." As she watched swaying couples in tight embraces, she longed to be on that dance floor clinging to a lover. As Mona debated whether to go down to the pool bar and order her first strega of the voyage with her welcome-aboard coupon, a dark-haired pixie bopped up the stairway and glanced around.

"Tess! Over here!" Mona called to her book publisher and best friend.

"Mona, all your hard work and planning paid off!" She bounded over, arms wide, and gave Mona a bear hug in a cloud of Make It a Stiff One hair gel. "The ship's crawling with authors, cover hunks, and *The Cutting Edge* reporters. They're doing a segment on us every night for a week!"

"Oh, yeah." Mona rolled her eyes. "They'll be crawling all over us for interviews. And some of the authors' moms and aunties showed up. You sure you didn't mention orgies in the ad?"

"Not in the ad, but I might've spread a small rumor. Speaking of hunks, my Moonmist Press authors are throwing a blowout for the cover models tonight. *The Cutting Edge* is going to cover it," Tessie gushed, her breaths coming out in spurts of steam. "And guess who I got to make an appearance at the last minute? Furio!"

Mona hoped the romance industry's most famous cover model *would* appear at the last minute. "How, in a chariot drawn by matched giraffes?"

"Okay, so he's a little overbearing." The wind blew her hair into her eyes, and she pushed it away. "He likes

2

to hog the spotlight. I'm sure he won't bring his life-sized book covers."

"Better yet, just ask him to send his hair, pecs, and cleft chin aboard," Mona remarked. "He can stay on land."

"I'll get him to serenade you," Tessie kidded. "He can't carry a tune, but I betcha he'll be carrying somebody out of there tonight."

Mona closed her eyes, and Fausto's image smashed Furio to pieces. "I'm waiting for my own gorgeous hunk. I haven't seen him since the day after my divorce, and my butterflies have butterflies." She glanced at her watch. "He said he'd be here when the ship pulls out."

"So, you're all dolled up for him, not the television cameras." Tessie rubbed Mona's faux ermine sleeve and gave the toe of her left snakeskin boot a nudge. "Speaking of hunks. Hubba hubba. What you got under there? A spank-me number?"

"Almost." Mona untied the scarf and opened the coat to show Tessie her goodies: a low-cut lacy cami that showed enough cleavage to get Fausto begging for more, and a short skirt. Wraparound. But she buttoned up when goosebumps started popping up.

"That'll speed up his launch mechanism." Tessie nodded with approval. "But ditch the religious medal. Nothing spoils a guy's view of perfect pushup boobs like Mother Mary watching him."

"It's Saint Paul, patron saint of authors. I wear it all the time. I sometimes forget it's on." She wound her scarf around her neck. "I just hope Fausto's aboard and hasn't extended his leave." Fausto Silvius, her on-again-off-again main squeeze, was the reason she'd wheedled with Apollo Cruise Lines for this romance writer's cruise. One of Apollo's shipboard doctors, he hadn't worked in six months because of a personal tragedy. A member of a despised minority, he'd been forced to lie low for a while. And Mona, born with the worry gene that ran in big Italian families, was scared to death for him. Her pep talk monologue of a few minutes ago didn't make her all that smug about her own safety either.

"He's due aboard to report for duty." Tessie raised her stenciled-penciled brows. "Why would he jump ship?" A sudden blast of wind off the Tyrrhenian Sea tousled her foil-streaked hair.

Mona pulled up her faux chinchilla hat over her ears. "Damn, it's nippy out here." Why couldn't she have arranged to meet Fausto in one of the thirteen bars? Or her stateroom with the thousand-dollar balcony? Her big idea, a rendezvous under the rising moon surrounded by twinkling lights, didn't include blue lips, a red nose, and stiff nipples.

"This is his first assignment since some of his family were murdered. So he might not feel he's ready yet." Mona dug out her Cherries and Cream lipstick from her pocket and ran it over her lips, using the case as a mirror. She checked out her face, one inch at a time. Mascara unsmeared, brows still in place, and her nose wasn't running. She had to admit she felt like a schoolgirl waiting for her date to show up. Well, it *was* a date.

Tessie glanced at a few passengers braving the chill to wave *arrivederci* to some poor souls left behind on the pier. "Don't worry, with you on the ship, he'll be on it. Trust me. He wouldn't pass up a wild ride with you on this floating passion pit."

"Let's hope so." She shivered with that familiar tingle of excitement, fantasizing about strolling the promenade deck with him in the wee hours. Or clinging to each other in ecstasy as the ship rocked and rolled...

But if things ended where she hoped they wouldn't, she'd have problems.

"Check out Pops over there." Tessie tilted her head in the direction of a well-built elderly gent in black tie and tails, shiny Oxfords clicking across the deck. "Now, why isn't he flashing a piece of blonde arm candy?"

"He's probably one of the dancers. They pay older gents to glide across the ballroom floors with single female passengers. I've talked with a few of these John O'Hurley clones, and the ones who get lucky brag about their conquests. To me, they're one rung down from overaged boy toys."

"Hmm, I wouldn't mind hanging on his rung." Tessie gave the *signor* a little wave, and he strolled over to them.

"Beautiful night, no?" He spread his arms, as if embracing the air, and took in a deep breath.

Mona noticed an Eastern European accent. "Gorgeous. Are you a dancer?"

"Yes, ma'am." He clicked his heels. "But I know none of your vild modern steps. My specialty is valtzes."

"Maybe I can talk you into a *tarantella* if we run into each other," Mona goaded.

He clutched at his chest. "Be still my heart!" His smile reached his eyes.

Pulling his lapels to his throat, he said, "Brrr, this makes my blood run cold. I bid you ladies *adieu* for now." He gave a bow, turned on a shiny heel, and pranced down the stairs.

"Not old enough for him, are we?" Tessie snorted.

"No, just not desperate enough. He was kinda cute, though, in a macabre kind of way."

Tessie shivered, hugging her arms to herself. "He almost made my blood curdle! He sounded like Dracula. Romantic, but a little creepy."

Mona nodded. "Looked like him, too. But let's not let our imaginations run away with us. You don't want an eight-second stand with an AARP veteran anyway." Mona gave Tessie a nudge. "You'll finally get to spend some one-on-one time with Quintus. That is, if we don't get too bogged down in massages, costume balls, and hunk bashes." Tessie had finally hooked up with Fausto's cousin Quintus, another shipboard doctor, after some detours kept them apart: work, travel, divorces...

Mona knew Quintus was planning on popping the question to Tessie on this cruise. Thrilled for her friend, she still fought a twinge of envy. She could be entering eternal bliss with Fausto if she weren't so skittish about...certain things.

Tessie fished her cigarillo case out of her purse, but a stinging blast of wind changed her mind. "We're very lucky, Mona. Eligible bachelors aren't easy to come by in our age group. I never dreamed I'd snag an Italian wine connoisseur who models men's undies on the side. Fausto and Quintus are real renaissance men."

"Oh, yeah, you can call them that, all right." What Mona needed to divulge to her friend in the next few hours, especially before the question pop, was that Fausto and Quintus weren't human. And neither were any of their gorgeous Italian wine connoisseur/model pals. They all shared a common gene.

Fausto, her longtime friend, fan, and almost-but-not-quite romantic interest *was* a Renaissance man. Literally. He was four hundred plus years old.

And undead.

Therefore, hence, and ergo—a vampire.

****

Fausto entered the doctor's office and looked around, breathing in the familiar aromas of disinfectant, soap, and the faint trace of medicine. A long-lost emotion rushed back—the feeling of being needed. But knowing his family was gone made it a bittersweet moment.

He sat at his desk and studied the inventory list. Someone approached, throwing a shadow over his paperwork.

"Dr. Silvius!" The staff captain, Paolo Brunetti, stood there, arms spread wide. Fausto went around the desk and gave his colleague an Italian bear hug, with the customary two-cheek kiss. "I can't tell you how sorry I am for your loss."

"Thank you," Fausto said. "I needed to get back to work. There's nowhere else I'd rather be right now." Not wanting to dwell on the condolences, he got straight to business. "As soon as Dr. Lombard gets here, we'll hold the drug count, and while you're verifying that, I can go over the hospital budget."

"Oh, before I forget." Brunetti opened one of the file cabinets along the wall. "This was left outside the door."

He took out a small cardboard box, Fausto's name typed on a mailing label. Thinking it was medicine or supplies, he pulled it open, but what he saw inside brought back all the rage of the last six months—and a new stab of fear.

****

Zanna Jones and her husband, Royal, sat at the bar after the art auction ended and the happy high bidders filed out. A woman who'd won a Peter Max for $2500 sauntered over on turquoise-and-lapis-studded heels and ordered a Long Island iced tea.

"Nice painting you got," Zanna commented, piercing the olive in her martini glass with the plastic sword.

"Thank you." A diamond bauble glittered on her right hand. "I'm doing a segment on art auctions on my show."

"Your show?" Zanna had seen this woman ditch her gown at the hunk bash and shimmy around like a whirling dervish. So she had her figured for a romance author.

"Yes, I'm Toi Brennan, co-anchor for *The Cutting Edge*, the newsmagazine show." She extended her manicured hand and gave Zanna's a quick, firm shake. "We're covering the writers' cruise for the week."

"Ms. Brennan, I've seen you." Royal leaned across Zanna and stuck out his hand to clasp the woman's. "My wife doesn't have time for television. She reads instead and likes certain outdoor sports."

"Me too!" Toi brushed a curtain of blue-black layered hair off her shoulder. "When I read, it's romances. That's why I'm here. I convinced my producers our readers would enjoy seeing a show about the conference, and it's an excuse to go on a cruise." She gave a semi-amused laugh that probably took years to perfect. "Are you authors, too?"

"Not on your life." Zanna tilted her head and gave it a slow shake. "We're here for another reason. We're members of the Fellowship of the Faithful. Ever hear of us?" Zanna needed to do some recruiting, and who better to go for than a professional gossip hound? This would make an even tastier treat for the sleazy tabloid show!

"No," Toi replied. "Is it a religious group?"

"It's more than that." Zanna began reeling her subject in. "We hunt vampires."

Toi's eyes lit up, and she leaned forward, nearly spilling her drink down her silk blouse. "You do? For sport, or is there a bounty on their heads?"

Zanna never blabbed too much too soon. But the Fellowship needed all the members it could get. If Toi Brennan proved worthy of joining them, that would come later. Yet she knew just how to spoon feed. "We devote our time to preaching the word against vampire clans, and if we come across a vampire, we try to save them."

Toi nodded, and Zanna could practically hear wheels spinning. "Why hunt vampires and not rapists or terrorists?" Now she sounded like she was in interviewer's mode, so Zanna got her guard up, with balled fists on hips and a ramrod-straight gaze.

"I'll tell you why. I became a hunter because when I was sixteen, a clan of vampires captured me, held me captive for days, and assaulted me, but I managed to escape." She conveniently omitted—for now—that she'd stabbed the life out of one of them before she jumped out a window nearly to her own death. "And vampires murdered Royal's daughter in New Orleans last year. If you didn't hear about it and report it on your show, maybe you should have." Her voice took on a biting, chiding tone.

Toi put down her drink, more interested in Zanna's story than her blend of seven boozes. She leaned forward. "Can we talk more about this?"

"Sure. We'll run into each other again, be sure of that. Come on, Roy."

Zanna exited the bar, brandishing a smug grin, her husband at her heels. She might have a valuable recruit eating out of her palm before this cruise was over.

****

Mona glanced at her watch again. Five minutes to five. She itched to spill all to Tessie, but they'd be pulling out at five, and Fausto should be here any minute. No doubt he'd be in one of his tacky disguises. He knew he'd have enemies aboard, and to throw them off the scent, he'd plod around like a typical American tourist on his first cruise, schlocky enough to blend right in, the exact opposite of what his nemeses expected. So she kept her eyes peeled for a gaudy Hawaiian print shirt, a droopy straw hat, baggy Bermuda shorts, and flip flops.

That would be the real test for Tessie—could she consider marriage with a vampire without freaking? Her finding out would pack a double whammy—her best-selling authors wrote vampire romances, and they were on this cruise, giving workshops on the sexy, mysterious, sexy, elusive, sexy, lascivious creatures. Mona smiled, her toes curling in anticipation of Fausto's kisses, his licks, his caresses—and the ship-rocking orgasms they shared.

Just as Mona's juices started to simmer, Tessie's eyes darted over to the side. "Don't look now, but if

10

this guy tries to pick either of us up, we'll say we're together. And if he doesn't believe that, we'll start smooching."

Oh, no, Mona thought. Not even here two hours, and some loser is trying to...

Clunky footsteps approached, a large familiar hand touched her shoulder, and she spun around to face a baseball-capped, blue sunglassed, scruffy-bearded sanitation worker.

"Yo, sista." He lowered the shades and peeked at her with his midnight blue eyes.

"Fausto! *Bello mio!*" She slid her arms around his waist, and they fell into an old-fashioned Italian rocking hug, nearly knocking each other over. "You made it! It's so good to see you!" She held him at arm's length and zipped her eyes up and down. "You look so"—she gestured with her hands—"so Flatbush! Nobody would ever guess you're the lifesaving hunk they'll all flock to when Mussolini's Revenge breaks out."

"Yoo gotta prob'm wit' dat?" His Brooklynese was flawless, too, but why not? He'd lived there for eighty-six years. But he only used the lingo when joking around or when some Joizey bum cut him off in traffic. He stroked the stubbly whiskers and rammed his other hand into his tatty jeans pocket, but it emerged from a hole. "This is the first time I've skipped a shave since I was ten." He now spoke in his regular voice, the plain unaccented American of TV reporters. "I thought of skipping the deodorant but didn't want anybody to think I'm French. And it's too cold for the touristy garb. I thought I'd go low-end Gotham instead."

"You're low end, all right. Make it more real. Cut into the line at the Chocoholics Buffet, and flip everybody the boid." She saw Tessie staring bug-eyed, not knowing what to make of this dude looking like he'd just shoved his way off the D train from Flushing Avenue. "Teresa Lionetti, you know Fausto Silvius. Fausto, of course you remember Teresa."

Before the third syllable was out of her mouth, Tessie broke in, "Please! Call me Tessie. Teresa sounds too much like a saint or a mother, neither of which I am and may never be."

He pulled off a ratty racing glove, and they shook hands.

"Nice to see you again, Tessie. That's the name of my favorite aunt. *Zia* Tessie makes the best pasta sauce south of Milano and said she'll take the recipe to the grave with her, but she didn't say whose. She'll never take it to hers, we know that."

Mona added *sotto voce,* "He's, uh—incognito for now, and I'll tell you why later." She'd explain the whole story, but only after a few Chiantis, with Fausto offstage. First Mona had to tell her that Fausto and Quintus were related and shared a rare gene of Ancient Rome. Contrary to best-selling lore, true vampirism was genetic. So she'd get bad news: Fausto and Quintus are vampires. And good news: they're not fanged, cape-swirling ghouls.

Fausto gave Mona a wink. "You've got some audience on board, ladies. Every man's floating fantasy. Toi Brennan from *The Cutting Edge* is even hotter in person." He glanced over the rail to the deck below and the crowded dancers, now wiggling to "Mambo Italiano." "Did every romance writer in the business sign up?"

"Registration is hopping!" Tessie jumped from one

over-the-knee boot to the other, flicking her scarf around her neck. "This was such a good idea of Mona's! We're gonna party like it's 1999. Again. Schmaltz it up for the television cameras. And maybe even talk about the writing business." She rubbed her palms together. "So, Mona tells me you're a budding medical thriller writer."

He gave his ever-modest one-shoulder shrug. "I wrote two partials when I was on leave." He didn't elaborate, but Tessie nodded her understanding. "They're on a thumb drive back home." He jerked his thumb in the direction of the ocean. "If you can take a peek at them, I'd be most *obligato*."

"Oh, I'm sure they're real heart-stoppers. Doctors write some of the best fiction." She pulled out her cig case once again and snapped it open. "Must be their ability to play God that gives them great imaginations." She fished in her bag for a lighter. In a flash, he whipped one out of his pocket and lit up for her.

"Grazie." Tessie took a long drag, and the wind whipped away the smoke when she blew it out. "Now I'm outta here, you two, so you can catch up. I need to help work registration anyway. Later, Mona." She turned to him. "Fausto, it was fun seeing you—whoever you're supposed to be." She flitted away before Mona could protest she wasn't intruding on anything.

****

Zanna Jones crept out from under the midship Paris Deck stairs. "That's her," she whispered to her husband Royal on her cell phone. "Tess Lionetti, the vampire peddler. Look at those boots on her. She must be easy, like the sluts in those trashy novels she publishes."

"Get her cabin number." Royal's voice broke up,

but she figured out his crackling words.

Zanna disconnected and followed Ms. Lionetti a safe distance away, tiptoeing on bare feet down the carpeted hallway, carrying her shoes. Zanna hurried up to the cabin door. Five three two eight. Good. Now she knew where the smut hustler was hiding. But not for long. When the ship docked in Naples tomorrow, they'd collar her before she had a chance to pig out on *pasta e fagioli.*

Zanna wanted to pursue the porn merchant ever since vampire "romance" movies based on novels got so popular. She did some digging and found out Ms. Lionetti was the CEO of Moonmist Press, the publisher of dozens of those trashy vampire novels. No doubt they'd make more movies out of them! But she didn't yet know if Lionetti was one of those cursed vampires. If not, she was a worthy catch, but Zanna's real target was Fausto Silvius, her ultimate challenge.

Time was running short for him.

****

Mona was thrilled to be alone with Fausto for this short time before he had to report for duty. They held each other, swaying gently, for the duration of "On An Evening In Roma." The wind died down, and content in his arms, she knew this moment wouldn't last long. When the song ended, a jolt shocked her. The metallic scrape of the hull and three loud blasts followed. The ship was pulling out.

As the lights along the pier slid away, he checked his watch. "My shift starts at six, but let's meet, say around midnight, in the doctors' private lounge, the *Salute.* It's on the Monte Carlo Deck below us, starboard and forward, past the fitness center. Knock and when someone opens the peephole, say '*parlo pianissimo.*' That's the code word for this cruise."

They sure were paranoid. "Like a speakeasy. Should I bring my own bathtub gin?"

"No, but homemade wine would help," he said. "I packed in a hurry and didn't bring any."

"How 'bout a can of Bud and a Krazy straw to go with your outfit?"

"I won't be wearing the outfit. I might not be wearing much at all. The lounge is very casual. You'll see just how casual it is when you get there." He gave her a smile that melted her toenail polish.

Jetlag dragged her down, but all the excitement wired her up. She clasped her hands around his and blessed her good fortune. She was on her first Apollo cruise, this rotten year was about to end, she was with fellow authors, hungry reporters, and one of her favorite people in the world.

What could go wrong?

Chapter Two:
Vampire Ball Busters

Mona forced a dose of cheer through her jangly nerves. Vampire hunters wouldn't attack Fausto and his friends on this ship. Security was tight. "Well, you're here, so does that mean you've been going out, and aren't confined to your house any more?"

Fausto shrugged. "Almost. I couldn't wallow in self-pity forever. And I knew seeing you would make it worthwhile."

She smiled and gave him a genuine Italian cheek pinch. "I'll cheer you up, *faccia bella*, you can count on that. You must feel safe." She gestured at the tacky duds. "I mean, relatively speaking."

"Don't let this scare you, but—" He glanced around over the rims of his shades. *Uh-oh.* Whenever he said "don't let this scare you," it sent ripples up her spine. "I got an ominous message at the doctor's office earlier."

"What?" She swallowed a lump. "What kind of ominous message?"

He looked away, shaking his head. "Nothing to get alarmed about. The hunters just want me to know they're here. After the initial jolt wore off, I said, 'Okay, I'm being stalked again.' But I'm used to it. It doesn't make me constantly look over my shoulder like in the old days. My family's murder gave me a reality

16

check. If they want me, they'll get me. I can't let it interfere with my work, or what little leisure time I have here. And you shouldn't either." He gazed at her adoringly and cupped her cheek, warming her entire body. "But you're still scared. All the blood's drained out of your face, and not in a good way."

He always knew how to read her. "I'm that pale?"

"A few days on Rhodes will take care of that."

He was right, but she glanced around. Again. They were completely alone. Below, the band packed their instruments away, the dance floor empty. She heard the hum of the ship's engine, vibrating floor, and her own breathing.

"Then I'll go about my business like everything's cool, and we'll have the time of our lives." She said it but didn't believe it. Yet.

"Oh, I can help you do that, all right." He winked and gave her his familiar half-smile that etched a crescent line beside his mouth. "How about talking to your psychic friend? She might put your mind at ease. Is she on board?"

"No, Julianna's not here, but Kylah is. She's a Druid and does Tarot readings. Would you like a session with her?"

He swept off the shades, which told her he couldn't be all that worried. Illuminated only by the spotlights on the deck rail, pinpoints of light shone in his eyes. "And tell her everything?"

"No, you don't have to tell her anything about your—about you. Chances are, she'll know anyway but won't judge you on it. She's a very good Tarot reader. Just take her reading at face value."

"Meeting a psychic isn't the best way for me to

keep a low profile."

She wished he didn't feel that way and hoped to change his mind someday, but not right now. She swore on January 1st that year she'd stop trying to make things happen before their time. Who was little Mona Rossi from the dot on the globe called TriBeCa to buck the universe? "Fausto, do you think the hunters following you are the same ones who—uh..." Her hands fluttered, and she hoped they could do the talking for her.

He nodded. "I know what you're trying to say. The ones who killed my family?" A ragged sigh showed his distress. "Oh, it's them, all right. The infamous Fellowship of the Faithful formed just days after my sixty-seventh great grandfather let it slip that he enjoyed feeding from his wife, and hunters are so widespread now, there's more of them than there are of us. But they have a lunatic extremist branch. We call them the Vampire Ball Busters. Wherever I go, somebody from that crew isn't far behind me."

"How do they know you're a vampire? You've always been so discreet about it."

"They've followed my family through sixty-seven generations, keeping tabs on us. They've been backed by the Catholic Church since the fourth century, so they have plenty of financial support. The mainstream hunters of the Fellowship, and by mainstream I mean as opposed to the Ball Busters, have regular meetings, and when they do corner one of us, the worst they do is give us a finger-shakin' scolding about being hell-bound if we don't give up this sinful lifestyle and join a local parish. What they don't realize is that most of us are already God-fearing Christians, and our 'lifestyle' "— he made quotation marks with his fingers—"is the way we're born. But if we were the spawn of Satan, why wouldn't we go to hell to be with our creator?" He gave an ironic laugh and shook his head. *"Pazzo."*

"So what makes the fringe lunatics—the Ball Busters—want to kill vampires instead of just converting them?" She moved closer, tingling as her arm touched his.

"The extremists have personal vendettas. Usually a vampire killed one of their loved ones—not one of us, of course, but vamps who've truly turned sour and bleed humans to death for the fun of it. So, they think we're all out to suck the human race dry, but that shows how ignorant they are. The Ball Busters who slaughtered my family wanted revenge because a sadistic vampire cult killed a hunter's daughter last year. The Ball Busters hunted some of the vampire cult members down and drove knives into their black hearts. But that's not enough for them. For vengeance they go after all vampires."

"But why did they kill your family if some cult murdered their daughter?"

"They go after whoever they can get. Their mission is to eradicate the world of vampires, so why not members of the ancient Silvius family? Enough of us are still around. Some of my relatives are easy targets. They're not careful. Like I am." He slid the shades back on.

"Do you know what these Ball Busters look like? The ones after you now?"

Another blast of wind blew his hair into his eyes, and she brushed it back as he drew her against the length of his body. She let out a calming breath, feeling safer. And warmer. Then hotter.

"I don't know who they'll be this time. That's why I always have to keep an eye out."

"My God, what a way to live." She shuddered under her layers of cashmere and faux fur. "It scares me. It makes me feel how vulnerable we all are."

"Yes, we sure are. In this world you must be vigilant. If you see something suspicious, report it. Ordinary citizens have to keep an eye out. I have to keep both eyes out." But his eyes were fixed on hers. She grasped his hand, brought it to her lips, and kissed it. He warmed her all the way through.

"Enough about me," he said. "What's going on with you? Have the police recovered any of those things your husband absconded with?"

"Ex-husband, as of two weeks ago. The divorce was final the day he went to jail."

"Congratulations. You're well rid of him. I still don't know why you didn't press charges. He's a criminal, plain and simple."

"He has enough problems being a gambler. After I got over the rage of coming home and finding the house almost gutted, and recovered from the shock of seeing the big gaping space where my piano had been, instinct told me what happened. Sure, he's a bastard for doing that to me, lying about going to work when he was going to the racetrack, taking off without a word instead of talking it out, asking me for help." She scowled in disgust. "But when he got arrested for embezzling from his company, and confessed to selling my things, I felt sorry for the both of us. Like we're both a couple of losers, and it's no wonder we hooked up."

"No reason to feel sorry for yourself, *cara*. You'll get through this. You're stronger than you think. And you're no loser." He squeezed her biceps. She made fists, her muscles tensing.

"But it couldn't have happened at a worse time. I married a gambler and a thief. My book sales are off. And I'm going broke, Fausto. My finances are sinking faster than the Titanic—oops, bad analogy. I'm hanging onto my self-esteem by a thread. The thread almost snapped the other day when the credit card company called me and said I was over my limit. I said, 'I know, but I'm worth it.' And I went out and had my hair foiled for the second time this month."

"Don't blame yourself because Ted is a gambler, or that your sales are off. The reading public is very fickle. Find another genre, and go with it."

"That's why I organized the cruise." She perked up. "To find the next big trend." She flexed her fingers. "Right now all that's out there is cold. We'd better go inside. It's getting too nippy up here." She got out her card key. "My cabin's on the Paris Deck."

They walked down the metal steps to the pool deck. The band was gone, the dance floor and bar empty. A shroudlike sheet covered the pool and hot tub. "We're the only ones on this deck," she said. "I hope. If you're not going to let hunters ruin this cruise, then I'll try not to. But you've had more practice than me."

"Don't get me wrong, I do fear them," he said. "But I can't live my life hiding from them or running from them. If they get close enough to confront me, or us, if we're together, I can protect us." He patted the slight bulge under his jersey. "But I don't go out of my way to taunt them." They entered the corridor. The glassed-in elevators distorted their reflections. A creepy feeling made her shiver. "Like here, for instance. I always take the stairs." He lowered his voice. "I don't want to get stuck in an elevator with some of them. They travel in packs."

So they took the dark narrow stairs, their heels clanging on the metal, down to the Paris Deck. "You are allowed firearms aboard, but how can a regular passenger smuggle any weapons on?"

"They manage," he said. "Remember, they have a powerful entity with big bucks behind them."

"Oh, yeah. How can I forget? The Church collects a fortune just with the money Italians pin to statues."

As they padded over the plush blue carpet of the narrow corridor, passing stateroom doors, she couldn't resist peeking into the open ones. A baby-boomer couple squeezed by. *What's their story?* she wondered. Did he rent a trophy girlfriend? Did she hide a bouquet of vibrators in her bra drawer? But that was Mona, typical writer, conjuring up character sketches of everybody, and no part of New York City crawled with more characters than TriBeCa.

But one more detail halted her—the big silver crucifixes they wore around their necks.

Crucifixes!

She grasped Fausto's arm and gestured wildly as the couple passed. Her heart pounded.

"They—they've got—" She thumped her chest.

"What? Breast implants?"

"No! Silver crucifixes!" The couple was out of earshot, but Mona still trembled.

"So? A lot of people wear those. This is an Italian cruise line, remember?"

"I'm keeping an eye out for those two," she declared. For all she knew, they were the zealots trained to kill now and ask questions in the next life.

She shuddered as the couple continued down the hall and out to the elevators.

"Calm down," he soothed. "A few days into the pampering of shipboard life'll mellow you."

"I hope so." She sighed, forcing it out of her mind. For the first time since daylight, her breath didn't come out as steam. Still, she was jittery and knew she'd be fighting jitters this entire trip. But Fausto's features relaxed, a smile flirting on his lips. She knew the disguise helped, but he never let his guard down completely. He'd once told her, "One of nature's imbalances is there are too many nuts and not enough nuthouses."

At her cabin door, he bent down and gently kissed her. She hadn't expected it, but let the kiss linger and followed his lead. Liquid warmth spread over her. She had to end this before she collapsed. It would be so easy to fall into his arms and let a rapturous romance sweep her away, if she didn't mind altering her destiny. But she wasn't ready to even think about that. She pulled away as her lips burned for more. "Fausto, I'm here to comfort you, to cheer you up. Not complicate things. We've been over this before."

"Who said anything about complicating things?" He didn't realize it wasn't her stiletto heels making her knees wobbly. It was the affection and desire burning in his eyes. "What's a little kiss?"

"There was nothing little about it."

"We're on a luxury liner about to sail off into the moonlit Mediterranean, we've missed each other, and we're sharing grief and pain and trying to heal each other's raw emotions. I wasn't reading any more into it

than that. But it looks like you were, romance author."
He tilted her chin up and touched her lips with his,
brushing her earlobe with his fingertips. She tingled at
the intimate gesture.

She didn't want this moment to end. Trusting
herself not to give in to him completely and become a
vampiress by evening's end, she asked, "How much
time have you got?"

"If fifty-five minutes is enough for you, it's enough
for me." They embraced, and he pressed his hard body
against hers. Her desire surged. "It would be a quickie,
but I'll make it up to you later."

"So you're asking for an invite in?" Her breath
came in short gasps as his tongue flicked over her
earlobes. How could she refuse a guy who considered
fifty-five minutes a quickie?

"I was hoping it would be your idea." His mouth
descended upon hers, his hands winding through her
hair, his tongue probing. A low growl escaped his
throat.

On wobbly knees, she forced herself to end the
kiss. "This'll be way better inside." She turned and
stabbed the slot with her cardkey, pulled it out, and
pushed the door open.

Pale moonlight and shadows bathed the cabin.
Mona and Fausto unzipped, unbuttoned, and
unsnapped, throwing coats, hats, sweaters aside. In their
underwear, they waltzed over to her bed, and her
heartbeat quickened as she tossed aside the life jacket
from this afternoon's drill.

He lowered her to the bed and unhooked her bra.
She let a smile play over her face, glad she'd worn the
bra that opened in front. Had Jezz, her nickname for her

sex-starved alter ego, been telling her something when she got dressed?

He grasped her hands in his, bringing them up over her head. Her thighs parted, and he straddled her. His lips blazed a fiery trail down her neck, between her breasts. Then he flicked his tongue over the sensitive buds until she shuddered with a wild wave of desire. Her thighs closed around him, and they moved together in exquisite agony.

They were just about to move to the next step when a loud insistent beeping shattered the moment. "Damn!" He groaned in frustration as he rolled off her. She shivered without his warmth blanketing her.

"What is it?"

"My pager." He groped around on the floor and held the pager to the clock's glow on the table. "The doctor's office, an emergency."

"And this isn't?" Months of pent-up desire shriveled, as though he'd doused her with a bucket of ice.

"I'm sorry, honey, it's one of the drawbacks of being a doctor."

"Another doctor can't cover for you?"

"An emergency's an emergency," he replied patiently, and began piling his clothes back on. "It must be serious to need two of us."

"Yeah, I know," she muttered, but remembered how grateful she was to the doctor who took her in when she broke her ankle and crawled to his office in agony.

Back in disguise, he bent over and gave her a light teasing kiss. "See you in the lounge at midnight. And maybe we can pick up this quickie where we left off."

He gave her fingers a lingering grasp. "Your eyes are like limpid poils, doll." He let himself out and tried the door to make sure it was locked.

She lay on the bed for a long time. It took a tremendous amount of willpower to make love with Fausto without letting him feed from her. One of these nights it would happen. And there'd be no turning back.

After thinking about it, turning over in bed, still unable to make that life-altering decision, she put it out of her mind for now, ready for some pampering. She unzipped her evening gowns from her garment bag, unpacked her moisturizer, neck firmer, toner, and cosmetics, and lined them up on the vanity. She set her hair products on the edge of the tub. A makeover always took her mind off whatever was eating at her.

She flipped on her vanity light and spotted a champagne bottle in the ice bucket. Someone wishing her bon voyage? Who could it be? She ran down her list of pals' names as she fumbled to open the envelope. But inside was far from a bon voyage wish.

A folded note fell out, and when she opened it, her heart lurched. It was a fax.

Mona,

I tried your cell, but you're out of range. I want you to have a blast, but I had a vivid premonition last night, and must warn you. Two shadowy figures are trailing you and Fausto. So watch your back. I'll let you know if I see any more details. Aside from that, enjoy the champagne and bon voyage.

Love,

Julianna

All her fears and jitters rushed back full force. What a way to start a cruise. With New York's most

26

respected psychic saying she and Fausto were targets for a couple of nuts. She sank into the chair, re-reading the warning. *Should we get off right now? Too late, we're already at sea!* What was the next port? Naples. A big enough city to disappear in.

There was a lot to be afraid of these days. But she wasn't going to flee her beloved New York and live the rest of her days hiding from psychos or whatever the terrorist *du jour* was.

"I. Am. Not. Running. Away!" She crumpled Julianna's fax and chucked it into the wastebasket. No wacko was going to chase them around. She'd keep her eyes open and watch her back, just like Julianna said.

She couldn't barge into the doctor's office and tell Fausto about this now. So, she wrote him a note to deliver on the way down.

She continued as if everything was wicked cool: laid out her black strapless with the slit up the side and decided on her four-inch-heel "boudoir slides" she'd won on an online auction for half the retail price. She showered, shampooed, blowdried, root-lifted, curled her long auburn hair into cascading ringlets and inserted her aqua contact lenses. After applying her foundation, blush, and trademark Cherries and Cream lipstick, she gave herself a full-length view in the mirror. Good. The bikini waxing was holding up.

She flipped through her underwear drawer, tossing aside thongs, briefs, bras, but her strapless wasn't here. She remembered packing it. Or did she?

"Oh, no." She couldn't wear the strapless gown without the strapless bra. "Damn! I knew I'd forget something! But why that?" She racked her brain for a solution. Finally, she got out her nail scissors and snipped away at the straps on one of her regular bras. It looked natural enough under the gown, but for good measure she taped the edges down with bandages.

Acting out her favorite proverb about life being short, she knocked the neck off the champagne. Nice of Julianna to remember that.

She sucked in her stomach and tucked in her buns, remembering Lana Turner's classic trick of walking like a quarter was between her buttocks. Especially since she'd read that high heels made a woman's ass stick out 25% more.

Before leaving, she took one more swig of champagne and sang the cruise song from that hokey commercial, "If they could, *hic!* see me now, I'm havin' such a ball, la-da-da-da-da *hic!* da..."

Now if she just could keep Fausto—and herself—alive.

Chapter Three:
The Naked Truth

At dinner, Mona admitted it: nothing would ease her fears, short of hunting the hunters and catching them. Tonight's show, a hilarious version of the Newlywed Game, cracked her up when the four couples, who fit together like old robes and slippers, guessed each other's answers about "making whoopee" in unusual places, evoking one couple's memory about doing the deed in a canoe that toppled over. But in between guffaws, she glanced over her shoulder between bites of pan-seared salmon with frizzi torti and crème brulee. But no crucifix-waving fanatics came tearing down the aisle.

Yet.

The cruise director came onstage gushing about how Apollo Cruise Lines loved having all these romance authors and *The Cutting Edge* crew aboard. Then he asked Mona to stand and take a bow as the coordinator of the production. She froze as the spotlight beamed down on her. A cameraman zoomed in on her. She glimpsed *Cutting Edge* anchor Brooke Hill, or Babbling Brooke as she was known to the world, rushing up to her with a mike thrust out.

"Mona, how did you get this great idea?" She flashed a set of crowns that probably cost her an episode's salary.

"Oh, I just wanted to let the public know how enjoyable romances are and to give the genre the publicity it deserves. Thanks for coming on board, Brooke."

Applause and cheers filled the theater as she bowed, turned, and headed for the ladies' room.

Her cabin boy nudged his way through the crowd and thrust an envelope into her hand. "It says 'urgent,' *signorina*," he warned in a lilting Southern Italian accent, "so I did not want to leave it in your room."

Her mouth dried up as if she'd gnawed on a cotton ball. She glimpsed his name tag. Marco DiBrizzi. "*Grazie*, Marco. You'll find an extra something in your envelope."

Trembling, she dashed into the ladies' room and locked herself into a stall. Her heart thudded in dread. She tore the envelope and held the document in her shaky hand. Oh, no, another fax from Julianna, shorter than the first one, but even more terrifying. Sweating, she held her breath as she read it.

Mona,

I sense danger. I keep seeing those two shadows, then a flash of metal. Then the image of a cross. I know it's a warning. Be careful. I'll tell you more when I see more.

Love,

Julianna

She read it again, knowing she had two choices—jump ship and get the hell home, or take her chances and trust Fausto to protect them. And she thought this past year had been lousy. Now it was going to end crapping all over her!

After splashing cold water on her face and

applying a quick retouch of Cherries and Cream, she read the note one more time, shoved the crumpled paper into her purse, and came back out with a smile frozen into place. No cameras, thank God. She blew out a long breath. Now she had to sit through the opening reception, when all she wanted to do was find a way to stop these lunatic hunters. Why not try to catch them and turn them in? If she could write about a heroine, she could damn well be one.

Partyers jam-packed the Tango Ballroom's vestibule, so Mona elbowed her way inside and found her name on a placard at one of the VIP tables. She sat in the red velvet chair and studied every sequined-gowned, faux-gemmed, strappy-sandaled author gliding in. Is *she* one of the hunters? Or is it *her*? Where's the husband? Hiding out somewhere, waiting to pounce? But the excitement, the welcome speeches, and the clamoring for autographs took her mind off it, almost.

At midnight, she had to tell Fausto about Julianna's newest vision. She doubted these sharper details would make him quit the cruise, but she hoped he'd still wear that cockamamie disguise, goofy as it looked. An image flashed in her mind—strutting through the ballroom, face concealed, hiding safely behind a mask. She had a hunch she'd end up wearing one before this trip was over.

The Diva Disco hosted the cover model blowout on the Lisboa Deck, the highest point on the ship. By eleven o'clock it looked like Chippendale's. Some of the hunks stripped down to their Speedos, and the women brave enough, or wasted enough, to shed a few garments bumped and grinded with them to the pulsating music. Colored lights throbbed in time to the steady beat, both above and below the opaque dance floor.

Mona would've been out there shaking her own booty, but her muscles ached in weary knots. Her eyelids pulled like soggy teabags. She had to force them back open a few times when they slid shut. She nudged her way to the bar and ordered the one thing she needed for another few hours of partying, black coffee.

At ten minutes to midnight, she found Tessie yakking with one of *The Cutting Edge* reporters about covering next year's cruise.

If there is a next year.

Mona tapped her watch.

"But we have ten minutes yet," Tessie pleaded, as a fan accosted the reporter.

"I have something important to tell you, Tess. Well, two things now. And it deserves at least ten minutes. Come on." She grabbed her friend's elbow and guided her two decks down to the deserted pool bar. The doctors' *Salute* Lounge, where they'd be going in a few minutes, was on the same deck. Her ears still rang from the music, and her feet throbbed, but this was her last chance to reveal Fausto's secret and Julianna's warnings. They pulled up bar stools, their bare legs glowing in the semi-darkness. Distant lights shimmered and faded as the ship swayed.

"Okay, what is it?" Tessie pulled out a cigarillo. "You're as white as a sheet."

Still? "Tessie, you've published a boatload of vampire books, and they're either Dracula knockoffs, or the opposite, a joke almost."

She arched a brow. "Well, they're humorous, but not meant to be a mockery. There's a lot of thin lines in

32

this biz, and that's one of them." She lit the cig and blew a stream of smoke out the side of her mouth.

But when Mona wiped her hands on her sides, licked her lips, and twirled her hair around her finger, all her usual nervous outlets at once, Tessie dragged the stool closer.

"What is it, Mona? You want to start writing them, too? Go for it, you'll do great. They're all the rage now."

"Thanks, but I'm looking for something original." She'd rehearsed all this on the plane but forgot what she'd memorized. She'd have to wing it, the way she wrote her novels, without an outline. It worked every time. Well, almost. Now she was tripping all over her tongue.

"Well, uh...you see, Fausto, Quintus, and their family and buddies are...not like the ones in the novels and the movies 'cause that's fiction, and they're way stereotyped, but he's..." She swallowed a lump, desperate for anything wet. There wasn't even a glass of melted ice on the bar. "What I mean is, they don't bite just anybody."

"What are you telling me, Mona?" Tessie's eyes widened, and a delighted grin spread her glossed lips. "They're vamps?"

She took a breath. "Not the Dracula kind. They're not even Transylvanian. They're Roman. A point in their favor, if you ask me, 'cause they love garlic. They don't sprout fangs or sleep in coffins. They're normal people. Well, almost."

"That's too funny."

Mona didn't smile.

"You're shittin' me, aren't you?"

Mona shook her head. "No, but I'm almost shittin' me. I was dreading this."

"You little wuss!" Tessie slapped her thigh. "I don't know how, but I knew you were going to say that. I had the strangest feeling, and when you said it, I felt it coming. Like an orgasm, it teases you for a few seconds, then just when it looks like it's slipping away, boom!" A dreamy smile followed a sigh. "Some things you just never forget." Her eyes focused on some distant point in wonder.

Mona mumbled a quick prayer of thanks. "I thought you'd start chewing your nails off at the very least. And jump overboard at the very worst."

She leaned over and gave Mona a cuff on the chin. "Hey, kiddo, we're Italian. Our culture is steeped in the supernatural: exorcisms, séances, giving every saint a specialty so none of 'em does double duty. Julianna regressed me to medieval previous lives so many times, I can write a saga that would put Downton Abbey to shame!"

"You lived previous lives in the Middle Ages? You never told me any of that."

"I didn't think you were into that sort of thing." Tessie took a drag and flicked an ash onto the floor. "You go to Julianna for readings on the future. You're always so forward-looking. You look to the future, when I mostly wallow in the past. But it's good to know that when I check out of here, there's a chance I'll have another go-around."

"So you can handle vampires?" Mona blinked, having trouble digesting all this. "I don't know if they live past lives, because once they become undead, they live forever. If loonies don't murder them."

"Of course I can handle it." Tessie adjusted the spaghetti strap of her gown. "Mona, I never told you this because I was afraid you'd think I was nuts, but now that I know that'll never happen, here goes." She took a breath and lifted her shoulders. "Julianna told me I was a vampiress in a past life. Some knight in the Middle Ages fed from me, and I became one of the undead. But I was arrested for a crime and left in a prison cell to starve to death."

Mona gasped. Her stomach clenched. "Oh, my God…"

"You know the one thing that can kill a vamp faster than the proverbial stake through the heart is starving. It's pure myth they don't eat food. Show me a dish of spaghetti Bolognese, and I'll show you a vampire who's willing to twirl it up and wolf it down." She blew out a breath, eyes closed in relief to get this off her chest. "So you can rest assured I have no qualms with vampires. They're no more scary than the Gambino crime family. Half of Mulberry Street, including my building, is still full of their bullet holes."

Mona let out a groan of relief, slid off the stool, and hugged her best friend tight. "Deep down, I knew you'd be okay with it, but that last shred of doubt clung like my gown, 'cause I'm sweating like hell."

"Where are your shields, girl?" Tessie asked.

"Home. I didn't think anything sweat-worthy would happen on this trip for me to bring them."

"I brought Kiss of Mint condoms," Tessie announced with a lifted chin and lowered lashes.

"You're the optimist among us," Mona said. "Assuming I'd be playing solitaire, I brought my Midnight Rider, a Pocket Rocket, and the Mermaid.

She's waterproof. In case we wind up bobbing around the Med in life jackets, I can amuse myself waiting to get rescued."

Tessie grinned. "Okay, you're off the hook for not bringing shields. But now that you know Fausto's aboard, I might borrow one of the Pocket Rockets."

"You won't need it—you'll be with Quintus. But in case you need a touch-up..." She opened her purse and took out what looked like a dainty bottle of pink nail polish. Handing it to Tessie she said, "Here's the latest Pocket Rocket. Waterproof, for those of us who hate to stay dry. The control's on the bottom. And it's new, so it doesn't have a battery."

"God, I hope it's new! Swapping guys is one thing, but I draw the line at vibrators."

"Speaking of which, I don't know Quintus well enough to know if he's into the group thing," Mona said.

Tessie slipped the Pocket Rocket into her purse. "He's Roman, so I'll give him the benefit of the doubt."

Mona shook her head in wonder. "That was the least of it. I was worried enough how you'd take them being vampires. Vampires aren't taken lightly, like the other Italian superstitions or curses. They're not your everyday scofflaws like CEO crooks. Vampires go against the dogmas of the 'good' religions. Heathen scum. Spawn of Satan. Evildoers." She whispered that last word, and it died in their surrounding silence.

"Yeah, all the forbidden stuff the 'good guys' fantasize about doing." Tessie took another drag. "Do they know you're telling me this?"

Mona twiddled the satin tassels on her purse. A drumbeat began pulsing from below them. "Yes, and we agreed it was better I tell you first, in case you didn't—" She swallowed, her parched throat constricting. "Uh, objected to their...let me put it this way. Fausto's friends all come with good references, but they have this quirky lifestyle, not like it's a choice..." She trailed off, knowing she was babbling, but she deeply feared what she'd have to tell Tessie next. "And then there's..." She took a breath.

"There's what? Don't tell me." She held out her right diamond-ringed hand, and her bangles chimed as they slid down her arm. "I know the kicker now." She took a quick puff, as if bracing herself. "They're all gay. Right? That's it, isn't it?"

"Huh?" Mona's contacts stung her dry eyes. "Nobody's more straight than these guys. There's an organization of hunters called the Fellowship of the Loyal or some upstanding name to make themselves sound legit. They hunt vampires to try and convert them. But a fanatic, lunatic splinter group has stalked vampires for the last few millennia, with the intent to kill them. The vampires call them the Vampire Ball Busters. And some are here." She waved her hands around for emphasis. "Aboard the ship."

Tessie's eyes widened. "Have you seen any of them? What's a Ball Buster look like? Do they carry pincers or wear medals or something?" Tessie took another puff and blew the smoke straight up. "'Cause if they do I'm in trouble." She fumbled around her neckline, pushed her emerald pendant aside, and pulled out a chain holding a tarnished oval emblem. "Saint Anthony, of course. The patron saint of lost things. I wear this so I won't lose my mind. But wouldn't you know it, this is my sixth medal in ten years. I keep losing them. I need to stock up when we get to Padua."

"No, they usually wear silver crosses. They can look like anyone, like you or me."

"They can't be that superficial, honey. Let's give them the benefit of the doubt." For emphasis, she hefted up her "Grand Tetons," her thirty-six D pair of silicones.

"Well, Fausto believes they follow him everywhere. He'll probably tell you about this later, but that's who killed his family."

Tessie's face dropped. She stubbed the cig out in an ashtray on the bar. "Oh, no, Mona. I'm so sorry. Were any of them caught?"

"No." She shook her head and squeezed her eyes shut. "They're still at large. And what's really scary is they're aboard ship." Mona took a deep breath before continuing. She pressed shaky hands to her thighs. Up till now, Tessie had found all this amusing. But this, she'd take seriously. "Now, don't panic, but Julianna sent me two faxes and told me she had visions. Someone is on the warpath right now, and she sees something bad happening to us." Mona snapped her purse open and took out the latest fax, handing it to her. "On the deck after you left, Fausto told me these Ball Busters are after him and his friends. And they're out for blood. Sorry for the pun."

As Tessie read it she nodded, deep in thought. "Okay, I'd respect any vision of Julianna's. I've heard about hunters. The topic usually comes up in church around Halloween. Everybody gets spooked. But I have faith those wackos who killed his family will be captured, too."

"It's time people realize that vampires are just like

the rest of us. But there are bad vampires, Tess. They do exist. They take sadistic joy in terrorizing their victims, and some even take enough blood to kill them. But the hunters' problem is they see *all* vampires as sadistic perverts." She shook her head sadly at the thought, hoping they'd shed that two-thousand-year-old cloak of cluelessness someday.

"I'm sure Fausto and his friends are being extra careful against these nuts," Tessie tried to assure her. "Do they have bodyguards aboard ship?"

"Not that I know of. He does a great job of getting on with his life, but I know deep down he's afraid of them, especially now. That getup he was in before was just a precaution, so they don't attack him when he's out in public. I'm so glad you didn't freak."

"Me freak?" She guffawed. "Honey, you're talking to someone born and bred on lower Mott Street. Unlike you in your upper west side enclave, I've been mugged more times than you can count on your fingers and toes, I'm from a clan of dock workers, and I was married to a New York cab driver who wasn't even a baseball fan. Even if I didn't have that super weird past life as a vampiress. So I'm going to quake over a few Bible-thumping goons on the prowl after our blood-slurping boyfriends?"

"They don't exactly slurp blood, but now that you put it that way—" Mona nodded, a relieved grin spreading her dry lips. Why had she been so worried about how Tessie would take this? Tessie was, as she always bragged, not just streetwise, but curbwise. "It took Fausto two years to tell me, out of fear I'd end our friendship."

"You? Ms. Libertarian, live-and-let-live Mona? He

should've known you better than that." Tessie tilted her head. "Come to think of it, I've been with Quintus a year, and he never told me, or even tried to take a nibble."

"I have a hunch he'll tell you before this cruise is over. You have to understand they're still in the closet for a reason." She smiled, thinking back on it. "I'll never forget when Fausto spilled his grand confession. I didn't blink an eye, and he appreciated that so much. He was almost moved to tears. But I said, look, I have atheist friends, Hindu, Muslim, and Buddhist friends. Why not a vampire?"

"Especially if they're the anti-Bela Lugosi horror movie kind. Movies aren't even like that anymore. That's just too campy for today's audiences." Tessie flicked her wrist. "And black-and-white film is *so* nineteen hundreds."

"You can't breathe a word of this to anyone, Tess."

"Of course I won't." She checked her watch. "But can I at least ask one of them if they'd be interested in publishing their memoirs?"

They left the bar and headed through the empty cafeteria, forward toward the ship's bow, the chill wind blowing through their hair. "No way! They're very secretive about it. Like the way it used to be for gays in the closet. Society is nowhere near ready for them, and they prefer it that way. It's enough they've got the Vampire Ball Busters after them, and we can't ever make it worse. The media would crawl all over them, making their lives hell. Especially here, with *The Cutting Edge* all over the ship. So, not a word. Not even to your diary. He'll tell you in his own way. I just wanted to give you a heads up, now that I know—"

Oops! She almost blabbed that Quintus was going to pop the question. She thought fast. "Er, you're going kinda steady."

Tessie closed an invisible button on her lips. "I'll keep my trap shut."

After too many wobbly steps, with the ship swaying, Mona gave up on the heels. Blingy as they were, they were eating her feet up. So, she bent over and slipped them off, wiggling her toes in blissful freedom.

"Why didn't you and Fausto ever conjoin?" Tessie asked.

"Fausto and I never made it because our lives are too different. I'm still smarting over my divorce. We travel so much, we'd never see each other. Sure, we make a little noise now and then. Keeps life interesting. But I couldn't ever become—" She ran out of breath, and Tessie finished for her.

"Yeah, I know. It's a big decision. Turning wouldn't bother me, if I loved the guy. Why should his alternative lifestyle stop you?"

"Well, Tess..." How could she tell her best friend how many times she'd tried? "Our shared interests and wicked case of the hots for each other isn't enough for me to let him turn me. I still need to wallow in the slop of my messy divorce. And to tell you the truth, I don't relish having my blood sucked, even by him."

Tessie nudged her in the ribs. "But isn't that the best part of it?"

"In the books and movies, it is. Let the romance authors write their vamp books and make light of it. Readers realize it's fiction, and that's okay. But this is real life. Think of what being turned would be like. My identity would be gone. I wouldn't be the same 'me' anymore."

They passed the fitness center, and Mona made a mental note to work out at least three times on this trip. Yeah, right!

"I've really been torn about this," Mona said. "There's also a chance I might like it too much and feel guilty if I got sucked into the forbidden temptation. You know what life as a vampire is like, Tess? It's erotic excess and freedom for the rest of eternity." Scary as it was, the fantasy warmed her entire body. Her face and neck grew hot and sweaty. She fanned herself.

"You've led a cushy life, girlfriend. That's why you're backing off from the erotic excess and the freedom and the unearthly pleasures. But when you've had a life like mine, it sure looks greener on their side. Or should I say redder?"

Tessie's open-mindedness reminded Mona to rethink spending forever with Fausto. But once again she slapped the fantasy down. "I love him to death, okay? Bad choice of words, but there are too many obstacles."

"Obstacles, shmobstacles." Tessie tugged on her gown, smoothing it out as they walked past the deserted gym and spa, the treadmills and ellipticals dark and still. "Obstacles are put in our way so we can kick their asses out of the way."

This gave Mona images of all the great times she and Fausto had spent together. They were both avid golfers, enjoyed the same operas, plays, and books...their shared interests went on and on. Yet every time he asked her to "come with him" she couldn't give in. Live for centuries, maybe for the rest of eternity as an outcast? A lifetime pass to a midnight buffet of blood? She shuddered. And it was *so* not her to obsess over her looks, but after half a millennium, she just knew she'd want a boob job. Give her ninety or a hundred years, she wasn't greedy. So, she was still unable to make the ultimate leap.

****

Royal and Zanna sat on the bed in their cabin, their hunting supplies spread out all around them.

Some were more traditional than others. Some were more effective than others. They never knew what worked until the time came.

Zanna slid Royal's medieval jeweled dagger from its sheath and ran the blade over her sleeve.

"Hey, don't, you'll dull it." Royal snatched his dagger away and held it up to the light, cradling the six-hundred-year-old blade like a newborn.

"Sheesh, it's not the Hope Diamond." She gave him a dramatic roll of her eyes. But she knew this dagger meant the world to him. His ancestor Percival Dudley used it to stab King Henry VI. Legend held that Mad King Henry was a vampire who'd killed dozens of women. Dudley had sneaked into Henry's prison cell and run him through. Ever since Royal learned that legend at age ten, he knew his mission in life. To follow in his hero's footsteps and be a savior. So, he joined the Fellowship of the Faithful. But when vampires murdered his beloved daughter Devon, he quit his job and joined the Fellowship's secret group of "eradicators" as they called themselves. Zanna spotted him at one of their clandestine meetings, started chatting him up, and she didn't need psychic talent to know they were soul mates.

"Finding these sinners and saving them from debauchery isn't enough," Royal said. "My intent is one simple act: revenge." He gripped the handle and stabbed at the air.

"I hear ya, Roy." She ducked out of the way and winced. "But watch where you wave that thing, willya? Well, getting Devon's murderers is a good start. Now we'll get all of them purged, to rid precious mother Earth of all that filth and vermin!" She waved her fist like a dagger. "But you'll have to help me nab Teresa Lionetti, you know," Zanna said. "Use the beggar routine. That usually works."

Royal caressed his dagger's handle. "Yeah." His lips spread in a sinister smirk. "My poor soul act tugs on their heartstrings. But I won't need to knock myself out this time. Teresa's an easy target." He looked up and gave her a nod and a wink. "Then you can zero in on Fausto. What's it been, three, four centuries now, the hunters've been after that Silvius clan?"

"They started as merchants in Henry the Eighth's time, I think, a dynasty of old sea dogs. Some Silvius vamps joined the navy, so an occasional hunter enlisted and tracked them down." She fingered the crucifix hanging above her breasts. "The military's not my calling. Cruise ships are much more my style." She glanced around the small cabin with its simple furnishings—bed, nightstand, desk, wall-mounted TV—hardly the lap of luxury. "A bad day on a cruise ship is better than a good day on land." She got up and strolled to the window. "I'm just glad my 'third eye' envisioned Fausto working this cruise."

"Why not?" Royal polished his dagger with a shoeshine cloth. "It's the premier Italian cruise line. It would suck anyone in with those swanky dining rooms, the fancy eats, and waiters falling all over you."

She nodded, gazing out over the horizon. "Yeah, Apollo's pretty crafty, getting these Lotharios for image more than any medical ability they might have under those Italian suits. I haven't been lucky enough to get Dr. Fausto yet. But I'll make this cruise his last," she vowed out loud, hands clasped in a determined appeal.

"Silvius might not be on this cruise." Royal laid the dagger on his pillow and petted it like a pampered poodle. "He might still be in mourning."

"My third eye is seldom mistaken. I had a vision of him on this cruise even before we got on it," she replied. "And after we catch Teresa and indoctrinate her, I'll get Fausto. I'm determined to make him a notch on my arm band."

"I wonder about that Teresa." Royal broke open a bottle of Scotch and poured himself a neat one. "I'd have thought she'd be with one of them. And she walks arm in arm to her cabin with a slob like that?"

"Maybe she was drunk. I'm convinced she's a vampire accessory. She publishes all Mona Rossi's novels, and they've made movies out of some. What surprises me is that Mona's going solo. I saw her at that reception, and she wasn't paired off with anybody. If Fausto's aboard, I figured she'd be on him like a duck on a June bug."

"Maybe Fausto's homosexual." He slid the dagger back into its sheath, replacing it on his pillow.

She sneered at his precious weapon. He spent more time pampering it than he did her. She gave herself a light slap across the cheek. "You shrew, you're jealous of an inanimate object!" she chided herself. At him, she nagged, "You're going to cradle that thing to sleep in your arms again tonight?"

"No, I won't need it yet."

He closed his eyes, rolled the Scotch around in his mouth, and swallowed.

"Ah..." He smacked his lips and let out a sigh. "Like liquid fire. It just about scorches my throat on the way down. Absolute ambrosia!"

She eyed his near-empty bottle. "Oh, well, you're entitled to a few pleasures since we quit our jobs."

"You nab this Fausto dude, and I'll buy you a whole case of whatever you want to drink. Just name it."

"Thanks just the same, but I can buy a case of spring water any time." Zanna pulled her bottle of silver polish from her suitcase. "Fausto's been hunted and almost caught several times but always got lucky." She unclasped the crucifix from around her neck. It had been blessed by the last three Popes at Masses outside Saint Peter's. "He's slippery. He's always managed to elude eradicators. He doesn't flit around, like his parents and siblings did." She poured the silver polish on a cloth and buffed the cross. "Precisely why I want to be the one to collar him. It'll be a huge achievement, and it'll get me promoted."

For eradicating a dozen vampires, she'd receive a promotion to second degree hunter by their superior, the Grand Nimrod.

"There ya go," Royal said. "After number twelve, you'll get your promotion, and you can rest easy. Retire and grow lilies."

"No, Roy, I could never just sit on the sidelines and bark orders." She held her gleaming silver crucifix up to the lamplight and admired it.

"Does Silvius have any bodyguards?"

"Not that I know of. I've never seen any of them with bodyguards. They're too arrogant for that."

"Then how much does he truly fear being killed?" Royal poured himself another neat one.

"He's probably armed," she warned. "We have to watch out for him. He's cautious, unlike his unwitting family. But that's the reason I'm after him. It's like capturing a cloud. And I want my twelfth to be the supreme challenge, to get me that promotion." She fastened the chain around her neck.

"You're wasting your time hunting him." Royal sloshed the amber liquid around in his glass. "Besides, I thought you were having all kinds of visions of that murder in Tuscany, and the police asked you to help find the dead guy."

"I did help them, as much as I could. But I can't see anything more specific than a shallow grave in an old bone orchard, so I'm not able to guide them. They want me to go back there when I can visualize the scene better. It's the first psychic vision of a murder I've had outside the United States, so maybe that's why I'm having a hard time focusing."

"Then go back to Tuscany and look around some more. They need you more than you need that promotion. Nab Fausto and his cohorts another time."

She shook her head, unable to concentrate on the recent murder of vineyard owner Sabino Musciatello, whose jealous girlfriend allegedly murdered him and buried him in an old graveyard. It was one of a string of similar murders over the last three years, and the Italian police had become desperate enough to request her psychic talents to help find the body, which could lead to the killer. But Zanna's vague visions made her shudder with annoyance. Was her third eye nearsighted on this one?

"Then if you can't help them find the murder victim, just concentrate on hunting Teresa. She's a way easier mark than Fausto."

"She's too easy," Zanna retorted, jutting her chin out. "When those eradicators purged Fausto's kin on that cruise, he was spared 'cause he was on another ship. So, that's my sign that this is my turn. My gift to the world will be Fausto Silvius, in his grave with a stake through his heart." She lifted her crucifix between her fingertips and kissed it. "It was only luck on his part he was spared when his family got wiped out. But there will be no more chances after I'm done with him."

"Zanna, he's dangerous. He's not worth it. Concentrate on Teresa. Even this Mona may be one of them. They're all part of the same clique. Did you see that workshop on the schedule called 'Creatures of the Night'? I wouldn't be surprised if the entire room will be full of them, including the speakers. You'll get your twelfth, and then some, if you play your cards right. But leave Fausto to the experts."

She stood and slapped her palm on the table. "Beggin' your pardon, sir, but I'm a mite more successful than you. In ten years, I've eradicated eleven vampires. Fausto will be number twelve. So, if I get two of them on this cruise, or even more, all the better. Don't go questioning my capability or my faith, because I won't let doubters like you undermine it. We spent the last year tracking down the vermin who killed your Devon. Now it's my turn. And Fausto is my ultimate catch." She wrapped the crucifix in a silk scarf and slid it into her faux leather bag.

He drained the last of his Scotch and loosened his belt to the last notch. "Let's catch this Teresa first and work on saving her. Humor me. Then, once she's ensconced in our orbit, we'll center on him."

"No offense, Roy, but I want to do this solo." She placed her stake, holy water, and foxglove in her hunter's briefcase.

He made a last ditch attempt to dissuade her. "What makes you think you can snag him yourself?"

"I have a trick or two up my skirt." Her eyes glowed like living jewels.

He chortled. "I hope you have a pair of fangs up there, cos you're no match for him otherwise."

****

Mona and Tessie reached the door to the doctors' lounge, with an ornate brass handle and *Salute* in discreet gold lettering. "Just don't call any of the guys drop-dead gorgeous," she warned Tessie as she knocked. "Although it *would* be apropos."

After a moment the square peephole slid open. "May I help you?" A pair of dark eyes peered out at her. The voice carried an edge of wariness.

She could hear Dean Martin crooning "That's Amore" in the background. "I hope that's a recording and they didn't bring Dino back to sing," she said to Tessie. "You never know with these guys." She whispered the code words, *"Parlo pianissimo."*

The door creaked open, revealing a mop of tousled blue-black hair, an inviting smile, and a cleft chin. As her eyes brightened in recognition, Tessie blew a two-note whistle behind her. Mona knew that whistle. It was her trademark mating call.

"Mona! Good to see you, *cara mia!*"

"*Ciao*, Quintus!" She fell into a bear hug with Fausto's cousin and oldest friend—and oldest was the word. He'd drawn the sketches for Nero's coins. He lifted her up like a garlic clove and twirled her around. He looked tanned and rested, his eyes as deep as the sea, hair in wavy abundance.

When he put her down, her eyes slid to what he was wearing—or not wearing. A simple toga wrapped around one shoulder and draped over his ripped torso, hugging him and not hiding much. So that's what Fausto meant by casual!

She turned to Tessie, already in a lip lock with Quintus. When they came up for air, he grasped her hand and kissed it, lingering just long enough to make Tessie's eyes glassy. "It's so good to hold you again. I can only go so long on dreams and nocturnal fantasies."

Tessie nearly swooned. "*Buonasera*, Quintus darling," she croaked. "And you're even more gorgeous in three-D than in your latest underwear ad."

Oh, yes, that's *amore*, all right. Mona let out a romantic sigh, glancing around the darkened lounge. Overstuffed chairs and low tables surrounded a curving bar. Several people held wine goblets, talking and laughing. The men wore those skimpy togas, and the women were in boob-hugging, midriff-baring loungewear. It made her want to strip off her gown and everything under it—almost—and strut her stuff. Fausto emerged from the bar area to greet her. Apparently a toga was too confining for him. He wore a simple loincloth and rope sandals. She got dizzy running her eyes up and down him and back up and down again. "Wow, you look...good enough to eat. Or drink."

"We'll see what to do about that later, *bella mia.*"

"Did you get the note I delivered?" she whispered.

He nodded before she'd finished asking. "Not a thing to worry about. As long as we're careful, we'll be fine."

How could he act so nonchalant, when one of them could...no, she refused to think about it. She took the crystal wine goblet he offered her. At least she hoped it was wine. "*Salute.*" He kissed her lips, and she took a sip as she continued to check him out over the rim.

As Fausto's eyes swept over her, she remembered the frustrating interlude in her cabin. She burned for his touch, his hand gliding down her stomach, circling, hot and tender, all at the same time. *Breathe.* No, she would not go there. She could never be a part of the Silvius clan. Be part of a legacy enshrouded in mystery? No. The less she knew about him and his family, the better.

She steadied herself and tried to tame her alter ego Jezz, who already had him in a lip lock, running hot kisses down his chest, teasing with her tongue, removing that loincloth one inch at a time as he throbbed against her...

He cupped her elbow and guided her over to some plushy lounge chairs before a row of floor-to-ceiling windows. His other friends came over to say hello; Adriano, Giorgio, and Castore, all Italian doctors, all vampires, all scantily dressed like ancient Romans.

She'd met these guys before, at Fausto's parties. Basking in their hand-kissing and rakings of bedroomy eyes over her with undisguised approval, she relaxed for the first time since being frisked at customs. They all looked hot and delicious in their skimpy togas. But Fausto, the loincloth barely covering his family jewels, was by far the hottest.

"Are all you guys working this cruise?" she asked, knowing if she didn't start the conversation, an orgy might begin any second. Orgy, forget it. She was too tired to play a piccolo.

"No, just me and Fausto," Castore replied. "These guys are taking a breather from their normal jobs."

Fausto opened a few bottles of Chianti Classico, wine being their favorite liquid besides the obvious. Contrary to another Hollywood fallacy, they also consumed gourmet cuisine, another reason they preferred cruise ships to hospitals. Fausto's arm draped around Mona's shoulders, and Tessie nestled in Quintus's lap, their gazes fused. It didn't take long for those two to get their pheromones fired up.

"How did you get the idea of this writer's cruise anyway?" Adriano asked, perched on the window seat, knees drawn up to his chin like a gargoyle.

Mona said, "I wanted to get Fausto back on board, get some new book ideas, and some publicity for the genre, so I contacted the cruise line and *The Cutting Edge*. And it all came together. I considered writing shipboard romance novels but didn't think that was too realistic."

"I'm convinced anything can happen in this life. Or any other." Tessie winked at Quintus, and he caught on. His eyes raked over her, lingering on her expertly arranged bust line.

"Oh, you'd be surprised how many romances start on cruises, and they last," he said. "My brother Sextus met the woman of his dreams last year, on the *Bella*

Regina Greek Isles cruise." He leaned over and topped off Tessie's wine glass. "By the time they reached Santorini, they were engaged. He proposed to her on a donkey."

Mona wanted to tell them that her quest to track down these crazy hunters was replacing her quest for book ideas, but it was too soon to bring all that up.

Apparently, Fausto didn't think so. "Tessie, I assume Mona told you about all of us." He gestured around at the others.

"Uh—" Tessie silently beseeched Mona, looking like a *Survivor* castaway after being voted off.

"Yes, Fausto, I just told her."

"*Bravo.*" He sipped his wine. "How do you feel about that, Tessie?"

"I'm cool. Being from Manhattan's Little Italy, I've seen it all. Not to mention smelled, heard, and tasted. I'm open—" She crossed her legs and let the thigh-high slit of her gown reveal a good stretch of flesh, making the bottom half of Quintus's toga look a little tighter. "—to anything."

Fausto said, "You know there are hunters after us, and some are on board?"

She nodded. "I know about hunters. And I'm pretty familiar with vampires." She didn't elaborate on that.

Mona took Julianna's second fax from her purse and handed it to Fausto. "I got another fax from my psychic friend Julianna tonight. Someone is out to get us." She peered around to each of them in the strained silence. "If we don't find them before they find us, one or more of us"—she licked her lips—"will die."

Chapter Four:
Bloodsucking Ghouls—Not!

As Fausto skimmed Julianna's fax, Castore peered over his shoulder to read. "Julianna Laurance sent you this?" His eyes brightened. "The celebrity psychic who told the Navy Seals where to find Binladen?"

"She's the one." Mona nodded. "We went to NYU and grad school together. I invited her on this cruise, but she was too busy. She's been giving me Tarot readings once a month for almost ten years. And I've— heh, heh, heh—proved her predictions wrong a few times." She lowered her eyes and clarified it with a sheepish grin. "That's what taking charge is all about. I just consult her to hear the good stuff in advance. 'Cause I like to celebrate ahead of time. Why wait? Life's short. For us humans, anyway."

"Julianna sees two 'shadows' following us," Fausto said.

"Of course they're hunters," Mona added. "I know Fausto's not that worried, but I had to tell everyone about it, since we're all in the same boat here. And that's not just a bad pun."

"I went to her right after my last breakup," Quintus said. "She told me I'd find the love of my life. Two years later I still hadn't. I was about to write her off as another crank, then I met Tessie." He kissed her cheek tenderly. "I sent Julianna a dozen roses, a thank you card, and a plane ticket to Tuscany with a key to my villa there." Tessie rested her head on his shoulder as their hands started to wander. Mona smiled to herself. *Oh, yeah, it'll be rockin', all right.*

As Tessie's fingers played with the hem of his toga, Quintus said, "Who am I to argue with the most famous psychic in New York? The weather asks *her* for a forecast."

Fausto handed the note back to Mona and waved it off as if to say don't worry about it. That simple gesture put her at ease for now.

"Consider that a good omen." Quintus gestured at the fax. "At least we know it's two people this time. I usually get some loser following me who looks like a reject from an Ozzy Osbourne concert."

Knowing two nuts are after them is a good omen? Mona doubted it.

"Now I have something to show all of you." Fausto stood and went behind the bar. He came back with a small cardboard box. "I wanted to wait till we were all together to show you this. It's proof they're on the prowl. Their sources must've done some digging and found out I'd be working this cruise." He opened the box flaps and passed the box around. The guys peered in, each registering mild disgust before passing it on. But Mona gasped in horror and dropped it on the floor.

It contained a dead vampire bat.

"Calm down, Mona, it's not a real one. The two-faced animal lovers didn't want to kill a real bat. And it came with a note. It says they know I'm here, and my time is running out. Just so you all know." He took the fake bat's body, tossed it in the air, and caught it. "But this shows how clueless these people really are. Bats make valuable contributions to the environment in the form of tree pollination and insect control. They don't just hang upside down and suck blood."

Quintus said, "Not only that, research on the anticoagulant in bat saliva resulted in a drug called Draculin, to treat heart patients. We have some aboard, don't we, Fau?"

"Sure do. We never say its name, though. Creeps some people out."

"Well, it sure is a fitting name," Tessie said. "Whoever coined that one has a sense of humor."

Quintus made a show of buffing his nails on the front of his toga. "Well, I don't like to bra-a-a-g, but—"

"It was you?" Tessie slapped her knee. "I'll have to get one of my authors to use that in a book. Is the name copyrighted?"

"You have my express permission. Just don't use my name, even if you do spell it correctly."

Mona covered her glass with her hand when Castore offered to refill it. What she really needed was another caffeine jolt. "All joking aside, guys, can you get the equivalent of air marshals on board?"

"We already have that, my dear," Quintus replied, a slight tension to his voice. "But the Vampire Ball Busters don't let bodyguards, security, or police deter them. They're covert, sneaky. They don't want to take out huge groups of people at a time. That would be committing a sin. No, they only want to purge the Earth of us heathens one at a time. And they have surreptitious ways of doing it."

"How?" Mona asked, nervously pulling on her left chandelier earring. Unlike the others, she knew zilch about this fringe of the Fellowship, on the far right edge of the mainstream church, yet able to wheedle support from them. She knew they were terrorizing a peaceful law-abiding group and hoped somebody ballsy enough would stamp them out.

"Stabbing in the heart, beheading, or starving, the only ways to kill a vampire. Permanently, that is." Fausto sat back down next to her. His bare thigh rubbed against hers. She tingled at the touch.

Plucking a few grapes from a bowl on the table, he said, "Some of them used to think the more traditional methods worked, drowning in holy water, silver bullets, garlic...especially garlic, till they realized we go through ten pounds of it a day, and that's just in one pot of puttanesca sauce."

"Remember that bearded Rasputin look-alike who was after us in Assisi, Fau?" Quintus casually draped his leg over the sofa arm and swung his foot back and forth. A stealthy glance told Mona he wasn't wearing any of those briefs he modeled on the billboards. "Poured garlic powder into your gas tank."

"Yeah, I parked wherever the hell I wanted for the next three weeks. No cop would come near the car." He gave his mildly amused half-smile. "*Pazzi.*" He tapped his temple. "All of 'em."

"Do any of them ever get caught?" Mona knew his family's killers could be on this ship, making her want to hunt the hunters all the more.

Fausto replied, "Some of the Ball Busters have been caught and prosecuted, but they're an underground group. It blows me away how ignorant some of the modern ones still are. They still think we change into bats, sleep in dirt-filled coffins, have no reflection...can you imagine these dudes with no reflection?" He gestured to his pals, who each took a surreptitious glance into the window. "They'd die!"

"Is that how old you are? Two thousand years?" Tessie prodded, with the curiosity of a kid asking a grownup about the olden days.

"Tess," Mona broke in, "it's not polite to ask a vampire his age."

"I'll be glad to tell her, Mona." Fausto turned to Tessie. "I was born in 1452, from a line of Roman vampires. The condition is genetic. I had no choice."

"Did you ever consider standing up for your rights?" Tessie asked.

He shook his head. "It's easier this way. We're hated because people think vampires kill, drain blood, rise from the dead." He sighed. "It's been easier just to live among ourselves, and we've managed for almost two thousand years, so why rock the boat now?"

They all groaned at the bad pun. As if to punctuate his words, the ship swayed underfoot.

"Our bloodline continued, and the genes mutated, so that when someone from our bloodline falls in love, he or she has a physical need to feed. It evolved out of the emotional need to feed. Now we maintain blood banks throughout the world, so we don't have to find a mate."

Mona's heart went out to him. She knew what it was like to crave love. Her ex was a guy who'd rather lay bets on horses than lay his own wife.

"What happens when you have a dry spell and you, you know, aren't getting any?" Tessie never quit when she wanted to dig to the bottom of something, be it a story or a bargain bin at Barney's.

"It does happen. A little more often than I'd like."

Fausto gave Mona's arm a few long, sensuous strokes, clasped her hand, and circled his thumb inside her palm. Liquid heat flowed throughout her body, to her pulse points and her pleasure points. She blushed when her eyes wandered to his tantalizing bulges beneath that skimpy loincloth. Was he trying to tell her that a few of his dry spells were her doing?

"But we can manage without feeding for a few months. When someone we love breaks up with us, we enter a state of hibernation. We sleep or simply lie in the dark. It's our way of dealing with the depression."

"We all have dry spells, like our human counterparts," Castore offered, sitting back and crossing one ankle over his knee. The front of his toga fell partly open, allowing Mona a peek at some of his merchandise. These Romans sure were open, she thought, taking a cocktail napkin and fanning herself with it.

"We draw from our blood banks in emergencies. The same way humans hoard bottles of water in case of drought, or eight pairs of black pumps to ward off the fashion police." He stared pointedly at Mona. She gave a coy little smile. "And contrary to another popular fallacy, we don't sink our retractable fangs into the necks of poor unsuspecting mortals." It was his turn to smile. His teeth were straight, white, and healthy, nary a point in sight. "Do you see fangs here? If we had fangs that went in and out like cats' claws, we'd set orthodonture back a hundred years."

"How long does it take for your lover to become a vampiress?" Tessie asked.

Mona knew she'd asked that for a good reason, and her mind began to wander. The thought of losing her best friend to the vampire world gave her a tightness in the gut.

"Someone we feed from will turn into a vampiress right after she drinks our blood," Fausto replied. "Van Helsing called it the vampire's baptism, but we're not that eloquent. In real life, we just call it—what do we call it, Quintus?"

"Depends on whose pop fiction you read or which shows you watch on the WB network," Giorgio said.

"Once she's swallowed our blood, she's reborn as one of us," Quintus said.

Mona nodded. These poor vampires, what a bum rap they'd gotten over the centuries. So, why was it so hard to let go with Fausto?

"We marry the traditional way, too, in church," Fausto said. "Hard to believe, but we're Roman Catholics. Although the Fellowship condemns us for that." He made the sign of the cross, accompanying his horrified falsetto.

Fausto squeezed her leg and ran his hand up her thigh to her panty line, lingering there. Wild thoughts flashed in her mind—stripping him, ravishing him, seducing him the way Cleopatra seduced Marc Antony...making him beg for more.

"How did your line survive all this time, with hunters after you constantly?"

That was probably the most intelligent question Tessie had asked yet. "I wondered that, too," Mona said.

"We only tell very close friends we're descendants of *the* Silvius family," Fausto said, "and we hide. As best as we can."

Oh, Fausto, Mona tasted the words on her tongue,

I'll never betray you! His plight tore her heart to pieces. She wished she could tell the world vampires had hearts, with no reason to drive a stake through them. But was she just as bad? Refusing to fall in love with Fausto because he was a vampire?

"And speaking of Christian marriages—" Quintus unwrapped himself from Tessie, sliding off the sofa and dropping to one knee. "I want my family and close friends to share this special moment with us. Tessie, I love you and want to spend eternity with you. Will you marry me?"

Her eyes popped and her jaw dropped. She swayed as if she was going to faint. She stammered as her mouth opened and shut. "I—I—I—this is so—"

"Just say yes, Tess." Mona reached forward and pushed the back of her head to make her nod.

"Of—of course I'll marry you!" The lovers fell into each other's arms, and everyone clapped. Mona imagined Fausto on bended knee before her, but the thought of a second marriage gave her hives.

"Congrats, bro," Fausto said. "You did all right this time."

Just then the haunting notes of "The Godfather Waltz" drifted through the room. Fausto gently brought Mona to her bare feet. The shoes stayed under her chair. "If you'll excuse us, I can never resist this one." With his hand splayed over the small of her back, he guided her onto the dance floor, colorful ceramic tiles made to look like a Roman mosaic. She curled her toes over the cool and soothing floor. Her arms wound around his neck, and she rested her head on his shoulder. They glided over the images of Roman lovers, olive trees, bougainvillea, and alpine pasque flowers. She should've crashed about four hours ago, but the music revived her as she and Fausto became one.

Another couple brushed by her elbow. She looked up to see Tessie and Quintus, arms locked around each other, his face buried in her hair. Giorgio then stepped onto the floor with a busty woman. One of the nurses, maybe? The white uniform hugged her figure, but it sure wasn't a nurse's uniform, showing thigh up to her lacy garters. "Who's the babe with Giorgio?" she whispered into Fausto's ear as the song ended and Al Martino's "I Love You Because" began.

"That's Rita Panepinto. She's from Venice. He met her through his brother Sextus. I think she's a ten-times-removed cousin. Although after that many degrees it's not considered inbreeding anymore."

In a flash of uncontrollable whimsy, Mona wished she was a member of the Silvius family. She and Fausto probably would have been married ages ago. She wouldn't have gone through that ugly divorce, and wouldn't be wondering where her next romance was coming from. But that was just another fantasy, like being one of those shapeshifters, or living in a world where couples mated for life. Or her new wish, capturing vampire hunters on cruise ships.

Tessie bumped into her, intentionally or not, she wasn't sure, but their eyes met for an instant, and Tessie smiled dreamily like she'd gone to heaven. Mona was thrilled for her friend but hoped she'd be around tomorrow for their first workshop, "The Future of Futuristic Romance." Since Mona wasn't sure of her own future as a romance author, or as an inhabitant of Earth, she needed Tessie there.

She melted into the musical Italian lyrics carrying

all the emotion of every love song ever written. She leaned into Fausto. His muscles moved with exquisite grace. She cherished these moments, the warmth of his body against hers. He grew hard against her through their few layers of thin fabric. His breathing became heavier as his arousal increased. He danced her over to a corner, dipped her at the song's finale, and guided her into a cabin with soft glowing lights set around a huge bed, and a private balcony. "Three cabins adjoin this lounge," he explained, "and this is the one I use."

She glanced at the door on the other side. "Is it locked?"

"It's locked and bolted. Don't worry. It's just us tonight. Now let's forget about those nuts, and play with these nuts for a while."

"The pleasure is all mine." How had she let this happen, and yet she couldn't stop herself. Her hands wandered down the length of his body and fondled him through the loincloth, feeling his erection surging. She splayed her fingers and found the only nuts she wanted to find for now. He moaned as she caressed him.

Placing his hand on her breast and feeling the thudding of her heart, he pressed her closer to him. "Mona, I want to make you mine in every way. Just like Quintus and Tessie will be soon."

"I still need to think about it..." she whispered as he planted feathery kisses on her neck, making her shiver with anticipation. Whether or not she was going to give herself to him tonight with reckless abandon, this was going to be a lot more Earth-shattering than a session with the Midnight Rider.

"You'll live a life you never imagined in your wildest dreams. We'd be together forever, never to part.

What can be better than that? Tell me what's keeping you from leaving this world and joining mine."

"Too many things, Fausto, we've been over this."

"But that was then, and this is now. You enjoy my company, don't you?"

His mouth descended upon hers lightly, becoming more insistent. Gasping for air, she broke the kiss to answer, "Of course."

"We have a lotta laughs together." He began tracing a finger down her neck and over each breast in a slow circular motion.

"A whole lotta."

His grin gleamed in the pearly lights. "Our lovemaking is wild and passionate."

She sighed under his touch, dancing flames beginning to ignite deep within her. "You turn me hard and soft at the same time."

"So does all this mean you're in love with me?"

"Let's not talk about falling in love yet." She stroked his chest, her lips on his earlobe, her tongue darting out and flicking it playfully, her breath matching his with increasing intensity. "Let's not talk at all right now." He already had her so hot and aroused and bathed in passion, her reasoning vanished.

He lay her down on the bed as he quickly slipped her gown over her head, slid her pantyhose off, and she wriggled out of her bikini briefs.

His lips and tongue were nipping at her nipples, erect by now, engorged with desire as she thrust her hips forward to meet his.

"Don't—don't feed from me yet, please..."

"I won't," he promised between kisses and hot blasts of his breath in her ear. His body covered hers.

Her legs parted, bending to wrap around his waist as they moved in an exquisite tempo. "Before I'd ever do that, I'd need to know that you're in love with me."

Their mouths locked together. She reached down, untied the loincloth, and flicked it off, exploring, stroking, and caressing him. His erection now throbbing, she arched her hips to meet his.

He moved to enter her. She thrust forward to meet him, to take him into the depths of her soul.

He teasingly pulled back out, and she writhed under him, whimpering in the heat of the intense fire burning inside her. "Say please."

"Fausto, I want you inside me. Please." He eased himself in and she arched her back, clinging to him with her thighs, determined not to let him go this time, her breath coming in rapid gasps.

Their bodies moved, slowly at first, rose and fell together as though they were a graceful piece of music. A million stars exploded. He plunged into her, and she rose to meet him, again and again. They gasped and groaned and cried out as they moved together, their bodies sliding in their mingled sweat. One body, one soul, of one earth, soaring to the pinnacles of one heaven.

She cried out, forgetting her vow, "Yes, I love you, I love you..." It felt so right on her lips, like a luscious delicacy, and he echoed her, "I love you, Mona, how I love you!"

But the nibbling on her neck grew stronger as his need intensified. She pulled back. "No, Fausto, not that. Please, not yet."

Instead his lips found hers, and their tongues mingled as they came together in an explosion that left them saturated in passion's heat and sweat.

As they lay side by side, arms and legs intertwined, the ship jolted. She jumped, startled. "Wow, did you feel that?" she whispered as it calmed once again and swayed gently, rocking them like a cradle.

"Feel what?"

"Like the ship hit an iceberg."

"The ship did nothing. That was aftershocks, *cara*. You'll be having reverbs for the next few days."

A glance at the illuminated clock on the nightstand told her it was two a.m. "I don't know how I stayed awake this long," she murmured. She shimmied back into her gown, but the pantyhose—forget it.

"You want to spend the night in my private stateroom on the Madrid Deck and have breakfast sent up?" He caressed her bare feet, her legs, her thighs.

She playfully pushed him away. "No, really, I think we'd better hold off on the overnights. I don't want to overtax you." That got a grin out of him. "What's your schedule like anyway?"

"Depends on how many people get Mussolini's Revenge." He went into the closet and slapped on the baseball cap and shades he'd worn on the deck. She was glad he was still being cautious, even though he seemed to have taken Julianna's premonition with a pinch of garlic. "That emergency before was one of the gentleman dancers with a concussion and a few broken ribs. He was walking across the pool deck, when one of the lounge chairs came crashing down on him from the sun deck above. It's impossible that a chair could have fallen off the sun deck, so we suspect foul play. But security went up there and didn't find a trace of anything out of place."

She recoiled in horror. "The poor man. I was talking to one of the dancers on the top deck just before you got there. He looked and talked—now this is going to sound absurd, but he had kind of an Eastern European accent, and Tessie said he looked and talked like Dracula. We were joking about it, and I was thinking, 'She'll soon find out what real vampires are like.' It's the ultimate irony. God, I wonder if that's him."

He nodded. "Sounds like him. Boris Nikolai. He likes to be called Nick for obvious reasons."

"Will he be all right?"

"Yeah, he'll be bandaged up for a couple days, but he's in good shape. It was those damn hunters. They must've thought he was one of us."

"Don't they do their homework before they decide who to stalk and attack?"

He shook his head. "The Ball Busters go after whoever looks like a vampire to them. That's why a lot of unsuspecting goths are assaulted, and some even killed." He leaned forward and touched his fingers to her cheek. "Don't worry, we'll be all right. Just remember if you're going to wear black, set it off with something pink to throw them off. Like a bow in your hair or a frilly ribbon or something that doesn't say 'I'll bite you if you don't kill me first.' "

She sighed. "It's amazing how you can keep a sense of humor through all this."

"I have to. I'm a doctor. And besides Nick's emergency, we had a sprained ankle, two bouts of bronchitis and eight cases of seasickness, barely ten miles out of port. It kept us and the two nurses hopping. Just wait till they start serving meals!"

He walked her back into the lounge. Music was still playing, and Tessie came out of the ladies' room.

"Have fun?" She gave Mona a nudge. "I didn't think I'd see you till at least Crete."

"You felt the ship jolt. What do you think?" She winked.

Tessie pulled her aside. "Fausto, can I borrow her a minute?"

"What is it, Tess? You look like you just saw a ghost. Or a vampire." Mona grinned.

"Mona, I just realized that Quintus and I were together in another of the past lives Julianna told me about!"

"Yeah? How do you know?"

"We were talking, and laughing, and—well, I'll give you the graphics later, but every minute that went by, I started remembering things, his gestures, the way he looks me up and down, the way he kisses, and it came back to me gradually. Before I knew it, I'd remembered. We were in England together. He wanted to feed from me, but I died of a chill before he had a chance to. If that hadn't happened, I would be a vampiress, and would be with him already. And now I have another chance!" She squeezed Mona's hands so hard, she nearly cracked bones.

"Ow! Hey, I'm very happy for you. So you're going to let him"—she could still hardly spit the words out—"feed? You sure you want to go through with it so soon?"

"Soon? It should've happened five hundred years ago. I know what I want, Mona. And maybe you should think about what you want, too." Just then, a scruffy guy come out from one of the adjoining cabins and lumbered up to them. "We'll talk later," Tessie said.

For a split second Mona thought he was a deck hand, but upon closer inspection—and that sure wasn't her idea—he came right up and slapped her on the back. Holy cow! "Quintus? Now that's a low-end disguise, even for the seventies." His hair was tucked under a newsboy cap. He slid his 70's-style mirrored aviator glasses down his nose and stroked his fake beard. "You look like you're ready to pull latrine duty—or you already finished a shift," she commented as he hiked up his acid-washed jeans and draped his arm around Tessie.

"Hey, ain't'chyoo my garbage man? Ya didn't hafta dress up for me." Tessie laughed, sliding a cig out of her case. He lit it with a match struck from a real book of matches.

"Hey, Mona." Tessie blew out a stream of smoke. "Maybe we should be in kitschy New York bimbo getups, if you're that worried. Does Naples have a Dollar Store?" she asked Quintus, but he gave a full-body Italian shrug, with shoulders, arms and hands, obviously with no idea what she was talking about.

"I already thought of that." Mona reached under her chair for her heels. But she knew they were going straight to charity as soon as she got home. She had to stop buying size sevens; she was an eight and that was that. "We'll be safe enough at the masquerade balls, but for the rest of the trip I'm going to follow Fausto's advice and not let these crazies ruin the trip for me."

"Good thinking. And I like you dressed much better as an Upper East Side Mafia princess than as a Flatbush *puttana*." Fausto gave her shoulders a squeeze.

"Pardon me, rent boy, I was gonna dress like a

Jersey *puttana*. There's a difference."

They left the lounge and said their goodnights to Tessie and Quintus.

Fausto offered to walk her to her cabin, but she wanted to wander off alone and sit on the sun deck under the night sky, to think over what Tessie had said: "... I'd succumb...it wouldn't bother me, if I loved the guy...why should his alternative lifestyle stop you?" Those words echoed in her mind all evening.

Fausto wrapped an arm around her shoulders. "If you think I'm going to let you wander this vessel at two a.m. with those lunatics out there, you're *pazza* in your pretty little head."

She liked it when he wanted to protect her. With any other man, she'd have felt like he was trying to knock her down a peg, but Fausto wasn't trying to build himself up to be the big savior. He already was her hero.

They walked up one flight to the promenade deck. She knew Fausto could protect them both, but for good measure, she always carried mace, and had a can in her evening bag. Her heels were still dangling from her hand. A four-inch stiletto could punch a lot of holes in a stalker.

Nobody was on the deck. Not a soul. The ship hugged the coast, and lights still twinkled along the shoreline. Beacons from small boats bobbed in the distance. The breeze caressed her like gentle breaths. The stars, flung across the sky, glittered and winked. She knew they held her destiny.

Ah, to sleep out here in his embrace. Fausto apparently had the same idea, because he wrapped her in his arms and warmed her.

"Whenever you're ready to let me make you mine, *bella,* just let me know. Give me a discreet signal if we're in public."

She inhaled his manly scent of afterlove. "This is a lot to think about, Fausto. Tessie believes she was a vampiress in one past life and knew Quintus in another. So, when I told her about you and Quintus being vampires, she knew she could handle it this time around. But I have to do more soul-searching to see if it's *my* destiny."

"Did your psychic friend ever give you any guidance on it?"

"She did tell me the next man I linked up with romantically would be the last one I'd ever be with. She said—" She tried to remember Julianna's exact words. "Yeah, she said forever. I just took it to mean forever as in as long as I'm breathing."

"You should know better than to think someone like her would throw a word like forever around casually. When a psychic means forever, it doesn't mean thirty years."

He kissed her tenderly. "But I'll wait for you forever, if that's what it takes. I'll never rush you or pressure you, Mona, because I know that becoming a vampiress isn't a decision you can make in a few months—or even a few years. But I can wait, because I have forever. And if you become mine, we'll both have forever." They went in and headed down the stairs. She peeked over her shoulder. Not a soul in sight.

Maybe Julianna was wrong about her warning.

Footsteps on the stairs one flight below put an end to her musings, and she peered down. Silence.

"What's wrong?" Fausto leaned over the railing

and took a peek around.

"I thought I heard something." Goose bumps raced up her arms. She shivered, suddenly cold. "I'm just being paranoid."

She muttered to herself, "Or am I?"

Chapter Five:
Predators Among the Editors

The last workshop of the day, "Creatures of the Night," centered around novels starring werewolves, shapeshifters, and vampires. As the leading trend in romance, four workshops were devoted to writing and marketing paranormals.

Mona attended, to see what these authors had to say about this wildly popular subgenre. Tessie was already front row center. People quickly claimed seats, shifting and gesturing, an excited buzz filling the room. Mona gave her a wave and sat in the back.

But she dropped her handouts when three tailored-suited, dark-haired, olive-complected hunks came through the door. Heads turned. Murmurs of approval hummed throughout. A smile spread over her face as the trio walked down the aisle, oblivious to the adoring stares, and eased into the seats next to her. She swiped up the littered paperwork from the floor.

"What are you doing here?" she whispered to Fausto, as Giorgio and Quintus flipped through their handouts.

"*Ciao*, babe. We're curious about these creatures of the night, just like everybody else here." He cupped her face in his palms and planted a kiss on her lips. "We want to see if they're as creepy and scary as everybody says they are. If they really do have fangs and come out of their coffins at night to suck blood, we'd better run and hide." He gave a mock shudder and covered his mouth with his hand. "Oh, horrors!"

She gave him a playful slap. "One of these adoring onlookers can be hunters, and you're not incognito. In fact, you're very cognito. Your grand entrance caused the old fashioned vapors, in case you didn't notice."

"What was grand about it? All I did was stroll in." He gave a casual shrug, like that happened all the time. And it did. "I'm not worried here, during the day, in a room full of people. So, one or more of them might be hunters or even Ball Busters. I wouldn't be surprised if they were. A 'Creatures of the Night' workshop would be the most obvious place to find one of us, wouldn't it? They're more likely to spot us here than at Bingo. But they won't do anything wacko in a crowd."

"Still, why look for trouble? I thought you were keeping a low profile since—" She caught herself, wanting to bite her tongue. "I'm sorry."

"No, it's all right. My family never exercised an ounce of caution. It's amazing they survived as long as they did. I'm careful, but I don't hide, Mona. I can't live like that. And you shouldn't either." He leaned forward and brushed her cheek with his forefinger. "Don't worry about Julianna's omens. She didn't say anything I don't know already."

Mona looked up at the dais where the moderator and the five speakers were now settling in, opening water bottles, and reviewing their notes.

She stared at the floor. His glibness rattled her nerves. "It depends on what they do. If they shoot us point blank, that won't be too easy to get out of."

"They don't operate that way, in big crowds.

Besides, shooting doesn't work." Fausto glanced over the handout. "Vampire lite lit? Now what in the name of Carpathia is that?"

"It's all the rage in the romance world, an offshoot of the low-end comedy novels, the antithesis of the dark traditional tales."

"Does that mean they're better or worse?" He flipped the page and skimmed it. "They portray us as buffoons, getting us into all kinds of slapstick rollicks, having us slip on banana peels and stale old gambols like that?"

"No, not quite that lowbrow. But romances have been lightening up. There's lad lit, hen lit, dick lit, something for everybody."

"Now there's bloodsucker lit." He scoffed. "How thoughtful of them." He tossed the handout onto the floor. "And all we get are three lousy stapled sheets of paper. No wax fangs, no garlic, nothing."

Just then, the moderator tapped her mike and introduced herself.

Each author spoke about her paranormal books and characters—fairies, shapeshifters, werewolves, and— vampires. Savannah Lee was the author of ten vampire romances, which Tessie's company had published. Her series hero, Helios Kostantakos, "Kos" to her fans, was every woman's fantasy, with his olive Greek coloring and his courage, a Greek warrior at heart, a descendant of Alexander the Great. Mona had to agree. Savannah knew how to make the legend come alive. But she stuck to formula. The fangs, the neck-biting, the dirt-filled coffin. Mona knew better—the nonfiction part of it. Mona glanced over at Fausto and the other guys. Their expressions never wavered between poker-faced and mildly bored. She couldn't wait to ask them what they thought of Kos and his adventures. She already knew they found the popular legends amusing, if not beneath their contempt. "They're just plain bogus," Fausto had once said. "Now I know how witches feel, when they're stereotyped as warty crones who zoom around on broomsticks." They were sure being polite, though—sitting through this, not storming out with agita.

When the Q&A session ended, the crowd headed for the dais and out the door.

"Well, guys? What did you think?" Mona asked them.

"I wish I could set them straight." Giorgio's eyes roamed the emptying room. Disdain crept into his features, hardening the poker-faced apathy. "They think we're all Dracula, with fangs and capes and Transylvanian accents. Hell, I've never even been there and wouldn't want to. None of us have." He cast a sideways glance at Fausto. "Unless *you've* snuck away for a bite."

"No way." He shook his head. "The food sucks, and the wine is even worse."

"It was Vlad the Impaler who started the whole thing. Now they think all vampires are like him," Mona said.

"And he wasn't a real vampire," Giorgio added, "but he sure gave the rest of us a bad name. Because of his shenanigans, Hollywood has us sporting fangs and sleeping in coffins. Folklore took over like the plague—okay, bad analogy."

"Movies gave us a worse reputation than Vlad or Stoker ever did," Fausto added. "A vampire dissolving in daylight was first seen in *Nosferatu*. Stoker never even mentioned that in the novel. Drac struts the streets of London in broad daylight."

"Yeah, they can't even keep their shams straight." Giorgio clucked his tongue.

Fausto said, "I was trying not to laugh when she said her hero's fangs emerge when he's ready to feed. Why doesn't he sprout a third head while he's at it? And the guy changes into a bat and flies around!" Fausto jabbed Giorgio in the ribs. "Hey, if we could do that, we'd never have to look out for the hunters! Just morph into Igor, flap our wings, and plop some guano on their heads!"

"Well, that's what's selling, guys." Tessie stuck her handout into her red "Romantic Cruise of the Century" tote bag. "Readers eat it up the way their vampires drink up blood."

"That's the only thing she did say that made sense," Fausto commented as they headed for the door. "Somebody found out about us a few thousand years ago and spread the truth, then it got more and more warped. What'll we be like in another thousand years? No body hair and two mouths, to suck blood twice as fast?"

"Maybe I'll write one," Giorgio said as they headed for the stairs. Tessie and Quintus, their arms wound around each other, wandered off. "My hero and heroine can travel to other planets and adapt to whatever the natives use as plasma. And I can top your futuristic dude, Fau. Mine will have evolved so efficiently, they won't even need fangs. They'll have stingers instead!"

"A combination pecker stinger," Fausto added. "They can screw and feed at the same time. Or they can suck on their plasma TVs!"

Mona closed her eyes and shook her head. "You guys should be writing all this down." Then she glimpsed someone familiar exiting the workshop room. "Hey, it's—" She grabbed Fausto's arm to get him to look that way. "That couple who passed us in the corridor, wearing those bright silver crosses."

She pulled him downwards and whispered, "They might be hunters."

He watched as the couple passed them, not giving Mona or Fausto or anyone else a second look. In a soft voice, the woman told her partner something about wanting a snack.

Mona grabbed Fausto's sleeve. "Don't these two look like hunters? They're just too clean-cut and righteous looking. And polite. They said hello last night and didn't elbow us out of the way when they passed in the hall."

He resumed walking toward the stairs. "Not everybody is from the South Bronx, Mona."

"Just don't forget I'm one of the speakers at tomorrow's workshop 'From Sex Kitten to Tigris.' "

He raised a brow and purred, "Yeah, I'd like to attend it, but I should be working, so I might call in with an unexpected case of Mussolini's Revenge!"

Chapter Six:
Temptation in the Garden of Tombs

Tonight, Tessie thought, *Quintus and I will fulfill our destiny.*

From the docked ship they strolled into the night, arm in arm, two halves unable to exist without the other. For years, Quintus had made her heart dance the tarantella. She regretted that it had taken so long to meet him in this life. But this vampire would want to turn her, changing her forever.

"In the mood for genuine Neapolitan *la pizza*?" He guided her across the street, holding her close. The joy of love tugged at her heart, and her bond to him strengthened, like they'd never been apart. "My favorite restaurant, Quaglia's, is around the corner. It's been in the Quaglia family for two hundred years, and I knew the original *Signor* Quaglia, such a pleasant, funny man. Always gave me free meals when I was here in town, treated me like a son."

"Are the Quaglias vampires?" As soon as she asked, she felt like a *fessa*. Heat flushed her cheeks. She had to stop assuming everyone he'd known for a few centuries was a vampire.

"Nah, just great cooks," he answered over a chuckle. She exhaled, relieved she hadn't offended him.

"Ordinary folk. Like I wish I were sometimes," he added, his voice flat.

She opened her mouth to ask him more about that, but the restaurant door beckoned them with painted purple grapes and wine jugs above the arched doorway. The aroma of garlic wafted outside.

Shivers of trepidation ran through her. "Quintus, if you don't mind, I don't have much of an appetite right now. Can we eat later?"

His raised brows told her that he'd never seen an Italian woman refuse a meal. "Well, sure."

She tucked her arm through his, and they kept walking. "What did you mean by you wish you were ordinary folk?" she asked.

"Like anything else, *cara,* it gets tiring. Eluding hunters. Taking ridicule from the ignorant who misunderstand us. The thought of never dying. Needing to feed from those we love, even though we don't always want to."

"I thought feeding was your exquisite pleasure."

"Not as much as you think. At times we feed because we need to, not because we want to. It's like being in the mood—sometimes your partner isn't." He caught her gaze and held it.

She wanted to stop blushing, and stumbled on the sidewalk, which didn't help. "Life's not always symbiosis, is it?"

He shook his head. "Life is a mystery. Even to us. Why are we invested with this power that lets us live for eternity? The biological reason is the way the blood plasma has mutated, but what's the spiritual reason our souls are earthbound forever? Our maker doesn't want us to join him in heaven? Sometimes it feels like we're cursed," he rasped.

"Your powers simply don't include knowing that

cosmic reason." She hesitated, not yet knowing how to tell him they'd shared a distant past. Maybe with some prompting, she could get him to remember it—and her. But it had to be at the right moment.

He suggested they find a quiet place under the stars, sending a thrill through her. As they strolled, she took in the sights and sounds. Colorful Christmas lights twinkled on balconies and on trees displayed in windows. Through the occasional half-open window, a television blared, a child cried, a tenor sang a love song with a guitar. A dog barked. A scooter zoomed down the street, the driver in front with his girl behind him, hands around his chest, her hair flying.

Tessie clung to his arm with her gloved hands, realizing how far away home was. Danger lurked everywhere in the dark alleys of this city, but his touch assured her safety.

They passed an old stone church with arched doors and stained glass windows. He stopped at the cemetery beside it. A cluster of mausoleums surrounded them. "It's a good thing the dead aren't buried in the ground here." He pulled open the iron gate, and it groaned on its rusty hinges. "In most of Europe, every few decades, they turn over the buried bones and crush the headstones to make room for more."

She shuddered. "Sounds morbid."

"Just practical." He led her down a winding dirt path to another gate and pushed it open. They stepped back out onto the sidewalk. "It needs to be done. There are a lot more dead people than live ones."

They strolled another few blocks in comfortable silence. She clung to him, ears perked for an approaching mugger. He made a sharp left into a narrow lane between two apartment houses. She tripped over the ancient cobblestones, and his grip tightened around her. "Careful." They walked down worn-smooth stone steps that led to a more secluded and shadowed graveyard. The old marble tombs were discolored, cracked, and weatherbeaten.

"This has been a resting place of my family for about nine centuries. I come here every chance I get," he said as she huddled into her coat collar. "Are you cold? Or just spooked?"

"A little of both." She was no stranger to séances that brought shaking tables, mysterious raps, and eerie voices from beyond, but strolling through bone orchards wasn't her thing. She wanted to meet his family, but...

He took her arm and coaxed her in. "Come on. It's safe. Nobody will bother us here. They only rise from their graves in the movies." His teeth gleamed in the last vestige of twilight and, no, not a fang in sight.

She always sensed the presence of restless spirits while walking through cemeteries, and went well out of her way to avoid them. They were a grim reminder of her impending end. But soon her fate would be forever altered. She grasped his hand, and he led her down a narrow dirt path past crowded rows of mausoleums, worn lettering carved into their stone faces.

"Is there a reason you're taking me through here, Quintus?" This wasn't her idea of a romantic setting, but she had to take his quirks with the good stuff. *The guy's a vampire,* she reminded herself. *Graveyards are their playgrounds.*

"I want us to share everything, now that we've finally found each other. I want you to see where some of my relatives rest, who never had a chance to enjoy being blessed as undead. This is part of me, Tessie, and I want you to be part of it all, too. I want you to enjoy what I enjoy. And I come here to be among my departed family's spirits, away from the deafening noise of the world. Listen."

She closed her eyes. The wind rustled through the dead branches. "I don't hear or see any sign of life."

"That's the whole idea. You hear nothing but the Earth's heartbeat. The quiet repose of hundreds of souls. The peace that comes with sharing the realm of the dead."

She knew she should've been chasing goose bumps from her arms, but enjoyed only peace and contentment. And burning desire to make him part of this life.

****

Earlier that same evening, Mona sat on Fausto's private balcony on the Madrid Deck. The rumble of the ship's engines died down to a quiet hum. The pilot boat had made its about-face and zoomed away.

She gazed out at the port of Naples. A sad nostalgia washed over her, but why? Terraced houses climbed up mountains, their pastel walls and tiled roofs glowing in the setting sun. The remains of a stone garrison staggered around the shoreline. Greeters on the pier waved and shouted. Even though cruise ships docked here all the time, natives still made a big deal out of it.

"When was the last time you were in Napoli?" he asked her.

"Freshman year of high school. My parents took me to visit some relatives. That trip was unforgettable because we went to Pompeii. I imagined how those poor souls must've suffered when Vesuvius erupted that day. Maybe that's why I feel kind of sad, looking out over Naples."

"Don't worry, *la donna Vesu* can't bury us here."

"I know that." She nudged him. "By chance were any of your relatives there when it happened?"

"Not that I know of. They never migrated far from Roma in the old days."

"We always considered ourselves Neapolitan," she said, "but one set of my great grandparents was from Sicily, so I go around bragging I'm Sicilian, 'cause it's just about the coolest place anyone can be from."

"Except Roma," he countered with a twinkle in his eye.

"All right, so your people conquered the world. Why didn't you try for the moon? You could've had a Colosseum and a Forum and a few bath houses up there for the last two thousand years." She turned and smiled at him, the slanting winter sun reflected in his eyes.

"Nobody to conquer. Too dry. And it's the worst climate for making wine. If vineyards could thrive up there, believe me, my Uncle Rocco would find a way."

The gangway was lowered, and disembarking passengers filled the air with cheerful chatter. "Will you have time to disembark for a while?" she asked. "It'd be great if you can take some time off so we can explore Naples together. I just realized, for the last six months, we've only seen each other under tragic circumstances. I want this trip to be an escape for you, too." So far it seemed to be working. She sure was living out *her* fantasies!

"I made sure I got New Year's Eve off, but I'll be on call. You're throwing one of your masquerade balls, aren't you?"

Excitement shot through her. "The 'Anything Goes' ball. Hey, can you have a tailor in Rome whip you up a pair of knee britches, a velvet coat, a ruffled shirt, and maybe a powdered wig, and courier it to the ship? The vultures'll never recognize you dressed as Casanova!"

"I can, but if my phone goes, I'll have to go dashing out on my white charger and save whatever damsel is in distress. I don't exactly want a repeat of our last *fuckus interruptus*. But it comes with the territory."

"Let's hope nobody gets too snockered, then. But what if one of the hunters fakes sickness to get into the doctor's office?"

He waved a dismissing hand. "They've done that before. They make complete asses of themselves. We can tell when someone's faking it. We politely escort them out, armed with Dramamine, since their bogus ailment is always seasickness. No imagination."

"That's more ethical than knockout drops, I guess."

"We've caught our share of hunters, too. We're not all a bunch of pacifists, you know." His eyes gave off a demonic little twinkle. "About a hundred ten years ago, I fought two of them off in Central Park, when it was still safe to walk there. I forced them to their knees and dragged them to the precinct like that. The sergeant, I'll never forget his name, McGlory, locked them up. In those days, they threw suspects in the tank first and asked questions later. I had my picture in the paper, just for personally bringing in two thugs. If only they knew the real story."

"How do you know they were vampire hunters and

not just muggers?"

"They had ancient daggers hidden in their pants. Your average mugger in those days couldn't afford a fancy weapon like that. But I sussed them out when they started yelling and spitting anti-vampire obscenities at me. There was no way I could expose them for who they were. I would've been laughed out of the precinct and branded as a loony. You know who the police commish was then? Teddy Roosevelt. Imagine explaining vampires to the likes of him."

"Why didn't you just kick them in the shins and leave them in Central Park?"

He turned to her and looked directly into her eyes, his gaze pinning her. "They were no match for me. I'd never harm somebody who's not my equal. Those two plug-uglies couldn't have beat a one-legged man in an ass-kicking contest. They sure messed with the wrong vampire." He let out a self-satisfied chuckle.

"You've had some life, Fausto," she sighed. Yes, sharing it with him for eternity was hers for the asking.

"Yeah, and it ain't over yet. I've got a long way to go. When I find myself grieving, I wish they could've taken me along with my parents and brother and sisters." His voice broke with emotion. "They'll get theirs," he vowed, like a prayer. "That's the only instance I'd consider killing. To get justice. Not revenge. Justice." His voice hardened.

"Darling, I'm glad you can discuss it so freely." She clasped his hand. "They'll get caught, I know it. You were left here for a reason, Fausto."

"I hope it's a good one." He leaned forward, she leaned forward, and their lips met in a soft, tingling kiss.

He left her side and returned a moment later with two full champagne flutes. "To the best New Year ever, and a new beginning for us both."

They clinked glasses, and she sipped. "I can sure use a new beginning." She hadn't meant to sound bitter, but she still seethed over her husband's betrayal. Absconding like a thief in the night was worse than if he'd run off with another woman. All through the divorce, Fausto consoled her, cheered her up, and convinced her to sign a prenup next time. Then his tragedy struck. Reversing roles, becoming his rock, made her stronger and put her abandonment into perspective. What was being dumped by a loser compared to the murder of your beloved family?

Through his grief, he was there for her. She couldn't have gotten through her own disaster without him.

"Mona *mia*..." He tilted her chin up toward him for another kiss. As his breath warmed her, she willed away the quiver that scampered through her. "We're in the most romantic place on Earth, and we're both single and free. I have this beautiful stateroom you can share with me. Why don't you say yes, and we can get on with our lives, I mean our life together?"

"You know why," she whispered, unable to find her voice. "I have too many reasons I can't become a vampiress. Way too many reasons."

"Your friend Tessie seems to have made up her mind. She and Quintus are inseparable. It's a shame they didn't meet years ago."

"It wasn't their time then. She's game for anything. She started Moonmist Press on her kitchen table, and when it nearly folded during the recession, she lost her apartment, but kept it up in a friend's garage, slept on a couch, and divorced an abusive husband. Becoming a vampiress would be like taking a vacation."

He moved his chair closer to her, grasped her hand, brought it to his lips and gave it a teasing, lingering kiss. "Don't knock it till ya try it."

She wanted to. Oh, how she longed to give in, spend the rest of eternity with him. It would be so easy. On the surface. They'd spend what little time they had together at his Palm Beach estate, or on the Grand Canal in his Venetian villa, when they weren't separated by careers and running from hunters. And could she ever raise a brood of vampirelets? No, marrying into the Silvius family was as dangerous as it was glamorous. "We wouldn't last, Fausto. You know that."

"You're too pragmatic for your own good sometimes." He took a sip of champagne and gazed out into the fading light. "Not to mention cynical."

"We have killers after us. Shouldn't we figure out how to get them off our backs first?"

"We'll never get them off our backs, Mona." He cut the air with his hand. "They've been after me for centuries, and they'll be after us when they find out we're together. So, we might as well be together. At least I can protect you then."

"When? The two months a year we'd see each other?"

"Would you consider coming with me on my tours of duty? You can write anywhere, can't you?"

She took a too-big gulp and looked for the bottle, so she could refill her glass. "That wouldn't work. I need my space."

She felt his eyes burning into her back as she walked toward the kitchenette. "Space? This stateroom is the second biggest one to the captain's. My Palm Beach place is eight thousand square feet. And my flat in Venice can give the Doge's Palace a run for its money. How much more space do you need? You want me to buy you the Taj Mahal?"

She shuddered. "God, no. The Taj Mahal is a mausoleum."

"I know." He gave her a smile that told her he knew. "But it's a great place to hang."

She took another gulp of her refill. She didn't usually go for fizzy drinks but needed to loosen up. Still, she walked a fine line. If she got too loosened up, she'd wind up wearing the four-carat rock undoubtedly stashed in his safe waiting to be slid onto her finger. She knew him. He was always prepared. One night, he'd confessed he was wearing a condom—and they were only dancing.

"I meant I need my own place to write. I vowed I wouldn't rush into another relationship, either."

"I didn't mean to rush you. You want another fifteen years?" His voice carried a teasing tone.

She matched his smile with one of her own. "You know what I mean. A marriage and a career are nearly impossible to juggle. It was tough even when Ted and I were getting along."

"How about some linguini *aglio e oglo*?" he asked. "My favorite restaurant in Napoli, Nicolino's, is only a few blocks from here. Nicolino's *aglio e olio* is the best in the entire boot. We can have pizza anytime back home at Baldo's." He winked, and she laughed. Baldo was a street vendor who gave free pizza to the hookers at the Holland Tunnel entrance while they plied their wares, but his pepperoni pizza was so good, people walked or cabbed to Lower Manhattan in rain, snow, or sleet for a slice of garlicky heaven.

She hadn't eaten since breakfast, and the champagne made her head fuzzy. She couldn't keep speculating about eternity together until she got some pasta and olive oil in her. "That sounds great, Fausto. I haven't had *aglio e olio* since I went off Atkins for the fourth time."

"I'm on duty at six." It was now four-fifteen. "Make sure I don't fall asleep afterwards."

"You've never fallen asleep after sex, so I'm sure you won't crash after a plate of *aglio e olio*."

As he slid into the Bronx getup, she wondered if Tessie was right and she should get herself one. Oh, the hell with it. She knew it was the bubbly talking, but she knew they'd never relive this moment. Their first trip to Italy together, and she wasn't going to let some kooks force her to dress like a stripper at the Bada Bing. But he gave her one of his coats and a baseball cap...just to be on the safe side.

****

Quintus and Tessie followed a winding dirt path to an ancient oak tree. Its twisted limbs reached at them like a deformed beggar. Its huge, hollowed trunk resembled a cave. "I sit inside this tree whenever I come here. It's been like this for hundreds of years." He gathered some dead branches and lit them outside the trunk's entrance. A small fire flickered into life, warming her. He led her inside the hollow, took off his coat, and spread it on the ground. He drew her to him. The earth beneath the fabric enveloped her with soft, inviting warmth. She no longer shivered with the winter's chill; just the earth's warmth, the heat from the flame, and his luscious body.

"What do you really think of me, Tessie?" He fondled her cheek with his fingertips. She tingled all over. "About who I am?"

"You're sensitive and sensuous and ooze magnetism and sexuality," she admitted, "but you're also a genuine human being." She winced at the bad choice of words, but let out a relieved breath when he seemed not to notice. She added quickly, "You are who you are. And I respect you all the more because of it."

His eyes captivated her, a rich hunter green mixed with flecks of earthy brown, the pure colors of nature.

"I'm sorry I didn't tell you sooner. I was waiting for the right moment. But Mona thought you'd take it better from her."

"I understand." She nodded.

"You really understand who we are? If we're going to have a future together, there's no turning back when we make that eternal pledge to each other."

She wanted to tell him that deciding had nothing to do with it. "Some things are planned for us without us having any control, Quintus. Like when we're born and when we die. When someone is murdered, it might look like it was at the hand of another, but I believe it's part of a plan that we mortals have nothing to do with. But you, on the other hand..." She fumbled, knowing she was putting her foot in it. Could she pull it out fast enough? "I mean, vampires have been known to kill—"

"We have no physical need to kill those we feed from. But like mortals, some vampires get carried away with their vices. That's why, when we fall in love with someone, we take as much as possible without harming her, and keep it in a personal blood bank. We never hurt the woman we love." He looked deeply into her eyes, and she knew—this was his way of telling her he loved her.

A surge of passion washed over her. "Quintus..." She snuggled up to him, her fingers toying with the buttons of his black silk shirt.

They'd agreed to wait. She was still the traditional, old-fashioned Italian girl. *What would it be like to slowly open this shirt?* Her lusty, forbidden fantasies returned, but more intense and immediate than usual. "You know when you meet somebody, and even though you've never laid eyes on them before, in person. I mean, you feel like you've known them all your life, or longer?"

"Longer?" His intrigued, penetrating stare unnerved her for a second. "Tell me more about the 'longer' part."

"This life is not the first time we've met. Your family with its special powers began sixteen centuries ago, and you've walked the Earth for almost five hundred, but how about before that? I've been here before this lifetime, when you were at the zenith of your youth. Think back to the Middle Ages, Henry the Sixth's reign."

His body lurched, as if a spark of energy jolted him. "My God, yes! I visited England as an emissary."

She further jogged his memory. "And your wife left you for someone who became very famous, right?"

He looked at her as if seeing her for the first time. "Yes. Cristoforo Columbus became a business associate of mine. He commissioned my shipping company to build a schooner to take him to Cipango, but he needed financing. So, I brought him to England on one of my vessels, to appeal to King Richard the Third. Cris boarded with me and my wife Bellona in a rented house. She won Cris over with her linguini and cream sauce. Cris was a chick magnet, the true swashbuckling romance hero. He swept them off their feet and onto their backs. Including my wife. She fell for his charm, he fell for her *finocchiona* and *panetone*, that Northern Italian fruit bread which I hate..." He grimaced, looking pained to continue. "She left me for Cristoforo Columbus." He showed no bitterness, no anger of any kind. If he had, it was a long time to carry a grudge, even for an Italian.

"I'm so sorry, Quintus."

He shrugged, splaying his hands in a "what'cha gonna do?" gesture. "It was five centuries ago. I've been over it for at least the last three. But how—how do you know about that part of my past? I never told a soul about it. I was a Richard the Third sympathizer. He had enemies all over the kingdom, and because of that, I didn't dare declare my allegiance. Not to my family, not to my lovers—" He stopped dead in his tracks. His eyes searched her, as if reading her. He drank in her features, caressing her cheek, running his finger along her jawline, over her lips. "Oh, Jesu, it's you! Angie! *Mia amore!* We are together again!"

"Yes, Quintus, I was Arcangela Valitutto then. I was there when your wife left you for Columbus, and I confess, I held a guilty sense of glee because you were free again, so I could have you. I was in love with you from the moment you set foot in England. Even before that. I followed you there."

He shut his eyes tight, pressing his hands to the sides of his head, and she knew he was reaching deep into his distant memory. "Of course I remember you. You comforted me, and told me I'd love again, and at that moment, I knew I had something to live for."

"Yeah, I was a convenient package. An Italian woman right there in Britain, crazy about you, willing to do whatever you wanted me to. Only I never got the chance."

"I remember now." He held up both index fingers. "You died of a chill, didn't you?"

She nodded. "On your boat. Waiting for Columbus to come back from the royal palace, so you could ferry him back to Genoa."

A sob escaped his throat as he encircled her in his arms and buried his face in her windblown hair. "Oh, my Angie. You came back to me. I'm so sorry about what happened. I never forgave myself."

"It wasn't your fault." His woodsy fragrance sent her back across five centuries, as if all that time and death and rebirth never transpired.

"I would've done anything to make you mine, Quintus. Even go to the New World with you if Columbus had let me."

"Oh, that wouldn't have worked. He didn't allow any women on board. He knew there'd be plenty in the New World. Why complicate things? I wouldn't have gone without you."

"And I died before you had a chance to make me yours. I thought it was too soon. I said, 'Wait until we get back to Italy, among our own people, and I'll be yours forever.' But I didn't have the chance. Not then. But now—" Their eyes locked. "I have another chance."

Her arms wound around his neck, and she brought his lips to hers. "From the minute I laid eyes on you even before Bellona left you, Quintus, I knew I wanted to spend the rest of my life with you. And I really believe Mona and Fausto are the same way, but she's too stubborn to make a go of it with him. They travel too much, she doesn't want to live forever, she says— flimsy excuses. She doesn't realize she probably knew him in another life, too."

"How did you find out you lived this other life?" he asked.

"I lived more than one, like most of us. But we never met again, until last year. Then I went to Julianna Laurance for a past life regression. I went back to more than one life during that session, let me tell you."

He clasped her hand, and their fingers intertwined as she settled into the crook of his elbow.

"Now I remember. Back then I wanted to take you to the woods where I grew up, outside Rome," he uttered. "I found a cave a long time ago, and I loved to go there as a child. I'd like to take you there now."

"How did you find it?"

"Exploring. And I'd like to do some more." His voice broke as he took her into his arms.

"I wish we'd gotten together earlier in this life," she confessed. "Being so busy with my career, and trying to make my bad marriage work, it was impossible. But when I saw that first underwear ad of yours—you, in your semi-naked glory, magnified two hundred times in the middle of Times Square—I said, that's it. I'm gonna get this guy, and keep him this time!"

He twirled a lock of her hair around his fingers. "When Julianna told me I'd meet the love of my life, I didn't know if it would take another five centuries. I wish she could've told me it was you."

"Psychics don't always get the details." She shook her head. "Sometimes you have to read between the lines."

"Oh, Tessie." His voice shook, ragged with emotion. "I loved you then, and I've been an admirer of yours for years—I mean recent years—and that's why I never told you about me. I was afraid I'd lose you."

"Lose me?" She ran her hand through his hair, falling like silk over her fingers. "I'm surprised every woman who goes near you doesn't sink her claws into you, or at least try."

He glanced away and hesitated. "A lot of them do. But for the wrong reasons. They don't know me inside. They just see what's outside. All the surface stuff that shouldn't matter. That's why I want a woman who sees beyond all that." He stretched out so that he was half lying on top of her. She wrapped one leg around him and the full lengths of their bodies met. "So, can we give it another go? Even if you keep your coat on?"

"This is fate, Quintus," she breathed in gasps as his hardness pressed up against her. "It would be against every law of the universe to fight it. And now, as then, I want you because you're you. We were put here for each other. In all our lives."

"Then let me make you mine, in every way. Finally!"

"I'm yours." She threw back her head and opened her soul to him.

Afterwards, he piled more branches onto the fire

and came back to her. This new strange sense of decadent freedom, out in the open, aroused her wildly. He lowered his head and gave her a light love bite on her neck, then began licking and sucking more intensely until pulsing blood flowed from her to him.

It was finally happening. The ultimate gesture of love with the only man she'd ever loved in all her lives. She'd waited two lifetimes for this, and now she was one with him.

And one of *them*.

****

Royal and Zanna sat in their borrowed black sedan across from the graveyard. "We can only take one of the lovebirds, so it'll have to be her," he warned her once again.

She ground her teeth in frustration and vexation. "All right! You seem incapable, so I'll get him on my own."

"We don't even know who *he* is," Royal snapped.

"Wake up and smell the garlic, Roy. Look at him. It doesn't take a psychic to see he's clearly a Silvius. Look at that nose, those cheekbones. If he isn't, I'll resign right now and enter Saint Lucy's Convent as a novice."

"Silvius or not, *she's* the easy mark. Just be ready to press pedal to metal when I grab her." Without a backward glance, he slid out of the car, the back door wide open. He practiced his "pity limp" on his makeshift crutch and ran his knuckles over his fake scraggly beard. Glancing down at his sweat-stained pants, he decided they still weren't ratty enough, so he caught them on a bare branch and yanked away, ripping the leg to shreds. Chilly air seeped through the threadbare corduroy. He shivered. *There but for the grace of God go I*, he thought, knowing how blessed he was. Every Sunday, he dropped ten dollars and a fistful of grocery coupons into the poor box.

Now for his next good deed, to persuade this misguided soul to cease glamorizing the lifestyle that killed his daughter. He'd guide this woman down the path of salvation. The weak-willed were always the best candidates.

The crunching of footsteps and voices, lilting with after-love playfulness, alerted him. He pushed his moth-eaten ski cap farther back to reveal the gash across his forehead, a real one, from last week's run-in with a vampire coward who'd fled. He took his bridge out of his mouth, leaving the few real teeth he had left. His slur, along with his pitiful plea, would evoke just enough sympathy. "I'm ready," he muttered. "Come and get it, vamp tramp."

As the lovers strolled past, arm in arm, Royal lurched forward, colliding with the tall Italian, nearly knocking him over.

"*Uh, scusi...mi dispiace...*" Royal staggered back and forced a sob through his throat. "I didn't see you," he continued in Italian, "my eyes are so bad. Do you have some spare change for a poor homeless gentleman for a hot meal or even a hot cappuccino. My stomach, it growls with hunger..."

As he spoke, he sidestepped his way over to Teresa's side, holding a grimy palm out, but keeping a safe distance.

The Italian reached into his pants pocket and pulled out a fistful of euros. "Will this do you, *signor,* for a while?"

Royal nodded, fingers wiggling greedily as he licked his lips and ran his tongue over his stubby teeth, gushing *"Grazie, grazie! Dio vi benedica!"* over and over.

Money in his clenched fist, he drew back, gave the Italian a punch in the solar plexus, and kicked him in the shins. When he staggered back, wailing in agony, Royal dragged Teresa, screaming and kicking, to the car idling at the curb, shoved her into the back, and jumped in, pressing a chloroform-soaked rag to her face.

"Go!" he ordered.

Chapter Seven:
Busting the Ball Busters

Mona soaked in the bath, inhaling the lavender-scented water, psyching herself for tonight's Loving Heart awards banquet and trivia contest, the Hens vs. the Chicks. She was captain of the Chicks' team, and they'd be battling the Hens, quizzed on each other's trivia. So, she'd studied a few Baby Boomer websites with Q&A's like "What was the name of the band Paul McCartney was in before Wings?"

Paul who?

And "What was the name of the music festival in New York State in the summer of '69?" She knew that one! Watergate!

The banging on her door jolted her out of her trivial pursuit, and she sat up. Oiled water and suds sloshed out of the tub. "Who is it?" Inching to her feet, she wondered how long it would take to sprint naked to the mace in her purse.

"Quintus. Open up, Mona, please."

Quintus! *God, no, something happened to Fausto!* Her heart hammered, and the *aglio e olio* she'd so gleefully savored an hour ago churned in her stomach. She grabbed her robe and yanked the door open.

His ashen face and darkened eyes startled her. "What's wrong? Is Fausto okay?" She pulled Quintus inside, wetting his sleeve.

"No, it's Tessie. She was abducted right from my arms."

****

Zanna and Royal stood over their captive, held up a crucifix that smelled of jasmine incense and chanted the Prayer of the Hunt.

"You're making a big mistake. I'm as human as you are, and that's a compliment." Tessie struggled and strained against the ties that bound her. She'd been in silk bonds before, but never this damn tight.

Zanna gave Royal a zipping gesture across her lips.

Royal fetched a scarf from the closet. He rolled it up and tied it around her mouth.

"What if she's telling the truth, and she's not one of them?" he asked Zanna as he tugged on the knot. "You can forget your promotion because we'll be shamed right out of the Fellowship. The Council will demote you and slap you with latrine duty on the graveyard shift."

"I don't care if she is or not, but the odds are in our favor. She was with him, wasn't she? They came out of that bone orchard cooing like a couple of love doves in mating season."

"Too bad I couldn't get him, too." Royal poured himself a Scotch and glanced around their borrowed villa in a quiet residential section of Naples. Track lighting illuminated the walls, bringing the murals to vivid life, giving the terrazzo marble floor a burnished hue. The villa belonged to a friend of one of their superiors, Father Farlinghetti. Royal called him Padre after his own father died. When the ship docked in Naples, Royal texted Padre that he needed a hiding place for a suspected vampire, and Padre texted directions to a friend's villa. *Nobody'll find us here*, Royal gloated with a spreading smirk.

"How can we conduct a useful interrogation if you keep this gag on her?" he ranted at his wife, busy typing on her iPad.

"We'll let her talk as soon as she promises not to do any more yelling and swearing in Italian. I'm afraid she's putting a curse on us." Zanna closed the iPad and slid a jeweled dagger from a sheath. She held it up, as if challenging Tessie to a duel. "See this? One peep out of you, and a vampire chowing on your neck will be a picnic compared to what I'll do. I'll say this much, you can kiss your head goodbye," Zanna rattled off her warning as she ran a finger across her neck. "Hear me, Anne Boleyn?"

Anne Boleyn a vampire? Tessie thought. *Small world. And Henry had her beheaded. All makes sense now.*

Zanna turned to her husband. "Take the gag off her, Roy."

He untied it and tossed it onto the floor.

Tessie's gaze met the dagger's deadly edges. Something told her she'd seen it before, long ago. Like an old song that recaptures a special moment, forever frozen in time by its melody or a penetrating chord etched into the heart's chambers, it evoked sadness from her distant past. The dagger's every detail was familiar to her, how the light caught the uncut rubies and emeralds in its handle, its gleaming silver blade marred with nicks and scratches. It winked and glinted at her as if trying to tell her something. She shivered.

A-ha! The memory flooded through her. Forcing the image from her mind made waves of pain shoot through her head. She'd been in this exact position once before. The same predicament. Falsely accused. And in just as much danger.

But not in this lifetime.

"Now." Zanna didn't move a muscle, the knife still and steady against Tessie's jugular. "How did you hook up with Quintus?"

"I met him on the ship," she lied, her voice barely audible. "We just met, and that's the truth."

"Where'd you get those love bites on your neck, a horny woodpecker?"

"I was—" She'd never been interrogated within inches of her life. She tried to reason through the fright and shock of being seized, thrown into a car, waking in a hard chair, and tied so she couldn't move a muscle. "I cut myself shaving."

"Shaving? Your neck?"

"Well, I *am* Southern Italian!"

"Spare me your ghastly bathroom routine." Zanna flipped a gray lock of hair off her forehead. "What do you know about Quintus Silvius, and how did you wind up in a deserted graveyard with a guy you hardly know?"

"He was lonely and wanted some companionship. It is a singles' cruise after all, and I'm single—" She didn't think she had to finish. How stupid were they if they couldn't figure out why she was with a babe like Quintus?

"And of course you know he's one of *them*." Zanna spat out the words like she'd bitten into a rotten peach.

"One of them what? He isn't gay. Okay, so he's a Yankee, but I can live with that."

"Don't mock us." Zanna twirled the knife in the air

and caught it by the handle. "In one swift stroke, I can make those phony breasts spurt like a Texas gusher." She grabbed Tessie's hair and forced her eyes to meet hers. "If you don't know what he is, I'll tell you. He's a vampire. One of the lowest life forms on earth."

Tessie smelled mint weakly masking the woman's pickled onion breath. "Oh, well...we didn't...the conversation never went beyond our mutual interest in vintage Campanian wines."

"How shallow." The husband leaned into her, highball glass in hand, and wagged a finger in her face. *She* was shallow? And what was he knocking back? Punch and whiskey?

"Look, you twit, I'm tired of your lies. My name is Zanna." The woman's tone didn't indicate the politeness of an introduction. She said it like the name had been invented for her by some Roman god once he realized Minerva was taken. "The first name ever created, means God's gift."

Tessie nodded. "Okay, so you're a Yenta. Were you born in one of those cold water flats on Hester Street?"

"God gave me the gift to banish sinners and psychic ability to locate them in my mind's eye, so I can confront and purge them. Now we summon you to contribute all you have to aid us."

Tessie half expected them to pass her a long-handled basket full of loose change and envelopes. "But I'm no psychic. I don't have any cash on me either. I'll have to make a pledge. Put me down for five bucks."

Zanna's eyes narrowed as she studied Tessie like a bug under a microscope. "You'll realize soon enough, we have been called, and now so have you, for a noble endeavor."

"If you're so noble, why don't you leave vampires alone and hunt down Al Qaeda cells?"

"Because this is my duty, to eradicate vampires and vampiresses for the harm they inflict on innocents when luring them into their lairs."

"So do telemarketers. But why me? I'm just your average Jane Doe. With a little more body hair." She hoped her experience working with agents would pay off at this crucial moment. If she'd ever needed to call on her ability to bluff, it was now. She conjured up a picture of her ex and said exactly what she felt about him. "He means nothing to me. I don't give a fat frog's ass about him. He turned out to be a jerk anyway. He's probably screwing somebody else right now."

Zanna went on, "We know you publish vampire books that are made into equally vile movies. They're an evil influence on the weak-willed. And we have the heart-wrenching, soul-rending proof! Vampires murdered Royal's daughter Devon. She died a slow, torturous death." Tears filled Zanna's eyes. "And vampires captured me when I was young, but I escaped with my life. I was luckier than poor Devon, robbed of her life by those bloodthirsty ghouls." Her voice broke. Royal tried to give her a highball glass, but she nearly knocked it from his hand.

"But that's only a handful of sickos!" Tessie shook her head, thankful Zanna had taken the knife away. She took her first full breath since being seized. "The books I publish are novels—fiction. Most vampires don't kill. They're not evil, they're just people. Their only difference is that they—they feed from each other. In private. As an act of love. And acts of love behind the closed doors of consenting vampires are nobody's business."

"Devon got ensnared in a cult and became one of them against her will," Royal spat back, spraying Scotch in her face. "Then they murdered her. Those perverts ripped my innocent daughter from me forever. We need you to stop them because you have a power that complements ours, the power of the media."

"So now, you'll do what we tell you to do." Zanna aimed the dagger back at her throat. They crept up on her and circled her like vultures around carnage. "If you want to live beyond tonight."

With widened eyes, Tessie looked from one to the other, her heart pounding. "Live beyond tonight? All right. Fire away. I mean, tell me what you want me to do. If it means saving my neck, then I'd better stick it out."

****

Mona's legs weakened. She gulped air and collapsed onto the couch. Quintus followed her into the sitting area of her stateroom and drew her head to his shoulder. "Calm down, Mona. We'll get her back."

"What happened?" She clutched his arms as terrifying thoughts assaulted her.

"We were coming back from a stroll...not just a stroll. We made love and...I fed from her, and she fed back from me. She's one of my kind now."

This shouldn't have surprised her, but it did. She didn't think Tessie would give in so soon. Sure, she'd loved him for a long time, in more lives than one, but Mona felt certain he had cajoled Tessie.

She narrowed her eyes at him, her anger growing as her heart thudded. "Why did you make her do something so...so..."

He threw up his hands. "I hardly made her, Mona. I didn't lift a finger. It was more than mutual, believe me. I'd never force myself on a woman, especially Tessie. I idolize her. She reminded me that we knew each other in the Middle Ages. During one of her past lives. She died before I had a chance to make her mine. So don't think I forced her into anything she didn't want to do. This is our destiny, and we're getting a second chance."

"If she comes out of this alive." She took a calming breath. "Tell me what happened."

"We were leaving my family's burial grounds. A beggar asked me for a handout. He punched me in the stomach and kicked me. Then he snatched her, and before I could fight back, they were gone." He laid his head in his hands and swiped at tears.

"Did you call the police?"

"Yes, they're on their way on board. I have to meet them at the hotel director's office. I caught a glimpse of the getaway car. It was a big black sedan, but they're probably miles away by now. I don't know how much the police can do."

"Oh, *Madonna mia*, help her." Mona trembled from her chattering teeth to her wobbly knees. "What if it's the Ball Busters? Will they hurt her?"

He shook his head. "She's not a target. They don't know she's one of us, and I'm sure she won't tell them. I can only hope they'll just pump her with questions and let her go. They want to know where we are—me, Fausto, the rest of us."

"We'll have to get her back ourselves if the police can't find her. We can't depend on the police." Her writer's mind whirring, she stood and paced the sitting area, taking long breaths to calm her racing pulse. She tried to lift a glass, but it slipped from her shaking hand. Instead, she grabbed the small pad and pen, scribbling to test it out. "Okay, tell me exactly what happened, and don't leave out a single detail."

****

Tessie couldn't believe what she was hearing. "You want me to what?" She knew what they'd said, but needed to hear it again, to make sure her mind wasn't playing tricks on her. Since she and Quintus united, nothing seemed real.

"Join us," Zanna repeated, calmly and patiently, like she was luring a child with a lollipop. "You have clout. You have the media at your disposal. You can preach the truth to the masses, instead of the falsehoods you've been ramming down their throats with those trashy books. You're guilty of spreading sin, and this is your chance to repent." She lowered the dagger by her side, and Tessie took a ragged breath.

"But I can't spend my life hunting vampires. There's nothing to hunt. They're harmless. Besides, what you're doing is illegal. You're nothing but a gang of vigilantes, and I don't mean the Guardian Angels."

Royal shook his head, tsked, and turned to his wife. "She doesn't understand what's at stake, pardon the pun. Life. Humanity." He once again faced Tessie and took another swig of Scotch. "Just your being here should make you realize this is now your calling. Everything happens for a reason, and we found you for the purpose of saving you. So that you can help us save the world."

She strained her neck, turning away from him and his stale breath. "No, you've got it all wrong! I'm not

108

capable of saving the world." Her destiny was with Quintus. She was now one of his kind, their souls forever fused, through the elixir of their past and present lives.

"You can do it, and you will." Zanna's eyes bored into hers. "If you can publish books glorifying and romanticizing that lifestyle, you can convince the world that vampires personify evil."

For a split second Tessie thought to surrender, promise to do as many books and public service announcements as they wanted. Anything to get out of this, to escape and return to her life with Quintus. Tears welled up in her eyes. He must be frantic! When Royal dragged her away, she didn't have a chance to look back. He could be lying dead on the sidewalk!

"What did you do to Quintus?" She didn't expect an honest answer, or any answer at all, but arguing with these maniacs was a waste of time. She'd think of some way out of this; meanwhile, she just wanted to think about him.

"Nothing." Zanna glanced toward the light, and Tessie saw a raised scar across her cheek. A jousting wound, maybe? "We couldn't handle the both of you at once. We'll get him later, now that we know where he is."

"How did you even know who he is?"

"The Fellowship has known him and Fausto and their cohorts for a long time. I realized I had psychic abilities when I was a child but never realized how valuable they were until I was older. When I joined the Fellowship, I developed my abilities with a gifted medium, and over the years I've honed them very well. Police departments call me to locate murder victims.

That's rewarding enough, but my heart is in hunting vampires." Zanna watched her husband take a sip of Scotch and roll it around his tongue. "But the Silvius clan is so established and seasoned, they've managed to elude us. They're crafty, switching ships mid-cruise, disappearing for months on end. But they're seldom more than a step ahead of me. This time I know we'll get them. It's the slippery ones who have the most to hide. They're the most harmful."

"If you're so psychic, why don't you know there's nothing harmful about the vast majority of vampires? They're God-fearing people!" she blurted, but then realized this was a battle of wills, and with them against her, she was outnumbered and outclassed. Maybe not outwitted, but still, it was them against her. Not only did they have the upper hand, a six-inch dagger waved around in it.

"Stop defending them!" Zanna smacked her palm with the dagger, rattling her junky charm bracelet. "You're brainwashed, don't you understand? You're a product of their conditioning."

"No, you are." Tessie heaved a deep breath. "Oh, forget it, why am I wasting my time? Not like I'm going anyplace." She gathered up all her energy and prayed. The police would find her. Sooner or later. And these righteous jackasses would be carted off to an Italian jail, where the meals were more like British fare. That alone would be punishment enough.

"You don't have much time left to waste. We need you just like you need us," Royal urged. "It's not like you have a choice here, Teresa."

She'd worn this tight low-cut sweater to look sexy for Quintus. Now she wished she wasn't exposing half of her Grand Tetons to Mr. Big here. Then Zanna approached her and did something that made her wonder what the hell was coming next: she took her hand and admired her red and silver striped nails. "I always wanted nails like this," Zanna said sadly, looking at her own chewed, ragged nails as she released Tessie's hand.

"You want them? Then untie me and you can have them. They're fake."

Zanna hesitated, as if deciding whether a set of fake nails was worth freeing her hostage.

"C'mon, Zan, it's not like I can jump out the window."

Zanna untied the bonds and Tessie peeled off one plastic nail after another until all ten were off. Zanna, with a look of delight like she'd won at Bingo, held out her hand as Tessie spilled the acrylics into her palm. "But you provide the glue."

Tessie saw Zanna's smug grin as she gave Tessie's nails a glance, looking no better than hers.

"I can give you an awesome manicure," Tessie offered. "All we have to do is find a drugstore."

"Tomorrow. After you've agreed to our terms."

A thought hit her like a smack across the face. She could get out of this and turn these fools' destinies around at the same time.

****

Mona looked over her scribbled notes, each point bulleted. "Old guy dressed like a bum, expensive gold cross around his neck, sloppy Italian speech. Fat. Woman behind a black car's wheel, saint on dashboard. A few things don't jibe here." Mona wiped her trembling hands and lifted the amaretto bottle she'd

111

bought earlier. She poured a shot and knocked it back. It warmed her instantly. "*Bibita*?" She held the bottle up to Quintus.

"*No, grazie*." He shook his head. "Just tell me what your writer's mind came up with."

She tapped the pen on the pad. "I'm working as if I'm creating characters for one of my suspense novels. If the guy was wearing bling around his neck, and he's fat, and hauled her off in a car, it's obvious he's not poor. He wasn't a bum. He was one of the hunters."

"Well, duuuuh." Quintus went for that shot of amaretto he'd turned down before.

"Look, you have to deduce the obvious first, get those out of the way. That paves the way for the more obscure clues. *Capisce?* The cross and the saint on the dash also tells us they're religious. So, chances are they're Ball Busters, not just members of that kooky Fellowship. And him being fat also tells us he's American, as does the crappy Italian grammar."

"How will that help us find her?" He spread his fingers.

"At least it's something we can tell the police. Maybe they can track these clowns through the airlines, see who's flown into Rome or Naples recently. If he's been living here, his Italian would be a lot better. Just ideas to begin with." She got her cell phone from the nightstand. "I have Tessie's number programmed in, but if she's being held hostage in some God-awful cave, she won't be answering her phone."

"At least we can let her know we contacted the police and we're looking for her." Quintus cracked his knuckles one at a time as she connected her phone and jabbed the buttons. Tessie's voice mail came on.

"Hi, Tess." Mona swallowed hard and cleared her throat. "Just sit tight. We'll find you, I promise. I love you, girlfriend." Not knowing what else to say, she disconnected. "God, I hope she's all right." She turned to him again. "What happens if she doesn't feed for a while?"

"A while can be up to two weeks. But when we don't feed from loved ones, or if we don't have a current loved one, we turn to our supply. We all contribute to it. That sustains us. The blood is all from the same gene pool, so to speak."

"What if you're isolated, like she is, and the gene pool isn't available?" She began digging in the dresser drawer for some clothes.

"She'll have to feed from whoever's available."

"She would be like the vampires you've been battling to disprove for the last two thousand years?" She pulled out underwear and a pair of socks.

"I'm just conjecturing here. It's never happened. None of us has ever been in that situation where we didn't have access to the family blood supply."

"No one has ever been marooned on a ship in the middle of the ocean, or on a desert island, or imprisoned?" He had to be mistaken. "You're from a long line of sea dogs. Somebody must have been marooned someplace."

"Not without falling in love. We do fall in love easily. That's part of our genetic makeup, too. In case you never noticed." He fixed his eye on her, and she let him know she noticed, all right.

"Yeah, you guys sure are hopeless romantics." She headed for the bathroom to get dressed.

"It's been bred in us, for survival, I suppose."

"So she might fall in love with her captor."

"Or he with her. Which is infinitely more likely."
He sank down onto her vanity chair and poured himself
another shot.

"Let's just hope it's a he." There she was, the
eternal cynic, just like Fausto always said.

"Oh, it was, all right. He's the one who grabbed her
from me. A lot of flab under those seedy duds, but built
like a brick...pizza oven. He sucker-punched me. I
didn't have a split second to jump him or throw my
weight on him or anything." He downed the shot. "I
wish I could've gotten the damn plate number, but it
was getting dark. He had a black sedan, though, I can
swear to that."

"If they don't find her, we will. Even if I have to
get Julianna to help us." She had no idea how efficient
the Italian police were, so it was safe to stay on the
cynical side.

"Yeah, sometimes psychics and cops solve cases
together. On television, anyway," he said.

She sighed. "Oh, if only I knew some mob
figures..."

He let out a sardonic snicker. "Yeah, when all else
fails, Cosa Nostra to the rescue."

"I'll get dressed and come with you to talk to the
cops." She went into the bathroom, finished drying off,
and pulled her clothes on, nearly breaking her legs, she
was shaking so much.

She grabbed her purse, laced up her running shoes,
and they headed down the corridor.

As they took the stairs, she halted in her tracks.
"Wait! I got it!" The idea was so sudden, it nearly
knocked her over. The connection fit together like the

pieces of a puzzle. Her mind racing, she dug her cell phone out of her purse. "What's directory assistance for Naples?"

"Eight-nine-two-eight-nine-two. Why?"

"I know some people in New York who have relatives in Naples, the D'Alessios. Two of the brothers run a restaurant here called Fratello's. If they can't help, nobody can."

"Why would they be able to help?" His voice was heavy with despair but carried a lilt of hope.

"Because they're a rather influential family, if you know about influential Italian families. I know I'm grasping at straws, but that family doesn't exactly respect every law of the land. They made a few of their own. They ran Staten Island in the fifties and sixties, and one of them, Greg, is an author. He writes sci-fi using his thinly disguised experience as backdrops for his storylines."

She connected her phone and punched the buttons.

Quintus nodded, his eyes shining. "I'd like to see her captors swimming with the baccala off the Amalfi coast. I don't know how good these D'Alessio brothers are at tracking down hunters, though."

She finally connected with directory assistance. "Napoli, Ristorante Fratello."

They automatically connected her, and she hoped her conversational Italian would get her though this. "*Pronto, sono Mona Rossi da New York. Vorrei parlare con Franco o Luigi, per favore.*"

"*Bella* Mona! This is Luigi. How are you, you beautiful rose among Brooklyn thorns?" He remembered her, all right. She also remembered him hitting on her in a classy kind of way, offering to fly her to St. Croix for a weekend on his chartered yacht, but she was still married. And like the gentleman he was, he'd accepted it, but made it clear the invitation was always open "when you crave a taste of *la dolce vita.*" She hoped he didn't think she was calling because she had a craving now. So, skipping the small talk, she explained Tessie's capture. Then she begged him, very politely, to help.

"Come to the ristorante, *cara.* Northwest corner of Via Antonio Lo Surdo. Across from Pizza Hut."

Mona and Quintus walked to the ship's reception area. Two policemen came out of the hotel director's office, and an assistant ushered them all into a stuffy room.

Too weak to stand, she sat in one of the two metal folding chairs. A fax machine and an old computer monitor provided the only other furnishings. She clamped down on her fear with gut-wrenching breaths as the police grilled them. They didn't play any games like good cop/bad cop but gave her overactive imagination a nudge. Did they consider her or Quintus suspects? She knew kidnappings were rampant in Italy, so by the police's way of thinking, Quintus might be in on it.

But he proclaimed his innocence and didn't protest too much.

With a warning to stay aboard during the investigation, the officers flipped their notebooks shut and left them alone in the windowless room.

Quintus wearily rubbed the back of his neck. Mona wished she had a masseuse working her neck, too. The tension was kinking her muscles. "Does Fausto know about this?" she asked.

"He's probably asleep. He's working a double shift."

"I want him to come with us." She stood, steadied herself, and opened the door. Even after a gulp of air, she fought the urge to collapse. "I don't think he'll mind if we wake him. You doctors are used to emergencies."

"Yeah, but I can't keep that emotional detachment now." He sounded desperate, and she gave him a reassuring hug.

They'll find her, she kept saying to herself, and would keep saying it until she believed it.

"Let me tell you something, Mona." They walked through the reception area to the midship stairway. At the foot of the stairs, he stopped her and looked straight at her. "And don't shut me up until I finish."

"I won't."

He led the way up the stairs.

"You might think we have a whirlwind courtship here, Tessie and I, but we've known each other a long time. And when we finally had some private time, we both knew it was for real, especially when she reminded me that we'd been together in one of her past lives."

She nodded as they climbed.

"So it wasn't just the consummation of our lust. We really love each other. We've loved each other through more than one lifetime. I know it can happen, so I think you should take a look at your relationship with Fausto. He's in love with you, *cara*. And although he managed to drag himself onto this cruise, he's still submerged in grief. He'll never need you more than he does now. Our loved ones can be snatched away in a minute. It happened to him, it just happened to me. So catch him while you can."

Of course he was right. Her BFF had joined the vampire world, and now her life was in danger. But Tessie had thought it was worth it.

So why can't I? Mona asked herself again.

"Quintus, you know I love Fausto with all my heart, but I'm not ready to make the ultimate sacrifice like Tessie just did."

"What makes you think it's a sacrifice? When you give yourself to someone you love, vampire or mortal, you don't lose anything. You gain so much more. Think about it, Mona."

When they reached the Madrid Deck, he led her down the corridor and knocked on Fausto's stateroom door. The poor guy had a heavy work schedule, and she hated waking him, but she needed him now more than when Ted had left her.

When he opened the door, her heart froze. His tousled hair looked as if some ardent lover had grabbed it in a frenzy of ecstasy. He wore pajama bottoms with no top, a splaying of silky black hair across his muscular chest. A shadow of stubble grazed his chin and upper lip. He blinked, and she fell into his arms. "What's wrong?" He held her, and his warm familiar embrace eased her frantic heartbeat.

"It's Tessie," Mona said.

"Tessie got abducted by hunters, right from under me." Quintus nudged past them into the sitting room. "I couldn't move fast enough to save her." He gazed out the window into blackness.

"Oh, *Madonna mia*. When did this happen?"

She eased out of the embrace, and he closed the door behind them. She saw the rumpled bed in the next room. Morbid curiosity made her peek. It was empty. Her shoulders lowered. Taking a relieved breath, she looked away. So what if he had a woman in there? She hadn't committed to him. Still, a tinge of jealousy niggled at her.

"About forty minutes ago," she said. "We're going to go see some people I know who live here. They said they'd try to help us. The cops just questioned us and told us not to leave the ship. I don't think disguises will work this time, with security so tight. But I may have a way to work around that. Fausto, will you be able to come with us?"

He glanced at his bare wrist. "What time is it?"

Mona checked her watch. "Almost eight."

He pressed his hand to his head, thinking. "I go on duty at ten. I'll phone one of the doctors to be on call if I'm not back in time."

"Oh, thank God there are enough doctors on board." She sighed in relief. "My friends run a restaurant not far from here, Fratello's."

He nodded sleepily and retreated to the bedroom to get dressed. "That sounds familiar. What's their name?"

She hung back in the sitting room with Quintus. "Franco and Luigi D'Alessio."

He came back out, wearing jeans and holding a pair of black socks. "The D brothers of Napoli? You know the D brothers? Why didn't you tell me?"

She shook her head and shrugged. "I only met them a few times. They're from Manhattan, friends of my father. They have a restaurant on Mulberry Street called Three Guys from Italy, but I phoned the local D brothers at Fratello's. Why do you ask?"

He perched on the edge of a lounge chair and

pulled on his socks, still looking at her. "They're a big mob family, Mona."

She rolled her eyes. "No shit, Sherlock. I know they run a few things around here and in Manhattan."

"Run a few things?" He shook his head and went back inside. He came out buttoning a shirt. "They practically reign over Naples. The family *capo* is Bruiso D'Alessio, or Dirty Neck Bruiso in the inner circles. He's in his seventies now, but the sons took over. The D brothers go on a lot of the cruises I work. You met one of them, Quin. Remember Ciro, the big loud guy on the Med-Black Sea run who kept singing "O Sole Mio" off key and bought everybody shots at the captain's table? He offered to buy the ship, but Captain Mangiano spent half the night convincing him it wasn't for sale."

"Oh, that was him?" Quintus grinned. "And what happened to Captain Mangiano? I never saw him after that."

Fausto didn't reply, he only gave Quintus a long look and opened his closet.

"I don't know who Ciro is," she said as Fausto took his coat off the hanger. "Just Luigi and Franco. They seemed like nice guys. Luigi was a real gentleman when I met him." She didn't blab more than that.

"And there's something else about them you probably don't know." He combed his fingers through his hair.

"What? What can possibly pack more of a punch than being in Napoli's premiere mob family?"

He looked straight at her and looked deeply into her eyes. "They're members of our family, too, Mona."

"They're—" Her jaw dropped, and her hands

fluttered. He grasped them in his and gave them a comforting squeeze.

"Yes, they're another branch of the Silvius tree. We don't see one another that often, but we're very well acquainted."

"How many of you are there in the world, Fausto?" Mona had never found out about his extended family. She had no idea the family tree was this vast.

"A few thousand descendants walk the earth today. We're distant cousins, but close friends. Most of us intermarry."

Quintus let out a low whistle. "Our family's bigger than I thought. Imagine, mob figures in our sweet innocent vampire clan. I hope they don't give the family a bad name." He forced a jocular tone.

"Because of them our reputation's in the sink," Fausto quipped, and it made her realize if the Ball Busters were after the D brothers for vampirism, they were after them for the wrong reasons.

"So, how are we going to get off the ship?" Quintus asked. "We're practically under house arrest here."

Mona smiled and took out her cell phone. "It pays to know people like the D brothers. And it pays even better to be related to them." She hit the redial button. "Ciao again, Louie."

Chapter Eight:
Trapped

Tessie knew she had to get Zanna out of there. If only she had a sugar jolt from sucking the cream out of a cannoli, her thinking would be razor sharp. Or dagger sharp, as she glanced at the gleaming weapon resting on its plushy pillow like a pampered pet.

"Zanna..." Her voice dripped with artificial sweetener. "I know where one of the Silvius clan is. And you can easily track him down because unlike the others, he flaunts who he is defiantly and flamboyantly."

"Who?" She twirled to face Tessie and moved in on her until their noses nearly touched. "Somebody I don't yet know about? It can't be. If he's flamboyant and defiant, I've either tracked him down to within a hair on his head, or already obliterated him."

Now isn't that a bit flippy, Tessie thought, *even for her*. "He's Fausto's half-brother, Justus. You've probably never had a vision about him because he's a recluse. He lives on his own Greek island. Sharing a cruise ship with two thousand people is slumming it to him. He has a hundred-twenty-foot yacht, the *Stunato*, docked there in the harbor. He doesn't look all that much like Fausto. Their mother was Swedish. He's..." Unable to get her imagination going, she described her ex. "...tall and skinny. Well, more like scrawny, with a droopy mustache. And speaks with a New York accent so thick, you can cut it with—" She stopped herself, not wanting to mention anything that cut. But she'd just cast one stone that, if this plan worked, would kill two birds. Well, one bird and one vulture. "But of course he uses an assumed name. Joe Bozzone." Her ex's name tasted like bile on her lips. She almost needed to spit...but this was the least of the tasks she'd have to perform.

Royal gave his wife an encouraging nod. "Can be the consolation prize, if you don't nab Fausto this time around."

Zanna tapped one of her chewed-up nails against a chipped front tooth. "It's a way to bide my time and hone my talents while waiting for the big payoff." She went for her coat. "But it doesn't mean you're off the hook, cookie. You still have two choices. One: join us. Two: or else." She turned to her husband. "I'll be back later, sweetums. Keep an eye on this chippie." She blew Royal a kiss and swept out with her carpetbag in a cloud of incense and Scotch—two mainstays of her virtuous cult.

"Oh, I'll keep an eye on her, all right. And maybe a hand..." He stepped closer to Tessie, leaning down to play with a tendril of her hair. "Very clever ruse to get her out of here." Scotch fumes assaulted her, and she strained to turn away.

"I don't know what you're talking about. Fausto's half-brother *is* on his yacht in the harbor."

"Well, either way, it grabbed her. Now we can grab each other."

This'll be easier than I thought. She didn't have much time, so she forced herself to get this sickening episode over with.

****

"It was nice of Louie to bribe some 'brothers' to let us leave the ship, wasn't it?" Mona commented as they approached Fratello's.

"These guys didn't get rich and powerful by being nice, Mona," Fausto answered.

Heading to Fratello's, they descended a flight of ancient stone steps, smelling the mustiness of ages gone by. As they rushed through the door, they entered a lively old-world style bistro. Arched brick passages surrounded them. Candles glowed atop red and white checkered tablecloths. Mona scanned the room for Luigi. "Come on, Louie, where are you?" Her fists clenched around her scarf. A band played "Volare." Serving girls delivered steaming plates of pasta. Dressed in traditional Italian costume of bright red or green skirts, laced-up vests, and circlets of flowers atop their heads, they brightened the cavernous room. Laughing, wine-sipping, hand-gesturing patrons sat at every table. Blazing torches threw flickering shadows across the stone walls, creating a medieval ambience.

Finally, she spotted Luigi talking to a willowy waitress. He dismissed her with a swat on the behind and approached them, kissing Mona's hand, then giving Fausto and Quintus bear hugs. Fingers of silver streaked his raven pompadour.

"Louie..." With trembling hands, she clutched his lapels, not wanting to rumple his black silk tie or disturb his Italy-shaped gold clip with a diamond chip where Naples was located. "They took her...in a car..." She gasped, her throat parched and painful.

"Calm down, *cara*." He turned and snapped his

fingers. Instantly, a waiter appeared with a glass of red wine. She thanked him and took a sip.

While she was catching her breath, Quintus explained what happened. "My fiancée, Tessie, got abducted by hunters tonight."

Luigi shook his head, swore in dialect, and clasped his hands as if in prayer, moving them back and forth. "Where from?"

"Outside my family's burying ground, in a black sedan," Quintus replied. "They're holding her somewhere. Do any of the hunters live around here that you know of?"

"Some of the priests and their cohorts have homes here. That's probably where they went," Luigi said. "The hunters have been in bed with the Church since Constantine's time. Then the Vatican jumped aboard. It's like one of those mob families." He turned to her and smiled. "It's all right, Mona, we'll find the *capodicazzi*. Come on." He led them out the back door onto a patio, past empty tables stacked with overturned chairs. An old garage stood between two scraggly trees. He pulled a door opener from his pocket, pressed the button, and the door slid open on rattling runners. Inside sat a white Cadillac and a small fleet of motor scooters. He gave them each helmets and lifted keys off wall hooks.

"My niece Vivianna can help you. Just follow me."

They strapped on their helmets, and she climbed on the scooter behind Fausto, leaning into him and wrapping her arms around his waist. She pressed her cheek against his back, shut her eyes, and snuggled into him, comforted.

"I want them found before they harm Tessie," she

begged.

"Somehow I don't think they'll harm Tessie," Luigi said. "The Ball Busters will pull their usual shenanigans: use her as bait to lure out the vampires because she's not one."

"But she is one," Quintus said. "As of a few hours ago."

"*Mannaggia la sfaccimma*," Luigi swore under his breath. "All right, what's one more complication? *Andiamo!*" Let's go!

Luigi revved up his engine and zoomed out of the garage. Quintus followed, with Fausto close behind.

"But they don't yet know she's one of us?" Luigi asked as they stopped for a light.

Fausto pulled up alongside him, and she said, "No. She fed from Quintus just before it happened."

"All right then. When Vivianna became undead, she developed clairvoyant powers," Luigi said. "That's starting to happen with the younger ones. They feed from the vampires of our bloodline and become infused with certain talents."

"How does that happen?" she heard Quintus ask.

"After being bled, the ones who take longer to wake up develop mystical powers as vampires. Some become clairvoyant, some can cast spells. Nobody's done scientific research on it, but we believe it's an element in the blood that's evolved over the centuries. It varies person to person, but Vivianna is highly gifted. And so are two of my *nipoti*." An air of pride raised his tone. "My younger one, Franco, is only ten, yet he reads Tarot cards like a seasoned pro. We keep it in the family because I don't want him exploited, but he hopes to become a detective. There won't be an unsolved crime in all of Napoli then."

"How many of us—I mean them—are like that?" Quintus asked. "Because no one in our circles is."

"Unless they keep it to themselves," Fausto remarked. "With powers like that, the Church would brand us as witches and start the witch hunts all over again."

"Vivianna doesn't keep it to herself." Luigi shook his head. "She owns a store called *Luna Lavanda*. She sells crystals, incense, jewelry, books on witchcraft, magic, all that paraphernalia. More Americans than Italians shop there. That's where we're going now. I thought of her right after you called, and she's meeting us there." The light changed, and they leaned into a sharp turn down a narrow side street.

"Why would they want Tessie and not me?" Quintus's voice echoed through the night as they whizzed past parked cars and over bumpy manhole covers.

"She's an easier target," Fausto called back to him. "They couldn't get both of you at once, so figured it would be easier to take just her. For now." Mona leaned against Fausto, hugging him tight. She knew they were all nervous wrecks, with only each other to lean on.

Luigi slowed to a stop at another red light, and the others idled beside him.

"I've always known if they want me, they'll get me." Quintus looked up at the sky and let out a breath of steam. "I can't run from them forever."

"They'll get me, too, eventually," Fausto agreed. "But once they do, it's up to us to protect ourselves. My family wasn't prepared. They thought they'd never get captured, because they were business tycoons. But their profile was too high. Despite the bodyguards and the electronic gates and the bulletproof cars, they flaunted their wealth. That drove the hunters wild. My family bringing outsiders into their realm infuriated them. I'm safer devoting my time to my profession, with as little leisure time as possible."

"You think they killed your family because they were rich?" Mona asked over his shoulder. "You never told me this before."

"Some of us are bigger targets than others. They'd kill wealthy partygoers before they'll kill a doctor, but they hate us all equally. That's why I know none of us is safe."

Just then the light turned. Luigi revved his engine and zoomed up the street.

He pulled up at a storefront on the ground floor of a swanky apartment building. An elegant sign reading *Luna Lavanda* graced the store's window. They chained their scooters to a lamppost and pulled off their helmets, hanging them from the handlebars. Luigi smoothed his hair, went up, and rang a doorbell. A buzzer went off, and he opened the door to an elegant lobby, a chandelier casting a gleam over the marble foyer.

A young woman galloped down the curved staircase, arms outstretched. She embraced Luigi with the customary two-cheek kiss. "*Ah, Zio Louie! Sono contento di riverderti!*" she greeted him in a singsong voice.

He turned and introduced his niece. "*Vivi, presento Mona, Fausto, and Quintus.*"

"*Molto lieta.*" Vivianna nodded to each of them and squeezed their hands.

Oh, no, don't tell me she doesn't speak English, Mona worried, but her fears, about that anyway, vanished when Vivianna started chatting in fluent English. "I'm so sorry to hear about your friend"—Vivianna turned to Quintus—"and your beloved, but I already have a feeling I know where she is."

"Ah, mille grazie, cara." Quintus clasped her hands and kissed them repeatedly. She didn't do anything to discourage him.

"Andiamo. Come with me." She turned and gestured over her shoulder. Her long blonde-streaked hair swung in time with her hips as she led them through her store, past counters displaying jewelry, gemstones, and shelves lined with books. A sweet flowery fragrance enveloped them. "What kind of incense is that?" Mona asked as they reached the back. Vivianna unlocked a door with a card key.

"Ah, that is the blend of twelve years of incense of every fragrance." She inhaled deeply as she pulled open the door. Mona glanced into the gaping maw at a steep stone stairway that spiraled downwards, as in a castle tower. Vivianna flipped a switch. A dim light flickered on, throwing shadows over the stone walls. "Follow me."

The air grew danker with every step they descended. Mona coughed. There was no banister, so she held the rough wall with her hand. A cold coat of slime wet her palm. She shivered as they sank into catacombs right out of a Poe tale.

The stairwell plunged on and on. Each step brought them closer to the bowels of the earth, mold growing in green patches. Mona pressed a hand to her dizzying head as they spiraled farther down. The thickening musty air nearly choked her. Gasping, she stopped to take a few gulps. Fausto, directly behind her, placed his hands on her shoulders, instantly warming her. "You all right?" he whispered, and she nodded.

Another deep breath spurred a coughing fit. The curving stairs grew steeper, more challenging to descend. She eased one foot at a time. *Please don't let me fall, please don't let me fall...*, she pleaded silently. Her legs trembled, her footing uneven over the crooked steps, the centers worn smooth from centuries of use.

"Where are we going, Vivianna?" Mona called, her voice echoing off the damp walls and dying in the passageway's depths.

"Where I do my readings. No need to worry, we're almost there," she answered over her shoulder. The jingling of keys rang out. Mona's imagination sparked flashes of guards dragging a screaming prisoner down these stairs to a cold, dark dungeon. She not only imagined, she *tasted* the bitter fear of impending doom. Sweat soaked her back. She shivered. As the catacombs grew frigid, she sensed a connection to a long-departed soul who'd paced these very steps on the way to a torturous death. She reached back for Fausto. His warmth seeped into her cold hands.

"You're freezing, Mona." She nodded, knowing that after they found Tessie, they could lounge on the deck sipping stregas and laugh about all this.

She struck that thought. Who knew when she'd laugh again?

Finally, the stairs ended and they stood on a hard earth floor. Vivianna lit a candle. Eerie shadows crept across brick walls that curved to form an arched ceiling, not much higher than their heads. Claustrophobia gripped Mona. Sheer panic flooded her. Her heart pounding, she gripped Fausto's arm. This wasn't Disneyland; what if they got trapped down here?

Vivianna lit more candles and handed one to each of them. "This is where I give my readings." Her whispery voice died in the stale air. Mona wanted to ask why she was whispering but didn't dare. A bone-chilling portent told her why: so she wouldn't disturb any lurking spirits. She sensed a hostile presence watching. As she glanced behind her, the hairs on her nape stood up.

Vivianna led them down the shoulder-width passageway. It made a sharp left turn. The darkness and earth entombed them. As they emerged into a larger space, Mona gasped at the horrid sight before her. Skeletons of every size lay flat or stood propped up. Torn, moth-eaten clothes hung from their frames, the remains of black funeral jackets, Sunday suits, and frilly skirts rotted from the ravages of age. Inches from her, the yellowed shards of a satin wedding gown and veil clung to an emaciated, mummified body. Detached skulls, their macabre grins daring her to come closer, lined a niche in the wall. Mona swayed and nearly fainted. Fausto steadied her, but her wobbly knees threatened to send her tumbling.

"Mona, Fausto, Quintus, this is the family burial chamber," Vivianna announced cheerily, like a Realtor showing a kitchen.

Moldy, damp and spooky, the chamber reeked of death. A terrifying fear crept up on her: *What if we suffocate down here?*

"We've been burying family down here since a hundred years B.C.," Luigi explained. "None of these

people died natural deaths. They were all murdered—
by hunters." His solemn voice triggered sorrow, as if
delivering a eulogy. He stood before a skeleton laid out
on the ground and bowed his head. "This was our
ancestor Leonius. He lived during Julius Caesar's reign.
Hunters murdered him at age twenty, and just as they
were about to burn him, family members rescued the
corpse and brought it here. But first they killed the
hunters and cast their bodies into the sea. He was the
earliest of our ancestors to die at their hands. Tradition
holds that his spirit watches over us. I've felt his
ghostly presence many times when a hunter was
nearby, giving me a mental push to flee, or grab my
weapon." He opened his jacket and revealed a holster.
Mona knew gangsters were always armed, but this
wasn't everyday Mafia business he was talking about.

"Sit on the floor, and make yourselves
comfortable," Vivianna offered. "I'll infuse you with
my energy, and together we can visualize where Tessie
might be." Vivianna sat cross-legged on the ground,
dripping candle wax into a holder and twisting her
candle into it. She gave candles to each of them. One
glance at her casual slacks made Mona glad she hadn't
put on her good ankle pants this morning, but she knew
she'd never wear these slacks again. Once she got back
to the ship, these duds were going overboard.

They sat in a circle, as if at a séance. She'd been to
a few of those, and heard rappings, thumps and bangs,
but chalked it up to special effects. A high-priced Park
Avenue séance could produce anything short of Conan
the Barbarian breaking through the wall.

"Hold hands, and close your eyes," Vivianna said.
Some irrational fear told Mona the staircase would

disappear, so she didn't dare close hers.

"Brrr, I feel a cold draft." Quintus shuddered, rubbing his arms. "It's passing right by me. The temperature dropped."

"That's the spirits," Vivianna explained. "They draw energy and take the heat from their surroundings."

Mona slid closer to Fausto, away from the cold spot, shivering, but not from the cold. This place spooked her like no haunted castle ever had.

"We are here to channel our energies toward you, Tessie," Vivianna chanted. "In order to rescue you, we need you to give us a sign that you have not been harmed, and can guide us to you with your powers of perception."

Mona forced herself to picture Tessie in her mind's eye, the mismatched blue and green contacts, the way she adjusted her "twins" under her tight sweaters, her high-pitched cackle. A few seconds passed. The packed earth beneath her was hard and uninviting. She sensed a hostility from the disturbed spirits. She ached to tear ass up the stairs, return to the street, and breathe clean air again. But without warning, she saw a scene in her mind, more vivid than a movie. She gasped. "I see Tess! She's sitting in an attic, her eyes are big with fright, her hands are trembling, she's gasping in short breaths." Mona's teeth chattered as she shared Tessie's fear and revulsion.

"I see her, too." Vivianna's calm voice filled the space. "She's with a man, and she's forcing herself to stay with him, although she's desperate to escape. But she can't. They're locked in."

"Is she all right?" Quintus's voice wavered.

"She's not harmed," Vivianna replied. "She looks

out the window, but it's shut. A woman locked them in. I think it's his wife."

Mona sputtered—because of Tessie or the stale musty air, she didn't know. But at that instant the hairs stood up at her nape. "Tessie's captor is a hunter!" she blurted out.

"Please, Mona, what does he look like?" Quintus begged her. "Can you see him clearly?"

"Yeah…I see a vague outline…he's corpulent, he's bald with a bad comb-over and tacky spray-on hair, his face is ruddy from boozing. I feel Tessie is horrified but knows what she has to do…" She gasped. "Oh no! She's gonna feed from him!"

Mona scrambled to her feet, her shoes sliding in the hard dirt, but Fausto planted strong hands on her shoulders and held her down.

"It's all right," Vivianna soothed. "She'll be fine. She'll feed from him, and he'll become one of us. He'll appear to die for a while, then he'll feed from her. She'll return to you, and those hunters will *loathe* having one of us among their cloister!" A sardonic, self-satisfied rasp escaped her lips. "Good girl, Tessie. That'll be one less hunter stalking us."

"Can you pinpoint with any more accuracy where they might be?" Quintus asked.

Straining in the flickering candlelight, Mona saw that his eyes pierced Vivianna. "Please, we need to find her before she gets hurt." He clutched her arm.

Vivianna shook her head, vexation creasing her features. "All I can see is that the house is next to a church. It doesn't have a steeple, though, like a traditional church."

"There must be a thousand churches in Naples."

Quintus's voice lowered in defeat. "We'll never find her. Nothing against you, Vivianna, but Naples is a big place. We'd better just rely on the police."

"*Aspettate!* Wait!" They all jumped. "I'm concentrating on the church. I see a basketball. But what's that got to do with a church?" Vivianna let out an exasperated breath, pulled her hands free, and pressed them to her head. She rocked back and forth, mumbling in Italian. "No, no, please don't tell me I'm losing my powers!"

Luigi leaned over and hugged her. "It's all right, *cara*, you aren't losing your powers. This is very difficult. Maybe you're concentrating too hard."

Mona's visions and feelings vanished. She prayed to Saint Anthony. "Please let us find Tessie," she begged the patron saint of lost things, hoping it applied to people, too.

"Basketball..." Luigi leaned forward, his face contorted with concentration. He shook his head in defeat, but snapped his fingers. His eyes lit up. "That's it! La Santissima Trinita Church was also a gymnasium for the school. I went to the first mass they held there. I remember it so clearly because I laughed at the circles and lines on the hardwood floor—it was a basketball court. My father backhanded me, telling me it was a sin to laugh in church. The house must be right near there."

Now everyone's eyes greeted Luigi's in response.

"Is it a crowded area?" Quintus asked.

Luigi nodded. "Every area in Napoli is crowded, but we'll find her. At least we've narrowed it down to a reasonable radius." He leaned over and gave his niece a warm hug. "Thank you, Vivi. You saved the day for these nice people."

Vivianna looked up and smoothed her hair from her face. "Oh, I don't know how much I helped you yet. We still have to find her."

"We'll take you with us. If that's okay with you," Quintus said.

"Of course." They all stood, brushing dust and clods of earth from their legs.

Mona curled her moist hands into fists, anxious to get out of there. As they headed single file for the climb back up the stone stairway, she kept her eyes downcast, averted from the gruesome sights. She'd never put much stock in ghosts or ghouls or anything that went bump in the night—if they existed, fine, as long as they didn't bother her. But this place creeped her out like nowhere she'd ever been before. She'd inhaled the dust of medieval torture chambers, traipsed through graveyards of witch-hunt victims in Salem, climbed the hill facing Vlad Dracul's palace at midnight, plodded across Gettysburg Battlefield in winter's howling wind...but never sensed a presence or glimpsed a shadow.

Now, after feeling the Silvius burial chamber's lurking spirits, she was a believer.

Chapter Nine:
Back For Seconds

Tessie glanced over at the villa's windows, thankful the shutters were open. Tiled rooftops reflected the moonlight, and to the right stood a squat brick building, an eyesore among the medieval architecture. Probably a gym. Instead of hurling herself three stories down, she could stick her head out and scream bloody murder. Would some kindhearted Italian citizen take pity and call Napoli's finest? She hoped these *paesani* were more willing to get involved than New Yorkers. Knowing Zanna would soon realize Joe Bozzone and his yacht didn't exist, she had to act fast.

With Royal ogling prominent parts of her anatomy, she'd have no trouble pulling off her repulsive stunt. "May I open that window please?" she asked in her sweetest honeydripper voice as he settled his behind into a creaking chair with a refilled highball glass. His twenty-gallon gut poured out of his shirt as he unbuttoned it.

"Windows don't open. They're built into the casement. You want a drink?"

She shook her head, her stomach knotted. *Please, God*, she silently begged. *Let him knock back the whole bottle and get so snockered, I'll step over him and haul ass out of here.*

But he shot that prayer straight to purgatory.

"Zanna locked us in here. Apparently she doesn't trust you. So don't think of escaping."

"Locked in?" A vague memory teased the fringes of her mind. She'd been locked in before. The same musty air thickened her lungs, the cloying dampness made her skin sticky. Sweat trickled down her back the way it had then. Familiar claws of claustrophobia clutched her throat. Her eyes roved the garret, and a horrible scene exploded through her mind in vivid detail. "We're locked in? We'll suffocate! We'll starve!"

"We will not. It's ventilated, and we have figs." He plucked one from a pile on a plate, gnawed on it, spat out the unchewed part, and pointed upwards to an intake vent. Whoever renovated this charming piece of real estate had the initiative to install A/C. "Come on, toots, let's enjoy each other's company." He gave her a gaptoothed smile that shriveled her nipples.

"Ooh, yeah, baby." She forced a velvety, seductive drone into her voice.

She didn't want to play cat and mouse, or drag it out. She just wanted to get this over with. But the buildup was as crucial as the outcome, just like a good romantic suspense novel. Without the romance.

"Roy, there's something unusual about my background. I lived several previous lives in the Middle Ages. In one life, I spied on King Henry the Sixth and his obnoxious queen for Edward, who became the next king. Edward was prepared to oust Henry from the throne and place him under arrest. I was a decoy where Henry resided, in Greenwich. But being my first assignment, I got careless about it. One of the servers saw me listening at the keyhole to Henry's chamber and ratted on me to a knight." He listened intently. "The knight dragged me to a dilapidated old house in London and locked me in the airless garret. Of course there was no A/C in 1475, and I wasted away there, with nothing but figs and lukewarm drinks for my sustenance. Like we have here." She gestured to the figs and Scotch bottle, leaving out one crucial detail.

"And what was the point to all that?" He yawned, hiking up his pants. "I don't need a history lesson."

But it would all make sense in the end. If her plan worked.

"When Zanna waved that dagger at me, I knew I'd seen it before. I was reliving that long-ago life. You see, Henry's knight who arrested me, Percival—Percy, he made me take the blame in his murderous plot. He held me at knifepoint with a dagger exactly like that one. It might even be that one. It's old, isn't it?"

"Yes, it's the dagger my ancestor Percival Dudley used to kill Henry."

She blinked in amazement. "I knew it. It's the same Percival. Did it ever occur to you that you may be the reincarnation of your ancestor, Percival?"

He shook his head. His gobbler chins jiggled. "Never. I don't believe in reincarnation. That's a temptation from Satan." He crossed himself, mumbling "In the name of the Father and of the Son..."

She wouldn't waste any more time telling him the whole story, but it came to her in a flash why she was here. Now she knew what to do. Mad King Henry had been a vampire. A bite from Percival Dudley...

Percival, her lover at that time, was a mercenary, hired to kill Henry. When she got arrested in that life, Percival fed on her and made her a vampiress in her prison cell, stabbed Henry in the heart, and framed her for the murder. While he ran off to support the newly crowned Edward, she starved to death in that cell. Percival Dudley cared only about money and didn't give a rat's ass how many lives he wasted. As she clung to life, weak and emaciated, she vowed retaliation. That's why she was here—to see divine justice done on Percival's reincarnation. She and Quintus were destined for each other—she'd died too soon in those other lives. She had to finish this one the right way.

"I don't believe any of that supernatural hokum!" Royal grabbed his Bible and held it to his chest like a shield. "The Bible condemns anything of the sort. Past lives, vampires, it all portents evil," he thundered, as if preaching from a pulpit.

"All right, Perc—I mean Roy," she said, her voice syrupy, her body language welcoming as she uncrossed her arms and legs. "I'll join the Fellowship and help you eradicate the world of vampires. But first we have some unfinished business." She stood and approached him, the dusty floor between them creaking. She braced herself for his octopus hands and slobbering tongue. But he slumped back in his chair. "What's the matter, Roy? Isn't this the moment you waited for?" she cooed, hoping that enough of the original Percival was in him to tempt him into succumbing. "You couldn't wait till Zanna left, so you could ravish me. Isn't that true?"

He shook his head, with a devilish gleam in his eye.

As she talked, she inched over to the table until her fingers curled around the dagger's handle. Its warmth seeped into her hand; its carvings and gemstones dug into her skin. "Here. You'll need this if you intend to guard me." She placed the knife in his palm, hoping to win his trust, keeping a firm grip on the handle. Then once she had him close enough...

She quivered, her mouth dry, about to take an enormous risk. But this needed to be done.

"I, uh..." He swabbed his forehead with his sleeve, stained with stale sweat. Gripping the knife with steady control, she backed him up to the wall. He crashed into a painting of the Amalfi coast in a gilded frame.

She closed her eyes, and imagining Quintus, pressed her lips to his, plunging her tongue into his mouth. Shuddering, her stomach turning, she inhaled his pungent sweat. She held the dagger against his throat with enough pressure to draw a trickle of blood. Then before he could react, she clamped her teeth to his wound and fed.

His eyes rolled back in his head, his face became deathly pale, and he slid to the floor like a sack of flour. She smiled in triumph, wiping her mouth with the back of her hand.

As she laid the dagger down, it glinted back up at her. "You did good, Diamanda." She stroked the weapon, remembering the name Percival had given it. "It took a few centuries, but better late than never."

Kneeling beside Royal, she pressed her fingers to his moist neck. The slow, thready beat drew a smirk from her. He still had enough life left in him to drink from her. Would it happen before Zanna got back? She let out a slow stream of air, rubbing her forehead.

She plucked a few figs and chomped down on one. Her teeth crushed the tiny seeds as she savored the waxy fruit.

She looked out the window into the empty street

below. A dim circle of light from a streetlamp illuminated a small area of sidewalk. Steady silence stabbed her ears. "Quintus, where are you?" she pled out loud. "I know you're frantic looking for me. Don't worry, babe, I'm all right." Her warm breath created a circle of vapor on the wavy glass.

She heard a low moan and turned. Royal put his hands to the stone-flagged floor, pressing with wobbly arms to sit up. Propped up on his elbows, he looked around and focused his glazed eyes on her.

"Now for the grand finale." She lifted Diamanda from its cushion, knelt before Royal, and slit a thin cut on her inside wrist. "Thirsty, Roy?"

He grabbed her wrist, held it to his lips, and gulped.

****

Vivianna's sports car cut a smooth path through the narrow winding streets. Fausto and Mona huddled in the back seat, their fingers interlaced. She silently prayed they'd find Tessie alive.

After too many red lights and sharp turns, Luigi guided Vivianna to a squat brick structure. "This is it. La Santissima Trinita Church." Fausto helped Mona out of the car. She shivered as her feet hit the hard sidewalk. A sliver of moonlight lit the cornerstone, etched with "1964," a throwback to a long-gone era, but very stark and modern in contrast to the classic styles surrounding it. The church had no steeple and wasn't in the shape of a cross. The only hint that it was a house of worship was the bulletin board displaying a mass schedule under a single bulb, which threw shadows on a crucifix above the doors.

The cold night brought back images of the

catacombs, quiet and still as death, the darkness enshrouding her.

She ached to scream Tessie's name, to pierce the darkness, to hear her voice echo until it reached her friend. This was all her fault. She sighed. If she hadn't run this crazy cruise and cajoled Fausto out of mourning, Tessie wouldn't be in this predicament. Right now she held Tessie's life in her hands. Shoving the guilt and fear aside, she vowed to rescue her best friend.

They stood on the corner looking up at the balconied facades flanking the church. Quintus turned to Vivianna. "So, where to first?"

"She's on a top floor, possibly a third or fourth floor of a dwelling." Vivianna looked at the higher-storied houses. "We'll have to try one at a time. I can see the inside of where she is, but not the outside."

"All right, Vivianna, we're going to put our psychic and writer's heads together." Mona faced the others. "This is what we have to go on. The hunters are religious fanatics. If they don't own a house, chances are they borrowed one from a friend who's very religious, maybe a priest. So, we'll try houses that have the biggest statues of saints in the front. Not the pocket-sized single-bulb night lights that sit on a window sill. The sturdy life-size outdoor jobs you can hang clothes on. Like that one." She pointed to a house two doors down. A Madonna statue, at least three feet high, beads hanging from her wrists, stood in a plaster arched shell. "That's a good place to start."

Quintus looked up at the top floor. "The top windows are dark, though. The whole house is dark. There's nobody home."

She noticed a brick townhouse two doors down, graced with Madonna and Child on the top porch step. But it didn't have a third floor. "Come over here, then." They followed her and looked the building up and down.

Luigi snapped on a pen light and read the names above the mailbox. "This is a two-family house. Mastropietro and Postretta live here, but there's no third floor."

Mona walked down the sloped driveway. "It has a garage! Luigi, help me out. If there's a big black sedan in here, we might have hit pay dirt."

"Good thinking, *sveglio*." Fausto and Quintus helped him raise the garage door, inching it up not to make noise. Hunched over, they scrambled through the three-foot opening but came right out.

"Well?" Mona pulled her collar tighter as Fausto brushed dirt off his hands. "A scooter, a kid's tricycle, and a convertible roadster. But no black sedan."

She was already eyeing the next house. A spotlight shone on a nativity scene in the patch of dirt that served as a garden. Manger, Holy Family, three wise men, donkeys, camels, sheep, the whole cast. Lights in the shape of a cross adorned the front window. The brass door knocker spelled GESU in the shape of a fish. But no garage. "Damn, where's that Benz?" she muttered. But a lighted attic was more important. The house had a third floor. She couldn't see an attic. Maybe Vivianna mistook her vision of an attic for a top floor. Psychics didn't see everything with HDTV clarity.

"This house is looked after," she commented as the others peered around it. The shiny tile steps leading up to the front door reflected the moonlight. "Expensive door and windows. This oak door, with its brass handle, must've cost a few grand. Whoever lives here has dough." Mona went up a step and slipped. Fausto grabbed her arm. "Damn, these things are slippery!" She clapped her hand to her mouth. "Oops, sorry, didn't mean to swear in front of Jesu Bambino."

"Let's go for it," Quintus rasped. "I'm breaking in." They followed him to the side.

Luigi said, "Try to do a minimum of damage."

Mona gave him a puzzled look. "What do you care about damage?"

"Hey, I ain't Paulie Walnuts. I got some class, ya know." They tried to push open the ground level windows. They wouldn't budge. With that, Luigi reached into his jacket, slid a handgun from a holster, and aimed it at the side door lock.

"*Aspetti*! Wait!" Mona grabbed his arm and pulled it back. "I have a better—and quieter way." She felt around in her pocket and pulled out her card key. "Sometimes these open more than ship cabins." She slid it between the lock and the door frame. *Voilà,* it unlatched! She swung the door open and stepped in. "Ladies first." She tiptoed into the house like a panther stalking its prey.

"*Ciao!* Anybody in here?" Mona signaled the men to follow her up the stairs with a wag of her wrist to the second floor landing. In the hallway, by the light of the kitchen below, a narrow stairway led to a third floor.

"*Sopra!* A third floor!" She grabbed Quintus's arm, guiding him toward the open doorway and the steps disappearing into the darkness above. Each step creaked as she ascended on tiptoe. With no banister, she grasped onto the walls. It reminded her of the stairway down to the bowels of hell they'd just been in, only in the opposite direction. It creeped her out. What kind of hell would she find up here?

She drew in a breath, the air mustier with every creaking step. At the top, a pull cord brushed her face like a ghostly finger. She jumped, thinking it was a spider web, but sighed in relief and yanked on the cord. A bare bulb blazed into light, and she looked around at an empty room, exposed beams and insulation telling her it was unfinished, probably waiting to become a spare bedroom someday. Her hopes plummeted as the dust billowed out. Nobody up here.

She turned to leave when a bat dive-bombed her with a squeal that made her blood curdle. She covered her head and stumbled inches from the stairs. Quintus held her up.

"What the hell happened?"

"Nothing, just a bat." She brushed imaginary cobwebs from her arms. "Strike one."

"You're right. *Andiamo*."

A door slammed. Mona jumped and grabbed Fausto's arm, her heart hammering. A college age kid in torn pajama bottoms came barreling down the hallway and rammed a fist into Luigi's jaw. Luigi spun and tumbled down the stairs. Faster than Mona could gulp a breath, she heard a sickening crack as Luigi landed in a crumpled heap.

The college kid gestured like a maniac and yelled in Italian, while Vivianna cursed and obscene-gestured right back at him. Quintus carried Luigi out to the car, Vivianna following.

Fausto nudged the kid out of his way.

"No! Don't shoot!" He splayed his hands and

blessed himself.

Fausto raised his arms. "I'm not armed. We're just looking for someone—"

"A woman named Tessie," Mona added, describing her with hand gestures. "Rather big—" She cupped her hands under her breasts and heaved. "Curly hair." She twirled a few of her own strands around her fingers. "American. Is she here?"

The kid stumbled backwards. By his glazed look, he'd been sleeping off a mega hangover. "I'm sorry I hit your friend, but we've had a lot of burglaries here. What was the name again?"

"Tessie," Fausto said. "Dark curly hair, wearing a fake fur leopard coat?"

"Chinchilla," Mona corrected him.

He shook his head and hiccupped. "*Scusi*, no."

"... American?"

"I dunno no *Americani*." He rubbed his eyes.

Fausto threw up his hands. "*Andiamo*." Mona grabbed Fausto's arm, and they trotted down the steps and outside, where Quintus was helping Luigi into Vivianna's car.

"Could be a concussion. He'll need to have the head wound looked at," Vivianna said as Mona murmured words of encouragement. Blood seeped through Luigi's white collar like a blooming flower, soaking his hand.

Sliding behind the wheel, Vivianna appeared dazed, staring into space.

"Just get him to the hospital," Mona said as Vivianna rammed her car into gear.

Mona stepped away from the car as it zoomed off into the night.

Once again they were on their own.

"One down, how many more to go?" As they stood on the sidewalk, Fausto looked at the array of shuttered windows and balconies.

"I just wish we had another psychic with us." Quintus fixed his eyes on Mona. "You aren't, are you?"

"No, but I wish I was. All I have are my skills as a writer." She dug her fingers through her hair, eyes shut, thinking. "Vivianna said the church was a basketball court. That might tell me something."

She strode across the street and peeked into one of the stained glass church windows. The dim streetlamps cast shadowy light on its interior. On the altar, a chalice glinted under the colored moonlight. Two rows of wooden pews formed a center aisle. She walked around the building and looked in another window. Same view, different angle. But not quite. "Look at this." She signaled to the men as she backed up until she was across the street. "From here, you can't see anything now that it's dark, but when the lights are on in the church, it's right in your face. They never took down the basketball hoop, and this house"—she turned and pointed—"is the only house it's visible from."

"I'll be damned." Quintus stood, arms akimbo, shaking his head. "Took a basketball court and made it into a beautiful church, altar, pews, stations of the cross, but instead of a choir loft, there's a damn hoop!"

"It still serves a purpose," Fausto said. "The congregation throws the money through there, and whatever lands on the floor, the church keeps."

Mona turned and stood back to get a good look at the house. "It has a small window way up top, and eureka, it's lit!"

Quintus rubbed his hands together. "That makes up for the lack of garage or Madonna statues."

"There's a driveway here, though." Mona knelt on the blacktop surface. Motor oil stains glowed in the streetlamps' milky light. "Whoever lives here owns a car. Looks like it's been leaking oil." She turned to Quintus. "Did the black car cough up smoke when they pulled away?"

"Come to think of it, yeah."

"Then maybe it's burning oil." She got to her feet. "Looks like we might have our house."

He rushed over to Mona and kissed her on both cheeks. "*Grazie, bella*!"

He dashed over to the nearest side window and gestured for Fausto to give him a hand breaking in.

She was aware they were committing a criminal act, and if that frat boy in the first house decided to call *la polizia*, they'd spend her long-awaited vacation in an Italian slammer. Which she doubted served *ziti bolognese* and Chianti Classico. But by now she was past caring. All she could think about was rescuing Tessie.

Fausto tried the front door. Locked, of course.

"Instead of breaking and entering, I wish we could just enter," she said. If only those myths were true and vampires could change into bats. But right now they were very human.

"You two don't have to come with me," Quintus said. "You can wait out here in the alley between the houses."

"No, I'm going, too." Her stubborn streak wasn't her best attribute, and she knew it would get her into trouble someday. This was the day. She shuddered. "I can't sit on the sidelines and let you face all the danger."

"I'll open this one." Fausto nudged his way forward and plucked a credit card from his wallet. He slid it between the lock and the door frame, wiggled it around and re-inserted it. But it still wouldn't budge. "Must be a deadbolt," he muttered.

He went around to the side and kicked in the first ground-floor window he came to. The glass shattered. She stood holding her breath, waiting for an alarm or a dog or a gun. Nothing but dead silence followed the tinkling of glass as the last shards hit the dirt below.

He reached in, turned the lock to the open position, and slid the window open. "You or me?" he asked Quintus.

Quintus gestured for him to enter first. "After you. Your night vision is better than mine."

"Oh, that's right, I keep forgetting how much older than me you are."

Under normal circumstances Mona would have laughed, but there was nothing humorous about crawling through the opening with its jagged glass. The aroma of garlic hung in the air. Fausto flipped a switch. The room flooded with fluorescent light.

"Please, God, don't let anybody be home this time except Tessie," she prayed, hearing the fridge's quiet hum as they took their first steps toward the doorway.

"Ciao!" Quintus called up the stairs. She held her breath. Nothing. She expelled a whoosh of air as she wiped hot sweat from her hairline.

As they shuffled toward the kitchen door, footsteps thudded above them. By now her nerves were shot. She didn't even have the energy to tremble. "Somebody's walking around up there."

Mona was the first up the stairs. She stood on the landing, looking for a trap door. Finding nothing, she cursed in disappointment. Opening the nearest door, she stared at an empty bedroom. Opposite was a bathroom. That left one more closed door. Heavy footsteps from above jerked her heart into a faster beat. A top floor!

She opened the last door to a narrow flight of stairs leading to the top floor.

Chapter Ten:
You're Just My "O" Type

Mona called down to the men, "I found a top floor!" and took the stairs two at a time. A wooden door on rusty hinges faced her. She gripped the doorknob and pushed. The door rattled but wouldn't open. Fausto and Quintus rushed up behind her.

"Move aside." Quintus stood back, turned sideways and rammed his body into the door. It burst open, rotted planks splintering around them. They charged into the attic. As Mona blinked against the darkness, shapes gradually took form. Fausto and Quintus stood behind her. The glint of a knife flashed. A blurry figure stood over a body on the floor. Mona gasped in surprise as Tessie whirled around and dropped the dagger. It clanged to the floor as she fell into Mona's arms and sobbed.

"Are you all right, sweetie? Did he hurt you?" Mona gently stroked her friend's hair, gathering it in bunches.

"I'm fine. Thank goodness you're here. And Quintus!" Tessie gave Mona a thankful squeeze and rushed into Quintus's waiting arms.

As Mona saw the cowering man in the corner, she knew what had happened. A sheen of sweat covered his pale skin. She approached her friend and spoke low into her ear. "Tess, did that skank try anything?"

Tessie shook her head, her chandelier earrings jangling. "He didn't have a chance. That's Royal Jones, a hunter. I just—" She gave Quintus a look that begged forgiveness, then faced Mona squarely. "I turned him. I had to, it was the only way out."

"It's all right," Mona soothed, and lifted the dagger off the floor.

"Where have I seen that knife before?" Quintus asked.

"In the Middle Ages. I'll explain later."

Fausto wrapped his arm around Mona's shoulder, gathered Tessie to him, and hugged them. "Just thank God it all worked out and you're safe."

Mona glanced down. The sight of Tessie's ragged nails drew a horrified gasp from her. "Tess, what happened to your nails? My God! Did you have to claw them in self-defense?"

"Oh, that." She held up her fingers, wiggling them. "His wife liked my fake nails, so I gave them to her." She dashed over to the window and peered out, up and down the street. "Speaking of the wife, we need to get out of here before she gets back. I sent her on a wild goose chase. I'll tell you all about it later."

"Did you turn her, too?" Mona asked, not sure she wanted to know the answer.

Halting, Tessie gave her a frosty scowl. "This ain't *The L Word*, girlfriend."

"So, he's one of us now." Fausto approached the world's newest vampire until he was within spitting distance. "Oh, well, we can't always choose who we let in." He eyed Royal up and down like a bottle of cheap wine.

"But he looks so—so harmless. He hardly

resembles a hunter. Of squirrels, maybe, but not vampires," Mona said.

Royal growled and rubbed his head with trembling hands.

Fausto said, "Chill out, pal, you'll get used to it. Blood has fewer calories than beer. You might ditch that spare tire hanging over your belt."

Royal pointed a trembling, but accusing finger at Tessie. "You'll pay for this!" His voice cracked in a harsh rumble.

"She already did," Mona replied calmly, tossing the dagger onto a table. "You just got the luckiest break of your life. So lie back and enjoy it."

"And you!" He brought himself to a sitting position and leered at Mona. Her flesh crawled. "You won't get away, either. You'll suffer if you let these ghouls turn you!"

Fausto's fists clenched, and he made a lunge for Royal.

"No!" She wedged herself between the two men.

"Let me at him, Mona." Fausto's breath was hot against her cheek. "No *cafone* talks to my woman like that."

From the short distance between them, the smell of Royal's fear smacked her in the face like rotting garbage. She turned to face the new vampire and got him to meet her stare. "Look, bro, you think you're really tough to go after vampires and wipe them out." She flicked her hand through the air. "Yeah, there are some bad ones who kill people, but the vast majority of them are good, God-fearing Christians. And you'll see that once you get to live with yourself. Then maybe you'll start thinking like a rational human being—er, rational person—er—" She turned to Fausto. "Help me out here. What *do* you call yourselves?"

"We're still people, for God's sakes. We don't lay eggs."

"All right, *people*. So don't threaten me with fire and brimstone because you're the one who's being tested now, not me."

"You're either a liar or sadly brainwashed," Royal rasped, wiping his thick neck. "They're no good. They're evil. For your own sake, don't let them turn you into one of them. I hate what I've become."

"Suit yourself." She shook her head and faced Fausto. Then she thought about what he said. Would she hate what she'd become if Fausto turned her? She might. That was why she couldn't make that fate-altering decision. But at least she wouldn't hate herself for the same twisted reasons Royal now had.

Quintus started for the door. "Let's haul ass outta here before the missus comes back. Hubby and wife will need to be alone and share a few things, like a hot drink." He smiled. "Besides, I'm lousy at dealing with pissed off wives. That's why I never remarried." With that, he gave Tessie a wink. "Until now."

As they turned to leave, Tessie called over her shoulder, "When Zanna gets back, you'd better tell her you're a vampire now. That's one of two things you just can't hide from a wife. The other is money. Happy sucking!"

As they rushed down the stairs, Mona got out her cell phone and called for a taxi. "We should go to the hospital and see how Luigi is doing before we head back to the ship," she said as they emerged into the cool night air. "I told the taxi to pick us up in front of the gym—the church. Just in case the wife does show up."

"You want to steer clear of that *zoccola*, don't you?" Fausto jabbed his cousin in the ribs.

"We have two choices if she shows up," Mona said. "One of you can turn her." She looked to Quintus who held up his hands as if to say, "This ain't *Queer as Folk*, girlfriend." Fausto shook his head, his hands cutting through the air. "Or tell her what Tessie did to her husband, and break the news that she'll be one of you before long, when he turns her. And I don't want to be at the business end of her hissy fit."

"She's gonna freak," Tessie said. "They became hunters because of personal tragedies. I feel sorry for her—for the both of them."

"I feel sorry for us," Fausto said. "Having somebody like that among our group kind of taints it."

"Snob," Quintus quipped.

"I know how to get back at him," Mona said. "Tell him he has to turn ten hunters for his initiation, starting with his wife."

"Well then, take some pity on *her*," Tessie said.

****

Just as Zanna figured, after tearing ass back to the harbor and peering around every yacht to see if it had that silly Italian name, she realized there was no Joe Bozzone and no yacht. She swore under her breath and kicked at an empty soda can in frustration. That scamp set her up. Furious, she boarded the *Romanza* and entered the dining room for her 8:00 p.m. seating. Why not eat a paid-for meal before going back to indoctrinate the wanton sinner? As the hostess ushered her to her assigned table, she glimpsed a waiter sliding a chair under Toi Brennan.

156

An idea struck her as she unfolded her linen napkin on her lap. If she could cajole Toi into mustering some media clout behind her and her fellow hunters, they could make life hell for vampires. The church would look like choirboys compared to berserking reporters!

Picking her napkin up off her lap, Zanna excused herself and sidled up to the media giant as she ordered her cocktail.

"Can I talk with you a minute, please?" she asked Toi as her dinner mates glanced over the tops of their menus at her.

"Sure." Toi stood, and they wound their way around the tables, waiters, and carts to the exit. They stood in a little alcove next to a twinkling Christmas tree.

"I know of another live show you can tape from here, even more transfixing than the writers' convention, that'll boost your ratings through the stratosphere!" Zanna licked the gloss off her lips.

Toi's mascaraed lashes flew apart, and her smoky-shadowed eyes nearly popped out. "Did you catch some vampires?"

"One. So far. And she's a very prominent figure among romance writers and industry mucky mucks. I'm not going to divulge any names yet, but with your help, we can expose her and maybe a few others. Think of what this will do for your show." She mimicked a voiceover teaser. "*Hunters capture vampires aboard luxury liner on writers' cruise!* Talk about rockin' the boat!"

"I'll tell the rest of the crew to switch gears for a while." She gave Zanna her cabin number, and they returned to their separate tables. Zanna nodded a polite hello to her dining mates, explaining that her husband wasn't feeling well. She picked up the menu, and in three seconds flat, the waiter served their usual cocktails and took their orders. She chose her five courses and engaged in the customary banter of eight strangers thrown together far from home.

But nobody knew the reason for her smugness—how famous she'd be and how powerful the Fellowship would become when Teresa started giving them vampires' names—and with a little more prodding, their heads on silver salvers.

****

Mona and Quintus went back to Fratello's for a much-needed round of drinks, but Fausto stayed in the taxi, promising to join them later. The hospital released Luigi with a flesh wound, his arm in a sling.

In the meantime, Fausto took the taxi to the other side of town, where a friend of his lived, Angelo Zolli. His family owned a jewelry store, but it wouldn't be open now. For Fausto, his childhood friend would open it.

He had to make a special purchase.

On the ride over, he closed his eyes and rested his head on the back seat as the cab whizzed through the empty streets. He ran through Tessie's ordeal in his mind, knowing how close she'd come to getting killed. He shuddered at the thought of something like that happening to Mona. His life would be over without her. He had to convince her to spend the rest of eternity with him. But would she?

****

Mona, Quintus, Tessie, Luigi, and Vivianna gathered at Luigi's private table. Luigi snapped his fingers, and the wine steward appeared. He ordered four bottles of Villa Raiano. "This is the best Campania wine, from a nearby medieval village. The Basso family, who owns the vineyards, sends it to me no charge. It's free advertising for them."

The steward performed the usual uncorking show, and Luigi did the roll-around-the-tongue test. When their glasses were full, Mona stood and proposed a toast. "To health—and safety. *Salute.*"

"*Per cent'anni,* to the next hundred years," Luigi added as they all clinked glasses. "But what's a hundred years to a vampire?"

They all shared a tension-relieving laugh.

"Anybody in the mood to *mangia*?" he asked, but hardly got an enthusiastic response. Only one hell of a trauma could make a table of Italians pass up an Italian meal. Even a wake was an excuse for a feast.

Mona sipped the fine wine, its musty tang warming her. She looked around the table at the people she loved the most—and some wonderful new friends. Mona still trembled as she lifted her glass. She'd very nearly lost Tessie. The thought of losing Fausto to a hunter filled her with grief. But the horrid fear never left her. It would be a repeat of her doomed first marriage. Goons had harassed Ted to pay his gambling debts. She spent many a sleepless night, frantic, waiting for the day he wouldn't come home. Shivering, she made the decision: *No, this life is not for me.* It was only fair to Fausto to let him know.

Tessie reached over to give her a hug. "You're more shook up than I am," she whispered. "It's all right. It's over."

But little twinges in her gut told her otherwise.

Seeing Tessie's capture filled Mona with fears she never knew she had.

Luigi snapped open a gold case, his initials monogrammed in diamonds, slid a cigarillo out, and lit it with a gold lighter. "Mona, any thoughts after tonight about making an honest man out of Fausto and joining our world?"

Her spine straightened and she stared straight ahead. She didn't want to look like he'd shot her between the eyes. Luigi sure didn't beat around the bush. Even when he'd asked her to join him on the yacht, there were no preliminaries. She had him figured for a wham-bam-there's-the-door-ma'am kind of guy.

"Uh, well, I—I need to think about it." Her taste buds bursting for more of that heady wine, she took a sip, then another.

"It's a beautiful life, *cara*. Just look at how happy Tessie and Quintus are."

She glanced across the table. They drank their wine, their arms interlocked.

Just then Fausto joined them but didn't take the empty chair next to her. Instead he beckoned a violinist to the table, dropped to one knee, and gazed at Mona with adoration. He held up a velvet box and snapped it open.

Oh, my God.

The diamond caught the light and dazzled in a rainbow of colors. Tessie gasped. "Oh, *madonne*, that's be—u—tee—ful!" Tessie stood and leaned over Mona to give the ring a good once-over. "Hey, that's some rock, girlfriend. I'll bet it can cut diamonds. Eat'cha heart out, J. Lo!"

Fausto cleared his throat. "Mona, my love, will you

marry me?"

Smiles burst out around the table.

Tears filled Mona's eyes. She loved this man so much but couldn't bring herself to accept this.

"Fausto . . . oh, if only we were alone." She looked around the table at her dear friends. Stars shone in Tessie's eyes. The ring winked up at Mona as if daring her to accept. "Can we have a moment, please?"

Fausto followed her to the empty banquet room at the back of the restaurant. She closed the door. Darkness enshrouded them but for a thin slice of light under the door.

She held his hands in hers, rubbing her thumb across his palm, her heart breaking. How could she tell him how she felt without hurting him? "Fausto, I've loved you for a long time, but seeing what happened to Tessie made me realize I could lose you at any moment. She's brave, far braver than I am, for doing what she did. It made me wish I could take the risk and marry you, but I just can't handle the possibility of not knowing if I'll ever see you again whenever we're apart, which will be a lot of the time. My fear is my biggest flaw. I'm a coward. I'm not as ballsy as people say I am. I guess I'm just destined to be a mortal and die like a mortal. I'm so sorry, Fausto. I'm just not cut out to share your life."

His eyes were downcast. She wouldn't blame him if he walked out now and she never saw him again. He snapped the ring box shut and slid it into his pocket. But instead of turning and leaving, he took a step forward and enveloped her in his arms. His trembles raced up her body. Her heart knew how devastated he was.

"You're no coward, Mona." He stroked her hair as she rested her head on his shoulder, knowing this might be the last moment they'd spend together. "But I'm going to win you no matter what it takes. I'm keeping this ring because I know someday you'll be proud to wear it. However," he sighed, "it will have to be your decision. I'll never force it on you."

In the silent moment that followed, she wondered if she'd change her mind someday. What could possibly make that happen? Recovering from her first marriage that almost broke her spirit? Going on a quest after hunters? Julianna never predicted her life would take such a drastic turn.

"Thank you, Fausto. Thank you for accepting me for who I am."

"Well, you've been accepting me for who I am. Not wanting to marry me is a lot more bearable than you chasing after me with a crucifix and drowning me in holy water."

They shared a light brush of a kiss, and he opened the door for her. "Come on, we'd better go back out there before they think we're snubbing them."

They took their seats at the table, but no one said a word. Tessie gave her an uneasy smile, but the way her friend's eyes bugged out, Mona knew she was bursting to learn what had happened.

Mona sat up straight and took a deep breath. "Guys, we've decided to hold it off for a while. Sorry we left you like that, but it came as such a shock to me"—she grasped Fausto's hand as Tessie looked at Mona's ringless finger—"but when we go ahead with any plans, you'll be the first to know."

She leaned toward Fausto, and as their bodies

touched, she imagined herself joined with him in his world forever. A thrill warmed her at the deliciously frightening thought. His world was the forbidden fruit—and everyone knew what happened to people who ate the forbidden fruit.

****

Zanna let herself into their cabin and gasped, dumbstruck, when she saw Royal sitting cross-legged on the bed, rocking back and forth, his head in his hands. A guttural groan came from deep inside him.

"Roy!" She rushed up to him, nudging his shoulder, but he didn't move. He seemed to be in a trance. "Roy!" She shook him hard. He finally dropped his hands and looked up at her, his eyes filled with tears. His sob of fear, horror, and regret stunned her. She took a faltering step backward, grasping the dresser for support. "My God, what happened to you? You look like you died!"

"I—I did, Zanna. That woman turned me. I'm one of"—he let out a choked sob—"one of them now."

Her heart contracted to the size of a tiny fist. "No, you can't be—it must be a mistake. She tricked you!" She stood rooted to the spot, paralyzed. She couldn't even touch him. Part of her mind refused to believe what he'd said, but physical contact left the taste of bile in her mouth. She spat onto the floor.

"It's no mistake." His voice dragged with defeat. "She sent you on that wild goose chase and bit me rather than let us save her. Look." He tilted his head back to expose the bite mark on his neck. "Now I'm condemned to eternity as one of those ghouls, forced to drink blood, to sleep in a sealed casket, never to eat a french fry dipped in ketchup again." He buried his face in his hands and wailed.

"No, it can't be." Some part of her mind was still in denial. A perverse thought hit her: *Denial is easier than facing the ugly truth.* She was in love with this man who now sickened her. Despite being branded lunatics, their actions served mankind and fulfilled their destinies here on earth. Her beloved Roy, the man she'd poured her heart to about her painful past and grief and loneliness, was among those she hated with her very soul.

Now it was all over. He was one of them. Forever on the other side.

How could she live like this?

"I...I need some air." She rushed to the porthole, pounded on it, spat out curses, but it stayed shut tight. If it opened, she would have jumped into the sea and drowned.

His frail voice reached her, but in her dazed state, she couldn't process his words.

"Don't turn your back on me, don't leave me, please, Zanna. You have to understand..."

He approached her from behind and placed his hands on her shoulders. She shuddered and tried to pull away, but he gripped her arms and held her to him. "I want you to become one of us now."

"No..." Unable to hear another word, she backed away, then yanked the door open and fled.

Chapter Eleven:
Motion on the Ocean

Fausto handed Mona a goblet of Villa Raiano from a bottle Luigi gave him. He had traded shifts with another doctor and was hers for the night. "*Grazie, magnifico mio.*" She propped her feet on his balcony railing and took a warming sip. Closing her eyes, she pretended she was his wife, together just like this every evening, sharing wine and the stars, belonging to no one but each other. Oh, how easy it would be just to say yes and fall into his arms.

"I want to toast us." He pulled up a chair next to her and clinked his goblet with hers. "To the woman I want to be with forever. And I mean forever." He took a sip, his lips pursing in pleasure.

"It's a beautiful thought, Fausto." But forever was a long time to uphold sacred vows, and she carried some heavy baggage from that last disastrous marriage. A sob escaped her throat as she imagined leaving him behind. She could at least help him where the hunters were concerned. That, and their love, would keep them fused. "I'm sorry, there's so much to think about. I'm having trouble thinking straight."

"You'll be your old self when you're partying at the ball." He plucked a grape from a bunch on the table between them and placed it between her lips. She bit into the tart juiciness. Right now this was the only feeding she wanted from him.

"Fausto, do you realize that crazy hunter woman could've burst into that attic when we were there and done God knows what?" She drew a deep, steadying breath. "That's what scares the hell out of me. Constantly fretting whether you'll come back to me alive." She took a thoughtful pause. "I lived that way once and never want to go through it again. Ted had thugs after him, when he owed them money. They'd drop by, looking like Tony Soprano's goons. Every bit as scary as vampire hunters. Last year I had to put up sixty grand he'd lost on a football game. If I hadn't coughed up that money, he'd be sleeping with the fishes."

He gave her cheek a reassuring caress. "You'll never know that kind of fear again. I know I can take care of myself—and you. I'm used to hunters, *bella*. I've been at it for five hundred years. To you, it's new, like the first day at your all-girl Catholic school, the struggle to fit into a clique, strange nuns. But you were okay once you settled in, weren't you?"

"Fausto, you can't compare Catholic school and nuns wi—" She cut herself off. "Okay, that's you. I've been thinking about this more and more, and short of doing what Tessie did, turning every hunter who confronts you, we can fight back. They want to purge the world of vampires. Well, I want to purge the world of them, too. But not drastically or violently. Tactfully and peacefully."

He blinked a few times. His thick lashes fanned over his dark eyes. "These people aren't known for their responsiveness to anything tactful, *cara mia*."

She took another sip. "It would be a subtle

approach, so they respond willingly. Like on *Survivor*, we have to use our brains to get Zanna and Royal kicked off the island first. And the media is the best place to start. Leak a tidbit here, a morsel there, and it gets beamed around the planet a trillion times, especially when they're having a slow patch, like when there are no sex scandals or runaway brides or avian flu to scare the public out of their wits."

"So you have to time your item between high profile crimes and diseases," he said.

"You can't out-time world news any better than you can out-time the stock market. I just have to draft my plan and go with it."

He hunched forward, resting his elbows on his knees. "Wait—what plan? We don't want this splashed on the news. We mind our own business. If they come after us, we deal with it. But we don't want to be spoofed on comedy shows. Then the political satirists will get wind of us. And as for the Supreme Court— hell, I don't even want to think about it. They'll take away our right to get married, for starters. You want to resort to exchanging vows in a 'civil union'?"

"You don't have to come out of your shell. I mean coffin—lair—whatever you want to call it. My cause will change hunter/vampire relations for the better. You don't have to go on Vampire Pride marches or become an activist or anything like that."

"But you're not even one of us. Yet. Just say yes, and we'll be joined tonight." He tilted her chin up with his finger and she looked him in the eyes. His gaze melted her. "Then we can talk about a cause."

The naked desire in his eyes made a stream of emotions engulf her—love, fear, and a flood of longing that matched his obvious need. Would being a vampiress strengthen her will to do this gutsy deed? Or make her complacent and accepting like he was?

"Fausto, it's your family who was killed. Why do I feel so much stronger about this than you do?"

"We'll never get rid of all hunters, just like we'll never get rid of all terrorists. Diplomatically, forcefully, or otherwise."

"But at least there's a war on terror going on. Kind of."

"And we have our own war on hunters." A gust of wind snatched his hair, and he smoothed it back into place. "Even some of the Ball Busters know better than to mess with us. Only the ones who have no sense of fear pursue us. I don't know if this Zanna woman is one of them, but we can't strike first. We're on the defensive, not the offensive. That would be against the unspoken vow we've all taken since the first vampire became undead two thousand years ago. We're peace-loving people. If we weren't, we'd be just like Hollywood warps us, and that would make us as two-faced as the hunters, wouldn't it?"

She sighed, realizing she was still shaking from tonight's ordeal, even though she'd taken a hot steamy shower and slipped into a cashmere wrap. She shivered, intent on talking this out. She was still running on adrenaline, her mind whirring, her heart pumping.

He gazed out into the night, the harbor lights twinkling in his eyes. "Please don't get involved. The woman who made me into a vampire, my first love Josefina, defied hunters, and they killed her."

The pain in his eyes sliced through her. "I'm so sorry, Fausto. When was this?" She wrapped her fingers around his cold ones, warming them with her love.

"I was young. About seventeen. She was a few years older. I can't bear that happening to someone else I love—and plan to marry."

"Marrying you is one thing. Your turning me is another."

"Well, Josefina is the one who turned me. If it wasn't for her, I wouldn't be here right now. She gave me eternal life, let hunters kill her rather than run away, and I won't ever let that happen again. It would be too painful. Those who don't learn from history are doomed to repeat it."

"I'm sure you didn't let it happen." She squeezed his hand. When he squeezed back, she felt fused to him. "Maybe she died so you could have eternal life."

He stared out into the night, his features pained. She longed to kiss it all away. "She took too much of my blood too soon. She thought she killed me, and I was dead for a few days. When I passed over and entered the spirit world, I met with ancestors from ancient Rome. I was enjoying myself, but she must've panicked because she gave me her wrist to feed from. I heard my family calling me, so I came back as one of the undead. Sadly, she never forgave herself for nearly killing me."

"What happened after that?" Mona asked, shedding her clogs and tucking her feet under her.

"She went to confession. Her confessor was a hunter who told her how heinous her sin was. Her penance had to be death. She laid her head down on a chopping block and let them behead her. Just because she was such a strong believer in what the Church convinced her was a mortal sin."

"The poor girl." Mona pulled her wrap tighter around her shoulders. "What a wasted life. You never have to worry that I'll do something that drastic."

"I'd just as soon you stay away from any controversy. We'll talk about your joining our world after I finally talk you into marrying me—and I will someday. But whether we marry or not, there's only one way you can truly be safe, Mona. We'd have to end this right now and go our separate ways."

She leaned forward and grabbed the railing. Her clogs almost fell over the balcony. He reached over and steadied her. He was right. Her choice was clear cut. Lose him altogether to escape possible danger from hunters? Or stay with him and risk watching the love of her life die. God, she was too young to be a widow!

"It's up to you, *cara*."

She pictured Tessie, in ecstasy with the man she'd loved over many lifetimes, but coming within a thread of losing her life. Whatever Tessie could do, she could do.

Or could she? Passing this test would tell her the truth—if she really was a heroine.

He brought her to her feet and kissed her, a deep, warm, loving kiss that communicated volumes more than words or any amount of pleading. She couldn't help herself, but falling more deeply in love with him, her earlier vows lay forgotten.

A wave of desire scampered through her, and she breathed a sigh as he planted kisses on her face, her neck, his tongue darting in and out of her ear, causing her to shiver with excitement. "Are you trying to start something?" she murmured, pressing her body to his, feeling its strength and growing hardness against her thighs.

"It's already started, *cara,*" he whispered and lifted her off her feet, carrying her from his balcony inside to the bed, placing her on the edge.

"I thought you'd be dead tired after everything it took to rescue Tessie."

"Remember, dead has a whole different meaning to our kind. And I hope you'll find out soon." He removed her sweater and let it slip to the floor.

She stepped out of her pants and slid her silk underwear off.

He laid her back on the bed and ran his hands down her muscular thighs, over the backs of her calves. His touch sent shivers racing up her spine. He dragged his tongue upward, sending her arcing off the bed. Raw desire raked through her.

When he reached her ankles, he tugged at the chain around her left one. "You're into ankle bracelets now?"

"Uh—not quite." She let out a light laugh. "It's my Saint Paul medal."

"What the hell's it doing on your ankle?"

"He can't see me from down there. I got tired of taking it off my neck every time—every time I thought we'd—"

"Saint Paul might not be able to see you, but I have a feeling he'll wind up jangling in my ear."

She thought about that a minute, and her heart raced in anticipation of the shiprocking ecstasy ahead. If Fausto enjoyed anything better than rum cake, it was going down on her. Her breathing quickened in expectation.

"I want so bad to make you mine in every way." He slid back up her body and teased her earlobe with his tongue.

She raked her hands through his thick locks, desperate for his touch, aching for the warmth of his skin next to hers. But he pulled away, stood at the foot of the bed, and gazed adoringly at her for a long minute, his eyes sliding up and down her curves, her breasts, and firm thighs as if for the first time.

"You are the most beautiful woman I've ever known," he breathed, shaking his head as if in awe.

"Am I?" she whispered, holding her arms out to him, trembling with emotion, yearning for him, but he stayed out of her reach. "That's quite a compliment coming from someone who's been through five centuries' worth of women."

"Do you want to take off my clothes?" He unclasped his watch and pulled his gold chain from around his neck, placing them on the nightstand. He put his Blessed Mother medal face down. "I have a pet peeve about guys who make love with watches and medals on," he said.

"And socks."

"Then you can take every stitch off me. It's no fun taking off your own clothes."

"But you wanted to make sure the Madonna wasn't watching either." She smiled.

"I've never been one for exhibitionism. Although chances are someone's always watching over us. At least we don't have to worry about Santa for a while."

"Oh, no, but I'm never naughty." She batted her lashes.

"Then I'd better change that right now. How 'bout I indulge your fantasies? You ever go to a male strip club?"

"Tessie dragged me to Chippendale's for my birthday a few years ago. I'll admit it was a guilty pleasure."

"This will be even better. And it'll save you a fistful of dollar bills." He slipped out of his shirt then tossed it away. He glided across the room and stood in the window, the moonlight casting a glow about his lean body, making him look like a god just descended from Olympus.

He pulled the undershirt over his head, then, barechested, strutted slow circles around her, flexing his arms, rippling his biceps as the beautifully developed muscles obeyed his every move. He strode over to her and brought her lips to his, letting their flesh touch, sending a wave of fire between them. He slid his thumbs into the waistband of his briefs and wriggled out of them.

He pulled away and twirled his briefs in the air before flinging them aside. Now completely naked, he plucked a long-stemmed rose from a vase on the dresser and approached her. "You think my hands are magic, wait till I tickle you with this. And don't worry, you'll feel a prick, but not from thorns."

He brushed her breasts with the very tips of the petals, causing her to squirm in delight as the delicate rose brushed her nipples. A rush of desire spread from the pit of her stomach and fanned out to her most sensitive nerve endings. He slid it down her body, over her abdomen, and along the soft sensitive flesh of her inner thighs.

Lighter than the softest caress of his fingertips, it teased and tormented in its subtle and fleecy gentleness, like a whisper of a breeze on her skin. She moaned in delight and arched her back, aching for him to come to her. He trailed a line back up her front with the petals' tickling ends, brushing over her breasts, then making one last stroke over her thighs.

He lay on his back and pulled her on top of him. She sat up and straddled him as he continued to stroke her with the petals.

"Let your hair fall over me," he whispered, his voice husky, his breaths coming in rapid gasps. She pulled the elastic from her hair, lowered her head, and let the silky ends brush against his chest, neck, and face. He wound tendrils around his fingers and kissed them gently, then pulled her down to him.

She tasted the sweetness of wine on his tongue as it met hers, probing, then becoming more urgent as their passion mounted. He was hard, ready; she eased him into her and rode him, enjoying this feeling of supreme command, controlling their movements, the degree of penetration. She teased him this time, easing him out, then plunging back down, causing him to moan in ecstasy with every thrust until their urgency culminated in waves of pulsating urgency.

They consumed each other, lost in the fervor of one beautiful body united with another, a desire bordering on indecency. She ground against him until his passion subsided and he begged her to stop, exhausted.

"Never," she insisted. She laughed wickedly, moved her head down to his flaccid penis, and teased it with her tongue. He gasped and fanned his fingers through her hair.

"What are you doing to me, Mona?" He groaned as she doubled her efforts, until once again he was hard, ready. She repeated the performance, riding him gently at first, then harder and harder until he cried out in blazing release, and she lay on top of him, her body spent.

If the hunters could see me now, she sang to herself, but immediately sobered. If the hunters could see her, they'd kill her. And then him.

Chapter Twelve:
To Vamp Or Not To Vamp

Mona rolled over and stretched. Her arm hit a cold empty pillow next to her. Fausto was working the first shift. Yesterday's events came rushing back to her uninvited. She pushed it all away—all except her night of passion with Fausto, and how Tessie was enjoying her new world.

She smiled when she saw last night's red rose resting on his pillow. She traced a velvety petal, inhaling its sweet perfume. She loved roses but—as sex toys? How deliciously wicked! This one was getting pressed into her scrapbook, and if it could brag to those shriveled up old prom corsages, what a tale it could tell!

She glimpsed the Cruise News on the nightstand. The front page article said they'd be pulling into the port of Messina, Sicily, in a little while. But after the above- and below-ground tour of Naples, she wasn't so hot to trot around more of Italy.

She put yesterday's clothes back on and headed to her cabin, looking over her shoulder the whole time. Nobody was after her. Whew…

Nobody lurked in the shadows, no footsteps followed her, no whispers drifted up from under the stairs.

In fact, she didn't see a single passenger from his cabin to hers. The corridor echoed a strange silence, only the ship's engines hummed in the distance. Ah, the breakfast buffet...everybody was stuffing their faces. She tossed on her little red dress and flicked some mascara over her lashes.

She entered the Botticelli Restaurant, breakfast in full swing, every table full. Her eyes swept across the room. Tessie sat at a windowside table with some authors. Relief washing over her, Mona rushed up to greet her friend. "Hey, guys. Tess, can we talk a minute?"

They exited the room among the clinking utensils and aroma of sweet pastries. Why not? Only a masochist would eat something sensible and healthy like grapefruit on a cruise.

She led Tessie to an alcove next to a twinkling Christmas tree. "So how the hell *are* you, girlfriend? What's it like to be a—" The words escaped past her tight throat.

"Just spit it out, Mona. *Vampiress.*" She nearly sang it. "It's awesome, for starters. A Sicilian priest is going to marry us at the stroke of midnight, to ring in the New Year! Of course you're going to be my matron—sorry, maid of honor."

That gave her a jolt no gulp of Colombian coffee could match. "Already? After all that happened? I thought you'd want to chill out in the spa for the rest of the trip, plastered with mud and seaweed, and a foot massage every hour."

Tessie laughed. "No, everything's cool, I have no regrets about turning that hunter guy. It all worked out in the end."

"Are you going to tell the police? I'd hate to think those crazies have somebody else holed up back there."

"Vampires don't rely on the law." She brushed a speck of lint off Mona's sweater. "Besides, with the hunter turned now, he has no incentive to hunt anymore."

"Who the hell knows what he's going to do?" Mona shook her head, glancing out the window. Laughter floated from the dining room. Everything seemed so normal.

"Forget about them." Tessie flicked her wrist. "We're gonna have a blast. I guess there's no way I can talk you into a double wedding ceremony. Then you can consummate your love in *every* way. Nudge nudge wink wink."

Mona couldn't begin to explain to her friend how much she'd love that. Nothing would be more romantic. But she wasn't ready to risk her heart—her body, yes, but she'd been hurt too badly. "No, I don't want to take your magic moment away. Besides, I'm still not..." She choked on her words. "I can't..."

"Mona, look at me. Do I look any different? Did I sprout a spiky pair of canines overnight?" She flashed a huge grin. "Am I talking with a Transylvanian accent? I don't have any ghoulish fantasies of neck-sucking these hottie waiters or crew guys in their starchy whites. I don't feel an urge to howl. I haven't added any Anne Rice books to my collection. I'm still me. Trust me on that. And you'd still be you."

"We talked about it more last night, Tess, and I have too many reasons. Bad vampires are out there, because their dark side comes out. Just like any human, some give in to it, some don't. And due to the crap I went through in the last year, my dark side sure as hell reared its ugly head. It's from all the welled-up anger because of the way Ted treated me and left me. If I become a vampire, I might be a bad one, want to hurt victims, because of my rage."

Tessie moved closer and gave Mona a quick hug. "Honey, there are 'bad' vampires in the Silvius family, too. They get carried away with the whole idea. That won't happen to you. It's not a dominant part of your personality."

"It has been ever since Ted went sour on me. To make himself look less like a loser, he put me down. 'You'll never amount to anything,' he always said. 'Your books suck.' And I believed him. That's when my sales started to tank."

"Okay, worse comes to worst, indulge your dark side, and go and gnaw the bastard to death."

Mona inhaled the rich coffee aroma, hoping that would give her a quick fix until she actually got a cup. It seemed to help—her mind cleared. "But the timing sucks. Giving in to Fausto, I'll give up my independence. Just when I'm turning a new page here, reinventing myself as a writer. And it's not a good idea to marry two weeks after a divorce."

"Independence shmindependence." Tessie frowned. "Quit making up excuses. These are Renaissance men we have. Not depression-era dockyard workers. Give them the benefit of the doubt already. So, if we won't be co-brides tonight, you're still my maid of honor, Cleopatra."

She sighed, knowing Tessie was right—for Tessie. "Of course." She nodded, but she wondered—where were the shipboard hunters lurking? Was Fausto safe in the doctor's office? Some *pazzo diavolo* could come in with a bogus case of the heaves and rush him right there and...

Swiping a hand over her eyes, she shook the thoughts from her mind. Tonight was her dearest friend's wedding, and she didn't want to spoil a thing. She knew what her dilemma was, and she'd have to make a decision soon.

Become a vampiress and risk death at the hands of Ball Busters, or stay human? Each meant doom in its own way.

"Come on. You can help me write our vows, romance author." Tessie took a step and looked down.

"What is it?"

"Something just crunched under my shoe. Cruise ships don't have cockroaches, do they?"

"Not Italian ones."

She bent down and picked up a small shiny object.

"Oh, my God." Tessie stood and turned it over between her fingers.

"What?"

"It's one of my artificial nails. Zanna is on the ship."

Chapter Thirteen:
The Real Bloodsuckers Are Here!

Zanna, sporting her new flashy fake nails, rapped on Toi's cabin door an hour before dinner, the tuneup hour, when women locked themselves in their bathrooms and glammed up for the evening.

The door opened to a blast of hairspray and lively chatter. "Yes?" A pretty blond boy toy raised his head a notch and sized her up. Then down.

"I'm Zanna Jones, here to see Ms. Brennan."

Before he could demand three photo ID's, Toi waved from the sitting area, her face plastered with a green mud mask. "Hi, Zan. Come on in, I've got a small makeup and hair crew here."

Small? Well, maybe for a big shot like her. Her suite was crawling with lab-coated hairdressers and makeup artists. The tang of mango-scented gel and mousse and more hairspray hung in the air.

Toi pointed to a chair at her vanity. "Sit there, hon, have a quick makeover. Emmett, give Zannie here a new face."

Emmett, who'd snooted her at the door, flounced over, plucked up Zanna's left hand and scowled at the purloined nails like they were the last thongs in a Victoria's Secret bargain bin. "I don't know about a new face, but these nails are outta here. They are *so* New Jersey!"

"How dare you," Zanna retorted, buffing the talons on her sweater. She'd lost one of the pinkie nails and sort of matched it to the others with some nail polish goop she bought in the ship's drugstore. "They're from Manhattan. Upper."

"No way. Nowhere above Ninth Street, honey. Lower. Definitely lower," Emmett quipped and began scrubbing her face with a loofah.

Toi said, "I've got the crew ready, Zan." Her lips barely moved, so as not to crack her mask. "I want to interview you for tonight's show. We're beaming it live, so review the questions." She tossed a list into Zanna's lap as a manicurist peeled off the nails.

"Give her something sophisticated, but BoHo," Toi instructed the nail artist. "And take those drugstore specials she's wearing and bury them at sea."

Zanna grew jumpy as she skimmed the interview questions:

Q: *Is hunting a part-time or full-time job?*

Q: *Can you quit, or is it a commitment for life?*

Q: *Do you move up in the organization only when somebody dies?*

Q: *How do you feel about vampires in the military?*

Things were more complicated now that her husband was a vampire and she couldn't stand to be near him. But she wouldn't blab that to reporters—those bloodsucking ghouls.

****

Mona stared at the fake nail. "So what now? Since you turned Zanna's husband, she's probably more pissed than a castrated bull."

Tessie glanced around, and Julianna's ominous warning to watch her back came rushing back to Mona.

Chills crawled across her skin like columns of ants. "I told Fausto I wanted to start my own anti-hunter crusade and use the media to back me, but he asked me not to. Then he told me about someone who died," Mona said.

"Oh, no. Who?"

"His first love, Josefina."

Tessie replied, "But he's right, once you expose these nuts to the media, they'll make a circus out of it."

"Who, the nuts or the media?"

"Both. Would you want the rag papers and the tabloid shows to mock us and hold us up to public ridicule to flash onto TV screens in twenty-four minute bites like a sitcom with no laugh track? I don't even trust *The Cutting Edge* not to go bananas if they get wind of this. As for the nuts, I'm lucky this is all she took off me." Tessie held up the nail to prove her point.

"I was planning to approach the more respectable networks."

Tessie screwed up her face like a Midwesterner driving past the Jersey Turnpike oil tanks for the first time. "It's all entertainment these days, kiddo. The line between what's fit and what's unfit to print has been way blurred over the years. It's better just to lie low."

"Okay for now. Let's go and start getting ready for tonight." She linked her arm through Tessie's and headed back to the dining room. "But first I need a java jolt. And one cannoli for each hip."

Tessie glanced at her watch. "Coffee, okay, but cannoli, fuggetaboudit. It's after ten. There isn't a cannoli on this ship that hasn't been chowed. The closest you'll get to a sugar fix is an Equal packet."

As they entered, a hand landed on Mona's

shoulder. She twirled around and just missed a microphone smacking her in the lips. Clasping it with a white-knuckled grip was Brooke Hill.

"Miss Rossi!" Brooke's heady perfume stunned her sinuses like a stun gun, stinging Mona's eyes shut. She reopened them to a bulky hulk, a camcorder perched on his shoulder. "We heard that you personally know some vampires who are aboard," Brooke probed. "Your public wants to know who they are!"

Mona backed away, bumped into a wide-eyed Tessie, and stared Brooke down, calmed by her caffeine deficit. "I can tell my public one thing." She lifted her head and spoke to the camera. "I don't know of any on board. If you think I have anything to do with them, your sources are misinformed. Go to Rome. Get an interview with the Vatican. The powers that be can give you enough dirt on vampires to propel you into Emmy territory. Again."

With that she hustled Tessie away, and they dashed into the dining room, the anchor and camera licking at their heels.

"But Miss Rossi—" Brooke pushed past the hostess and bumped into a cart piled with dishes. "It's already common knowledge you're intimately acquainted with several vampires. Can you tell us who they are? Are they sexy hunks like in romance novels?"

She twirled to face Brooke. "No, for the third time. I don't know any, and if I did, I wouldn't tell you about it. You're here to cover the writers' convention. So just do your job."

Brooke projected a practiced stage laugh and turned to her cameraman. "There you have it. She denies what we've confirmed, but we'll get to the bottom of this. We'll be reporting live from the *Romanza*, and at the New Year's Eve bash, I promise we'll get some vampires to open up. Once they're out of their coffins, there's no telling what will happen!"

Mona and Tessie grabbed the farthest table for two and sank into their seats, heaving huge sighs. The crisp white-jacketed waiter greeted them with a smile, filled their coffee cups, and handed them menus.

"Who the hell tipped them off about this?" Tessie's eyes darted around, but the chattering diners ignored the media vultures. Nothing short of hitting an iceberg would disturb mealtime.

"Zanna, who else? Now are you convinced we have to fight back?"

****

Fausto ended his shift the next evening at 5:00. Dressed in oil-stained plumber's overalls, a baseball cap, and galoshes, he knocked on Mona's cabin door. No answer. He checked the Cruise News, but all the writer workshops were finished. Where could she be? The gym? The spa? He turned and loped back down the corridor.

He passed a priest carrying a crucifix and a bottle of holy water. "*Buon giorno*, my son." The priest gave him a nod and held up a hand.

"*Buon giorno, padre.*" He couldn't hide the puzzled look. What was a priest doing on board? Nobody was sick enough to need last rites. Yet.

He headed for the piano bar next to the Theater L'Opera, but such a huge crowd jammed the entrance, he barely got to the top step.

"What's going on?" he asked another passenger who was craning his neck to see.

"They're taping a live television show. Something about vampires."

Fausto froze. "Holy *merde*." He tore down the stairs, ran across the deck one flight below, and bounded up the forward stairs to approach the theater from the stage entrance. He peeked out at the stage to see Babbling Brooke Hill interrogating a woman. Every seat in the audience was filled, and people packed the aisles. Cameras and spotlights lined the stage.

"Why did you become a vampire hunter, Mrs. Jones?" Brooke's voice boomed through the theater. "Moralistic reasons, or did vampires physically assault you?"

"Vampires captured me when I was a teenager," the woman replied. "They didn't just assault me, they nearly killed me. My mission is to stop them before they take away more innocent souls."

He didn't stay to hear the rest. Damn it, now they had the media on their tails. If the Ball Busters weren't enough.

He found Quintus in the private lounge soaking in the hot tub. He shucked off the disguise and eased himself into the bubbling hot water. "Did you see the spectacle in the theater that's packing the house?" Fausto asked him.

The Hooters version of a Roman slave woman brought a glass of wine and a plate of grapes.

"No, what is it? Nude lesbian gladiators?"

"Nothing that good. One of the hunters is giving an interview to Babbling Brooke of *The Cutting Edge*. That's it." Fausto heaved a frustrated breath. "We've been exposed."

That harked back an ironic guffaw from them both,

considering they were in full view with everything hanging out.

"Not necessarily." Quintus plucked a few grapes. "They don't know who we are. Keep wearing the disguises, and we should be okay."

"That's not the point. That show's already being beamed all over the world from here. It's just a matter of time before they find out who we are and make our lives hell."

Quintus lowered himself into the water up to his neck and leaned back. "Well, what do you propose we do, *capo*?"

"Mona's been badgering me about starting an anti-hunter crusade. Show the media who we really are, and slowly, over a few decades, they'll grow to accept us, instead of all the hate crimes and vampire bashing."

"It's hard to undo two millennia's worth of hate in two decades," Quintus said.

"Well, somebody's gotta do it. You want to spend the rest of your life—which is a damn long time—running?"

Quintus shrugged. "So they expose us, and then the whole world'll hate us instead of just a handful of nuts. I'm not too crazy about the general population either, but I won't have time to fight back. If you do, go for it."

He cuffed Quintus on the chin. "You've become a real softie, cuz."

"Not really. I'm just mellowing with age. I'm not the youthful warrior I once was. I have everything I want at this point. Finally marrying the woman of my dreams. She's one of us now. So, we'll just go *ptui* to the cameras and ride off into the sunset. You bite Mona in any of the right places yet?"

"No. She's still not ready."

"Bite her in her sleep," Quintus suggested. "Kind of like the tooth fairy. Leave a quarter under her pillow, and she'll get the hint something happened."

Fausto shook his head. "Nah, that's not my style. She'll come around, but it doesn't look like it'll be soon."

"Well, for your sake I hope it is soon. She's not getting any younger."

Fausto rolled his eyes. "*Mama mia*, Quin. She's all of thirty-four."

"The clock's ticking, bro." Quintus rested his head against the tub's edge.

Fausto nodded, understanding Mona's reluctance, but refusing to rush her. Turning a loved one was the ultimate gesture, the most romantic and sincere expression of love a vampire could share, but forcing it cheapened it. Mocked it. How he wished he could get to that heart of hers and set it free. "Maybe those kooks can make themselves useful after all," he muttered.

"What?" Quintus turned to look at him.

"Nothing, just talking to myself again. Sometimes myself comes up with useful answers."

****

Mona got so involved with helping Tessie write her vows, she didn't hear her cell phone beep.

"Hey, it's for you." Tessie handed her the phone.

"What is?"

"Your cell. Didn't you hear the opening bars of 'New York New York'?"

"No, sorry, I was in a writer's trance." She took the phone. "Hi, darling. Sorry, I'm so into writing these vows, you'd think they were mine. Oops, I—"

"Never mind, yours will be better," Fausto said. "Did you see the circus going on in the theater?"

"I was there for about two minutes and couldn't take it anymore. That's Zanna, the hunter wife, giving the interview. As long as she's there and we're in Tessie's cabin, we're safe, but what happens when she prowls for us again, leading the way for the media now?"

"We'll be in costumes tonight, so we'll have time to think about it. You going to be tied up with the bride until midnight or what?" he asked.

"No, we're just finishing this up." She laid the pen down and flexed her fingers.

"Good. Come to my stateroom when you're finished. We'll have a soak in my hot tub together."

"Mmmm." She licked her lips. "Sounds like good clean fun."

"Yeah, it'll be good fun, all right. But not clean. I mean, I don't use soap there. *Ciao*, babe."

She disconnected and gave herself a brief telling-off for breaking her vow to cool it with him. However, the thought of a frolic in the hot tub with him gave her a delightful shiver.

She turned the notepaper around for Tessie to see what she'd written. "I know the 'eternity' part would be hokey if you were still human, but it sure fits now."

Tessie gave her a big hug. "Hey, thanks so much, girlfriend! I'm so glad my best friend's a romance writer. How will I keep a dry eye during this?"

"You won't, so make sure you have your old standby, waterproof mascara."

"Of course I do. If the ship sinks, I have two waterproof necessities. Mascara and your borrowed

189

Pocket Rocket."

"Hey, speaking of something borrowed—keep the rocket on you during the wedding. Now all we need is something old, something new, and something blue."

Tessie lowered her lids and let out a wicked little laugh. "I told Quintus no hanky panky till the wedding night and have been putting him off, so I'll have something blue, all right. A certain part of him."

****

Mona whisked off her bathing suit coverup and stepped into Fausto's hot tub.

"Yo, this is a Roman cruise," Fausto warned, gesturing up and down her bikini-clad curves. "The only suit you're wearing in here is your birthday suit."

"But—" She shrugged. "Why not?" and slipped the suit off.

"Now that's more like it. You can't wear apparel in my private spa. That's my number one rule."

"I still have to get used to Roman decadence."

"Become one of us, and we can do it every night. Just like my ancestors, most of whom are still alive. They mate like horny teenagers."

"Yeah, five hundred years old and not even middle aged," she hrrumped. "Where's the justice?"

His dark chest hair glistened in the glow of the multicolored lights surrounding the tub. He was as exquisite as the naked marble statues all around the private doctors' lounge. Especially the one at the entrance, as nude and gorgeous and graceful as Michelangelo's David, but with one difference: the statue was fully aroused.

"What's the name of that Italian stallion at the entrance to the lounge with the huge boner?" She slid closer, thinking how much Fausto measured up to that statue in every way.

"Nobody, just an average guy."

"An average guy? You can hang a shower curtain on that thing."

"Average for a Southern Italian. And guess who the model was?"

Her hand found him, rigid and hard, and she began stroking him. Her stunned eyes questioned his smiling ones. "No way."

"Have I ever disappointed you?"

"Of course not, but—"

"They always look bigger in marble. But not half as much fun. Now...where were you?"

Chapter Fourteen:
This Ship Rocks!

Zanna slowed her pace as she approached her cabin, dreading to enter. Heavy footsteps echoed behind her. She dragged her sweaty palms down her pant legs. The thought of her husband curled her lip into a sneer. Self-loathing burned her throat. How could the man she promised herself to disgust her like this? But she hated those vampires even more. *Thank you, media, for putting your power behind me.* Her gratitude relaxed her.

Brooke and Toi brimmed with slimy confidence that this show would get the highest ratings of the entire year. Reporters waited outside the doctor's office, mikes and cameras ready for action, for Dr. Silvius to begin his shift. And once they unearthed his big secret, he'd be the ticket to Zanna's promotion.

Meanwhile, there was Teresa to deal with. Zanna grinned, licking the Vaseline off her lips. When they demasked at the stroke of midnight, showing the ugly visages to the shocked world, this was one ball she was sure to bust.

****

Mona brought Fausto back to her cabin to show him her Cleo costume. "You didn't manage to get the Cassanova duds, did you?" She unzipped her garment bag.

"No, but I'll be in costume tonight. I'm just not going to tell you what it is right now. It's somebody more notorious than Cassanova. I'll give you a hint: a famous writer had a field day with him."

She stopped in mid-zip. "Hamlet!"

"Nope. Fugget it, sista, I ain't tawkin'."

"How will I recognize you?"

"You will, but not right away. Just look around. I'll be lurking in the shadows," he warned, with a menacing tone and his mysterious slice of a half-smile.

"So you really can change into a bat!"

"That is way cliché, not to mention campy. I wouldn't even if I could. No, you'll just have to watch out for me. If I don't see you first and make a lunge for you." He sprang forward and captured her in his arms, enveloping her in a crushing bear hug. Giggling with delight, she wound her arms around him and they rocked back and forth.

"Okay, okay! I surrender!" He gave her a mouthwatering kiss and finally let her go.

"But how about the Ball Busters? And now, *The Cutting Edge*?" She laid out her gauzy costume on the bed. "I don't want anything ruining Tessie's wedding."

"And I'm sure Tessie doesn't either. Now that the media knows vampires are aboard, we'll have to do our best to dodge them. The hunters are another matter. But like I said, they're too wussy to do any harm in public. As long as we stay in costume tonight, we'll be okay."

"But costumes or not, Zanna knows who Tessie is and knows she's a vampire now. She probably thinks I'm one, too. We're bound to run into her. She's probably after us right now. So they're the two shadowy figures Julianna told us about."

He sat in her vanity chair and poured a shot of amaretto. "With Zanna's husband one of us now, I have a hunch she'll have a change of heart. When she's over her initial hissy fit, she'll let him turn her."

"Or snuff him out, before he commits another of her imaginary crimes."

"Either way, she's got issues, and I doubt she's in the mood for any costume balls. And they can't get in without a costume." He poured the dark liquor into the shot glass.

"Does she need one? She liked Tessie's fake nails enough to steal them, how normal looking can she be?"

"Don't sweat it, she won't show up." He dismissed the idea with a wave of the shot glass. "And if you're going to look like Cleo, I expect you to act like her, too."

She cocked a brow at him. "You mean express deliver myself to your door wrapped in a Persian rug?"

He sidled up to her and gave her arms a leisurely caress. She hummed with delight. "As long as the rug's all you're wrapped in."

"I don't know, these cabin boys do have limits, even at two bucks a day."

She slid the plastic off her costume, a cleavage-revealing, belly-baring number that would cover less than her face mask. He let out a low whistle. "No wonder Marc Antony and Caesar tripped over their tongues to get to her."

"Not exactly appropriate for the maid of honor at a wedding, but it's a costume ball first and a wedding second."

"Just wait and see what the bride and groom will be wearing," he remarked. "Quintus was always the flashier of the two of us."

"He likes to flash, all right." She remembered his family jewels display in the lounge. "But they're head over heels for each other. A really good match. She's not exactly the girl next door, either."

Fausto glanced at his watch. "We can out-flash them and get married naked in a tub full of champagne right now, before dinner. Worlds more romantic than your first wedding. I recall your telling me you married Ted at City Hall on his coffee break with his garbage truck idling at the curb."

She tensed, and once again her heart ached as she sighed. "Oh, darling, of course it's romantic and madcap and wild, but"—she wrapped her arms around his waist and leaned into his warmth—"as much as I love you, I just got through with one marriage to a man who's always got someone after him. I couldn't handle it. I don't feel capable of success at another marriage. I'm no good at it."

He rested his chin on the top of her head, and she felt his heart thumping. She sensed his hurt. "I can't force you into anything before your time, Mona."

They hugged and swayed for a long, comfortable moment.

"But if and when the day ever comes—" He forced a smile and nodded toward her costume. "I hope you'll at least wear that."

"How about a compromise? You can take it off me tonight."

"It's a deal. Now how about ordering dinner up to my cabin and dining on the balcony?"

"Sounds delicious. I have to meet Tessie at ten to help her get ready."

She looked forward to making it up to Fausto, spending a few leisurely hours with him, dining in private, maybe another frolic in bed. But when she opened her door, a huge globular microphone in her face made her stumble backwards.

****

Holding her breath, Zanna slid the card key into the lock, pushed the cabin door open, and peeked in. Royal wasn't there. She breathed a sigh of relief. All she wanted was to change her clothes and fetch her hunting items.

As she opened her briefcase, the creaking door jolted her. She spun around and froze. Husband and wife stared at each other like two strangers.

"Zan, I was walking around the deck, thinking..." Royal moved toward her.

She cringed. "Don't take another step, Roy. I don't want to be near you. You represent everything that made my life hell." She held up the crucifix, but he didn't cower or run away. She threw garlic cloves at him, and he kicked them under the bed. Why weren't any of these things working? She opened the vial and flung holy water at him. He wiped it off and came closer.

"You're supposed to be repulsed!" She held the crucifix at arm's length between them.

"I am, but not by that stuff. So, either they're all a bunch of crap, or I'm immune. But it's probably both, 'cause I sure as hell don't feel any different since any of this happened."

She inched the cross to her side, but kept it facing him. "You don't...want to suck the blood from my neck or crawl into a coffin?"

He let out a tired laugh. "No. When I need to feed, I will, somehow. But I'm not going to force you."

She shook her head, her mouth hanging open, unable to understand why he was saying all this—unless..." I don't believe you. You're trying to trick me just the way that Teresa woman tricked you. But I'm not buying it."

"I hate what I am, too, Zan. But I have to live with it and make peace with it. And the irony is, now I understand what they've all been going through for two thousand years. Maybe some vampires enjoy being who they are, and some hate it. But they all live with it. And you can't understand how a vampire feels unless you've lived in one's fangs. Figuratively speaking, of course. My bridge didn't sprout points after a soaking in denture cleaner."

"So you're going to"—she shivered, nearly dropping the cross—"give in to all those evil urges?"

"I don't know if I'll have any urges. I've been turned for almost twenty-four hours now, and I haven't had any urges. I don't want to bite you, for instance." He kicked another garlic clove under the bed. "Hell, I don't even want to kiss your hand."

She gripped the cross and brought it to her chest. "I can't handle this, Roy. I've got the biggest tabloid show on earth here and have exposed the vampires on the ship. Reporters are with them right now, convincing them to quit hiding and reveal themselves, so the world will know what it's up against. Priests are aboard, ready to perform exorcisms. But I didn't tell them about you. How can I possibly save face if they know my husband is one of them? They'd have me branded as a hypocrite."

"Well, then, maybe you are one anyway." His voice dragged, sad, defeated. "Because like it or not, I am what I am now. And I have to live with that, even if you can't." He turned to leave.

"Wait!"

He glanced over his shoulder. He looked so dejected, his shoulders slumped, his clothes hanging off him. His gut wasn't even busting out of his pants. He'd lost weight. Or that tramp sucked it out of him.

"Where are you going now?"

"To get sloshed," he answered. "Blood isn't the only thing we like to drink. I still like my shots of Scotch. Thank God for small favors."

"We can't go on like this, Roy. I've devoted my life to hunting vampires. Maybe you can live with yourself, but I can't. I—"

She dropped the cross, and it thumped onto the carpet. Sobs choked her. "I love you, but how can I stay with you after what's happened? I'll never forgive Teresa, and I'm trying not to blame you, but— somehow I feel it's your fault, too. You let this happen. I love you but I hate you!" She slammed her fists into her sides.

He placed his hand on the door handle. "Well, if you think I'm that weak, then you don't want me anyway. Goodbye, Zanna." He opened the door and walked out, closing it behind him.

Now she had another vampire to eradicate—if she wanted to. Fausto was her ultimate trophy, but she had her safety to think of. Roy was married to her, and when he was ready to suck blood again, he'd go for the most familiar and convenient source—her. If she didn't stop him first.

****

Mona tried to push the door closed, but reporters and cameramen barged into the cabin. An intense beam of light stabbed at her eyes.

"What the hell's all this?" Fausto sprang to his feet.

"Are you Dr. Silvius?" A tailor-made-suited Brooke Hill thrust her mike at him. "How long have you been a vampire, sir? Can you tell us how it happened? Who sucked on you to make you this way?" Not skipping a beat, she said out of the side of her mouth, "Get a closeup, Harry."

Fausto nudged her aside, bounded up to Harry, snatched the camera and smashed it against the wall. Heart pounding, Mona stepped back, hand flying to her mouth to hide her grin. *Knock 'em dead, Fausto!*

"Now get the hell out of here before you really make me mad." Fausto's fists clenched, his knuckles bloodless. "And trust me, my bite *is* worse than my bark."

Brooke held up a string of garlic, and he swept it from her hand, tossing it onto the vanity table. "Thanks. I was running low."

She gasped, staring at her empty hand like he'd torn her bling off. "Dr. Silvius has obviously decided not to admit to the world his true origin and orientation. For now he prefers to stay in the closet. But we will get the truth!" She spoke into a micro recorder. In a flash, it joined the busted camera.

"That's it. I'm calling security to kick you all off this ship." By then they'd backed out, leaving Fausto enough room to slam the door. He turned and leaned against it, swearing in Italian. His clenched fists struck the wall. His hair fell over his forehead.

Mona approached him, smoothing the stray locks back. She planted a row of kisses on his neck and opened his fists. "You did great. Certain celebs could take a few pointers from you."

"No, he couldn't. I should've punched that *cafone* out, not just smashed his damn candid camera." He heaved a deep breath, pushed himself off the door and splashed amaretto into a glass, taking a huge gulp. "Those *figli di puttana fottuto cretini*. Now they'll never leave us alone."

"So you're famous now. You have everything a movie star has. Gorgeous looks, tons of money, homes all over the world, a ripped bod, talent, brains— everything but a movie deal—for now."

"Hell, I don't want a damn movie deal. I just want them to leave us alone. We've survived all these centuries minding our own business, now one crazy *chiaccharione* opens her mouth and they're crawling all over us. We're reduced to tabloid fodder. Now I suppose we'll be tailed like friggin' NBA players." He drained the glass. "You have any crackers?"

That came out of left field. "No, why?"

"To spread that garlic on. I'm starved, and I can't wait for room service."

"Even if I did, I don't have a garlic press."

He whipped his key ring out of his pocket. There, swinging from a chain among his keys, was a gold garlic press. "An Italian coke spoon. I'd wear it on a chain around my neck but don't want to look too flashy. After all, it *is* eighteen karat."

She found the room service menu among the pile of Cruise Newses, evacuation instructions, and shore excursion itineraries. "What say we have dinner right here? In bed?"

"As long as you serve me the appetizer right now." And he proceeded to strip everything off and toss it on the floor—garlic press and all.

He looked every bit as good—and aroused—as that stud statue in the lounge. Oh, she wanted him!

"We can be like this forever, if you decide to become mine..." He rolled back onto her and ground his hips against her. She gasped in wonder, burying her face in the thick hair as he moved down the length of her body, causing her to arch toward him.

"I don't just want you to be part of my future. You *are* my future," he whispered. "Forever."

"Forever is a long time, Fausto. It makes my brain hurt to imagine the concept of infinity."

"Just take one day at a time, and don't think about it. That's what we do. Some might consider living forever a curse. But to me, it's a gift. Have you seen how happy Tessie is?"

"She seems happy."

"You should know. You're her best friend."

"But she's a different kind of person." Mona ran her fingers down his jawline. "To her, this is another big adventure. I don't know if she realizes she can never go back."

"I've never met a turned human who ever wanted to go back. It's always been a one-way ticket."

"But it's so—so permanent." She thought back on all the decisions she'd made, some she considered life-altering at the time. But there was always a way out. There was even a way out of her sucky marriage.

"Yes, that's the real test of character. If you can live with a choice like that. Because there's no alternative."

She wanted to tell him she was still young, she had time to make up her mind. But he had forever, and she was afraid to ask how long he'd wait for her.

She had to make up her mind before too long—after all, a year to her was a thousand to him.

Chapter Fifteen:
A Vamp and a Scamp

The port of Messina twinkled, and the stars twinkled back. But Mona didn't get off the ship. Warm lassitude oozed through her from the wild lovemaking and four-course dinner Fausto ordered.

She still tasted the buttery garlic bread she'd dipped in the rich tomato sauce. Tangy mozzarella fattened four ravioli. She ate till her belt dug into her waist. For dessert, she promised she'd take one bite of a sweet cream cannoli. That led to another bite, and another—and no more cannoli.

She got her costume ready to bring to Tessie's. But first she peered up and down the corridor for stalking reporters. Not a soul in sight. She dashed down the stairs, hiding behind her garment bag.

She rapped on Tessie's door, but no one answered. "Tess!" she stage whispered, in case any vultures were in the cabin next door or hiding in the air vents. "Tess, open up, I've got my costume."

Still no answer.

She glanced at her watch. Where the hell was Tessie, four hours before her wedding?

Just as she turned to make a quick getaway, the door opened. She squinted into the dim room and took a step forward. The sight before her eyes jolted her. Good God, this couldn't be her best friend! Tessie's eyes swelled from crying. A ratty robe hung on her like a sack.

"What happened?" Mona rushed in and closed the door, bolting it. "What's the matter, and why aren't you getting ready for the wedding?"

Tessie turned and scuffed toward the bed in her fuzzy slippers. "There isn't going to be a wedding."

****

Fausto entered the doctor's lounge, the only place on the ship he could spend a minute in private, now that they knew who he was and where he worked. He was sure they were tracking down his stateroom number.

The empty lounge zinged him with relief, everyone either at dinner or on shore exploring Messina's ancient charm.

He headed for the spa in the corner, shucked off his clothes, eased his body into the hot bubbling water and smiled, remembering his and Mona's rapturous lovemaking in his cabin hot tub. His arousal heightened as he fantasized about her luscious body, his fingers sliding over her curves under the hot water. Aching for his lover, he fought the urge to march to her cabin and tear her away from her preparations. He drew a deep breath and sank deeper into the tub so his growing desire wouldn't surface. If he wasn't so deeply in love with Mona, he'd be having a fling with a theater dancer—or two. But Fausto didn't want any more flings—not with the love of his life right here on board.

He closed his eyes and rested his head against the spa's edge as the humming motor lulled him into a pre-sleep trance. "Ahhh," he sighed. Finally, after five hundred years, he was truly content—well, not quite. Not until Mona agreed to be his.

****

Mona sat Tessie down, poured her a glass of strega, and thrust it into her hand. "Why is the wedding off?"

Tessie sniffed and took a sip, then another. And one more. "We got off the ship and were strolling down the street, arm in arm, just about to go into a bistro, when along came Brooke with a camera crew, surrounding us and hammering us with all kinds of outrageous questions: Can you suck another part of the anatomy besides the neck to get blood? Do you have an orgasm when you're feeding? Do vampires go through menopause? Quintus blew them off, or tried to, but they wouldn't let us move. He got his cell phone to call the police, but Brooke grabbed it, threatening to call everybody on his call log and interview them. Then he got his Italian up. He took a swipe at the cameraman, who clocked Quintus with a piece of equipment. It was dark, I couldn't see what was going on, but there was a lot of shouting and punching. Then two cops zoomed up out of nowhere, and the cameraman accused Quintus of assault and battery."

Mona stomped around the cabin thrusting her hands out in sharp gestures. "Damn! Why did that crazy Zanna *diavolo* have to open her trap to the media? And they call vampires bloodsuckers!" She paused and considered her friend. "What happened then?"

"The cameraman was on the ground, so he had all the credibility. The cops cuffed Quintus and hauled him off to the police station to book him. Oh, my God!" She leaned over the counter and pressed her face into her arm. "Who knows what'll happen now! We'll have to get married in a stinking jail cell and spend our wedding night on a metal bed hung from chains!"

"No, you won't," Mona promised her. "He'll be okay, I swear."

Tessie plopped herself on the bed and kicked her slippers off onto the wig that trailed on the floor—she was going to the ball as Lady Godiva.

"Look, Tess, I'll tell Fausto what happened, and we'll bail him out. It's not like he murdered anybody."

"No, but—" Tessie took a gulp of air and wiped her nose. "I kind of rushed ahead of myself."

"What?"

"Brooke kept spitting questions and shoved Quintus's cell phone down her front, so he"—she sniffed—"he lunged for her, tore open her blouse, and—oh, my God, I can't believe this happened—he bit her!"

"No way!" Mona's head spun with the sudden rush of blood. "He turned her?"

"She has to feed, and then she'll be completely turned."

"Where is she now?" Mona asked.

"Unconscious in the sick bay." She tossed her head in that direction.

"Why didn't you go with Quintus?"

"They wouldn't let me." Tessie gulped air. "They escorted me back here with Brooke and told me not to go to the station until tomorrow. My husband-to-be is in Sicilian Sing Sing!"

Mona balled her fists. "I'll get Fausto, and we'll work this out. Just stay put. I'll be back."

She headed for the lounge, knocked, and when the peephole opened, Fausto drawled, "Gimme the password, babe."

"Fausto, let me in, I have to talk to you."

The urgency in her tone got him opening the door fast. "Hey, gorgeous, in a hurry to get naked and join me for a—"

She cut him off. "Quintus is in jail. Not only that, he turned Babbling Brooke."

He rubbed his eyes as if it hadn't registered. "Run that by me again. And in less than a thousand kilometers a second."

When she repeated it, he headed for the spa and grabbed a towel. "I'll post his bail. He's been in Italian clinks before, but as far as Babbling Brooke goes, I only wish she'd stayed human. She doesn't deserve to be one of us."

Mona gave a grunt of disgust. "She doesn't deserve to be human either."

As he dried off and threw on his clothes, a knock sounded at the door. "What's the password?" she called out.

"I don't know, but I'm Royal Jones."

Royal! She opened the door, and he stood there, looking more dejected and miserable than when they'd left him in the attic. His shoulders slumped, his head hung down, he couldn't look her in the eye.

"What are you doing here?"

"We've been passengers on the ship since we left Rome, Mona." He raised his head and met her eyes. "Our mission was to hunt down vampires, and Zanna was after one in particular. I'm sure you know who he is. But things are very different now. And I need to talk to one of the vampire men, to get some things straight in my mind, about my new life, how to handle things. Because right now I'm suicidal, and I can't very well cut off my own head."

Fausto approached them and gripped the door, ready to slam it shut. "Can't this wait, Jones? It's a bad time. We're in the middle of another crisis here."

Just then, Royal pitched forward, pushed from behind. He stumbled through the doorway, his hands on Mona's shoulders, making her stumble back. She thumped against the wall as Zanna burst in, wielding a dagger like an Amazon in the vanguard of battle. "You! All of you!" she shrieked. "You ruined my life, ruined his life, and now I'm going to make sure you get what's coming to you!" Her hair flew out behind her in snakelike snarls as she lunged for Fausto.

He grabbed her wrist and held it above her head, squeezing. Her fingers splayed wide and dropped the dagger. It clanged to the floor. "Look, lady, I don't want to touch you, because if I do, I'll kill you. Just crawl back under your rock, and nobody'll get hurt."

"No!" She began beating his chest with her free fist. "I'm going to purge you from the earth. You're a curse to mankind!"

Mona dashed over to the bar and swiped a corked wine bottle. With one swift move she swung it in an arc and smashed it over Zanna's head. Red liquid and glass shards went flying in all directions.

Zanna swayed and crumpled to the floor.

"No, Mona! That's not wine, that's blood!" Fausto shouted, but nothing registered. Royal lunged for his wife lying on her side, but instead of helping her, he lowered his head to the floor and lapped up the dark liquid like he was marooned in the Sahara.

"Why's he doing that?" Mona backed away from the macabre scene.

"He's starving, he needs to feed," Fausto replied.

"He didn't have anybody to feed from. His wife's not turned, and he was desperate."

Zanna sat up, dazed, saw her husband slurping blood from the floor and let out a horrified scream.

Mona knelt next to her. "It's all right. He needs to feed. But these vampires prefer to feed from loved ones. Let him feed from you."

"No!" She scrambled away, slipping on the blood spreading over the floor, seeping between the tiles. "I can't let this happen!" She reached for the dagger, but Mona grabbed it first. She got to her feet, gripped the hilt, stood over Zanna.

Royal looked up with a savage look, his face smeared with blood. "Zanna, next time I won't be able to feed. If that happens, I'll die. Please, let me feed from you."

She shook her head, wincing in pain. "No, never. You're monsters, all of you!" Zanna made a move to kick him but plopped back down.

"Zanna, please, let me turn you," he begged. "It's the only way we can continue to live together."

She struggled to her feet and scuttled backwards, breaking into a run at the doorway.

Roy bolted after her, but Mona clutched his sleeve. "You'd better clean yourself up, bro. The way things are going on this cruise, a bloody face'll get you tossed overboard."

Dazed, he stood still while she dabbed at the blood with a wet towel. "Now go get 'er. You'll convert her, don't worry," she assured him. "You did okay recruiting Ball Busters. Just use those same powers of persuasion on her. And a lot of begging won't hurt."

"I've got begging down to a science, but I'm

expecting the worst." He turned and chased his wife down the hall.

Fausto hung the "in service" sign on the outside doorknob. "I gotta run to the doctor's office to get some hydrogen peroxide to clean up this blood. Meantime, don't let a soul in here. Even if it's the captain. If anybody insists, it's being cleaned and will be open in ten minutes." He dashed out the door, and she locked it after him.

She went over to the spa and dangled her feet in the cool water, going over everything that just happened. Her heart hurt for Royal. If she were a vampire, she'd have let him feed from her. She surprised herself. For the first time, the thought of being a vampire wasn't so revolting. She could be helping someone right now.

She let Fausto back in and asked him, "Now, how do we get Quintus out of the clink in time for his wedding?"

Dousing the tiles with peroxide and throwing towels on the floor to sop up the blood, he said, "We'll go down there and see what bail is set at. But I might have to exert some influence—by that I mean offer a few bribes or turn a few cops. I wonder if any of them are hot babes?" He gave her a wink and a cocky brow.

She pinched his arm. "Quintus can do that himself. He already turned Brooke. Just do whatever Italians do to spring their *paisani*. Tessie is frantic!"

They took a taxi to the precinct where the police held Quintus. It reminded her of what she'd read about the Tombs in nineteenth-century New York, a dank cavern where criminals, especially immigrants, were held without bail, starved and maltreated while awaiting an unfair trial presided over by corrupt judges.

A draft chilled her to the bone as they approached the captain, sitting at a beat-up metal desk. Another cop sat on a stool eating a cannoli. They were watching a laptop tuned in to *The Cutting Edge*, live from the *Romanza*. Did the whole world stop to watch this damn show?

Fausto addressed the captain in Sicilian dialect. The captain fired back a few choice phrases, which got Fausto slamming his fist on the desk. Catching a word here and there, she mouthed a silent prayer, then another as the conversation heated and hand gestures cut through air. She made out the words "solitary" and "uncooperative." It sounded like Quintus wasn't being a model prisoner, and he wasn't even in prison yet.

She thought of Tessie, back in her cabin, pacing the floor, bumping into the couch and table of the cramped quarters.

Fausto said something about *avvocato di fiducia*, lawyer. The captain shook his head, stubbornly refusing to budge.

She knew the Sicilian system didn't have a monopoly on scruples, but to arrest a man and deny him access to a lawyer? Had Quintus done something Tessie didn't even know about?

The captain came around the desk and clutched Fausto's sleeve. She tensed, thinking *oh, no. Now Fausto's going to join his cousin in the catacombs!* "Please, don't fight!" she begged him.

But Fausto turned to her, scratching his chin. "What made you think we were fighting? The captain here, Angelo, knew who Quintus was when they brought him in. They've been watching *The Cutting Edge* tonight. He wants to be turned because he wants to start a special police detail of vampires, to bring violent hunters to justice and educate the public on how dangerous they are. He's wanted to be turned for a long time, but now that things are getting out into the open because of the show, he feels this is the best time. Quintus doesn't want to do it, so they locked him away until he changes his mind." He added *sotto voce*: "Quintus might have good reasons for not wanting to cooperate, but I can tell you the biggest one—he isn't into turning other men."

Mona nodded, facing the captain. "*Signor*, you want something from Quintus?" she asked in her halting Italian. His blank stare told her that she'd better get Fausto to interpret. "Fausto, please tell him what I just said."

With him translating, she explained how they could work this out. "You want to be a vampire, captain?"

He nodded. "And your friend isn't getting out of here until I get what I want."

"Well, that's easier than posting bail," she said, but shut Fausto up before he could relay that. "Listen to me. I think I can arrange it, if you let him go."

Angelo shook his head. "I get what I want, then I let him go. But he no give me what I want."

"All right then. Come with us back to the ship. Would you be willing to let a beautiful woman turn you? She was just turned, and needs to feed. Let her feed on you, and let Quintus go."

Fausto translated for her as the captain nodded and licked his lips like he was about to bite into a footlong salami sandwich.

"*Benissimo!*"

A half hour later, they climbed the gangway onto

the ship, and Angelo flashed his badge to gain admittance. Two *Cutting Edge* reporters lurked around the metal detector, mikes and notepads at attention.

A pushy young thing in a designer knockoff snapped on her recorder and fumbled with the mike. "Miss Rossi, are you and one of the alleged vampires lovers?"

"In America, we're innocent till proven guilty, and I *am* dating Dr. Fausto Silvius. But vampire or not, he does give great neck. See you at the ball."

"But Miss Rossi—" The stringer nipped at her heels, clutching Mona's shoulder as she climbed the stairs. "Are you going to be a vampire, too?"

"No, tonight I'm Cleopatra. Try me again at Halloween. You might catch me as Elvira."

The stringer abandoned Mona and pounced on Fausto. "Dr. Silvius, is it true your cousin Quintus was charged with assault and battery on one of our cameramen? Do you have any comment on this?"

"Yeah. You ain't seen nothin' yet." Fausto gently nudged her aside. "I have a sick patient to attend to, and Miss Rossi isn't giving any more comments."

With that tone of authority, the stringer nodded reverently, made an about face, and fled into the elevator, clutching the recorder to her breast like she had Saint Francis of Assisi's meatball recipe in there.

Before parting with Fausto and Angelo at the doctor's office, Mona said, "I hope to have good news for Tessie soon." She told Fausto, "Send Quintus to her cabin as soon as he's sprung."

"*Certo, cara,*" Fausto assured her in that velvety voice that turned her to molten lava. He caressed her cheek, leaned over and gave her lips a lingering kiss that made her toes tingle. "After we tend to Brooke, I'll head back to the spa for that nap I didn't get before. It'd be nice if you join me there."

"I'll be there," she promised him, wished Angelo luck with his new life, and hoped everything would work out for these two tonight. Who was she to question the stars that shone over Sicily?

****

Fausto and Angelo entered the doctor's office. It was empty. Dr. Lombard sat at his deck mousing with a laptop. "How's Brooke Hill doing?" Fausto asked.

He released the mouse and looked up. "She woke up twenty minutes ago, telling me she had a raging thirst. I gave her water, but she turned that down. I gave her orange juice, she pushed it away. She said she needed blood. She made a lunge for my neck, but I fought her off and gave her a small bag of plasma. She tore it open and sucked it dry. You'd better attend to her. This is your area of expertise."

"Thanks, Doc. We'll take it from here." Fausto led Angelo to the back, where a row of hospital beds were lined up. Brooke lay in the first bed, eyes closed, wavy blonde hair splayed over the pillow, her chest rising and falling steadily.

The captain halted in his tracks. "That's the woman who's going to turn me?"

Fausto nodded. "Sure beats Quintus feasting on you, eh, Cap?" He approached Brooke and nudged her shoulder. "Brooke." She opened her eyes and fixed them on Fausto, then on Angelo standing beside him. Fausto introduced them, and they stared at each other for a long moment. Fausto could feel the electric charge between them. It could've lit up the whole ship.

She opened her arms and drew him to her like a magnet. "Come 'ere and gimme a piece of neck, Cap," she purred.

Fausto caught Angelo by the arm before Brooke sank her teeth into him. "Wait, isn't there a little matter of your end of the bargain?"

Fausto handed him his cell phone. Angelo called the precinct and issued the order to release Quintus and erase any record of his arrest.

"*Grazie*. Now I'll leave you two alone. Call room service if you want dessert." Fausto slipped out and closed the door.

****

"Seems like it's the tenth time I've done this today," Fausto muttered as he shucked off his clothes and tossed them onto a chair next to the spa. But he smiled dreamily as he remembered at least one of the times wasn't for a solo soak or a routine shower.

Rippling water bubbled around him. Just on the brink of slumber, he heard someone step in. Opening his eyes, he focused on a full-breasted, hourglass-shaped blonde. She sat so close, their thighs touched.

He couldn't make out her features in the dim light. But he knew she wasn't one of the nurses, and none of the doctors' squeezes were this hot. She wasn't any crew member he'd ever seen, on any cruise. So who the hell was she?

"I've never seen you here before." He stared at her luscious body. "How did you get in?"

"I have the right connections," she purred. "And everybody has his price."

"You're a crew member? I don't know you, do I?"

"But I know you, Dr. Silvius." Her voice was as

215

warm and sweet as honey. She splayed her long tapering fingers across his thigh and began working her way to his groin region, which was on the verge of throbbing.

"Hey! What the hell—" He slid away, but she slithered right up to him again, like she was adhered to his skin.

"Take a closer look, Fausto. I'm Lucrezia Borgia. Your almost-divorced wife from the year 1485, the first of October, to be exact."

He nearly jumped out of his skin. "Oh no, *Gesu Cristo*. How did you know I was here? And how did you get here so fast?"

"Sicily isn't all that far when you own a twin-engine jet." She snickered. "Those ignorant reporters, thinking we can turn into bats. Even if I was, I'd only be halfway over Naples by now. I thought you'd been killed with your family six months ago. The news reported 'the Silvius family' on a ship, and I naturally assumed you were with them. I thought I was a widow and went to apply for the Imperial Vampire Widow's Benefits. But I saw the live show *The Cutting Edge* is broadcasting from here. When I saw you were alive and well, I thought we must pick up where we left off."

"How did you get on board anyway?"

She smiled, showing perfect white teeth. "The easy way. I bought a ticket." Her familiar scent of heady gardenia-rose sent him back centuries. He remembered how delicious she always smelled and tasted, and felt frozen in time. Her lips glittered, full and inviting. "Incidentally, I offer my deepest sympathy for your losses. Your family was a cut above."

"Save your sympathy. What do you mean widow?

We're not married anymore. I filed for a legal divorce in England. Bishop Stillington signed the decree."

"Apparently His Excellency wasn't all that excellent. He overlooked one small detail—we weren't British subjects, so the divorce was never legal and valid."

He wanted to climb out, but his clothes were about six feet away, and he didn't want her to see what kind of effect her presence was having on his involuntary reflexes.

"Then we'll make it legal and valid now," he declared.

"Oh, no. Now that I know you're alive, I want you back with me, and you must agree we have a lot of living to do—among other things." She found the essence of his engorged manhood and wrapped her fingers around him. He thought he'd burst right there. "I see it hasn't gone down since last time."

He couldn't move a muscle, especially the one she had a firm grip on and was now stroking with exquisite mastery. She sure learned a lot in five hundred years.

"Let me go, Lucrezia, this isn't the time or the place."

"You want me to let go? Leave you alone? Never come back?"

"Yes, yes, and yes," he replied through clenched teeth as her other hand joined in and began teasing his sensitive underside.

"All right then. But I'll have a few things to say to the reporters lurking outside the door dying to burst in here. And I don't think your mortal girlfriend will be happy to see us naked in a spa beamed all over the world either."

"What the hell are you getting at?" He was losing his senses as her hands brought him higher into orbit.

"Leave that insipid human, and come back with me. We'll live in my Como villa, and no one will ever find us. Or I'll tell *The Cutting Edge* and the world what you really are—and I'll tell your girlfriend that you have a lawfully wedded wife."

Chapter Sixteen:
Digging Up The Past

Mona sat in her cabin, sipping an amaretto on the rocks, her hair in hot twisters. The sight of Roy lapping up blood haunted her. She stared out the window and focused on the distant battlements to purge that horrid scene. *Please, Zanna, come to your senses,* she sent the huntress a silent telepathic message, *let Roy turn you.* Where was the trust in that marriage?

And that brought her back to herself and Fausto. Why couldn't she take the plunge, marry him, and let him turn her? He knew about her checkered past, her disastrous first marriage, her hopes, fears, and dreams. In turn, she knew about his devotion to medicine, his passion for eternal life, his trustworthiness...oh, yes, she knew her Fausto. She also knew he was waiting for her in the lounge. A thrill scampered through her.

She unrolled the twisters, fluffed and sprayed her hair, opened her door and, checking the hallway for reporters, dashed to the stairway.

She rapped on the lounge door, and the small square slid open. "It's Mona, for Dr. Silvius. He's expecting me."

A doctor she recognized from the other night let her in. He slipped away and she stood there, alone. She glanced around, puzzled. No one sat at the bar—no Italian love songs crooned from the speakers. Was

Fausto even here?

Oh, was he ever!

Her eyes landed on the spa and her knees buckled. She grabbed onto the wall as if someone kicked her legs out from under her. There sat her beloved Fausto, a blonde bombshell hanging all over him. Mona's blood boiled.

Think straight! she told herself. Is he drunk? Is he drugged? Is he sick and she's a nurse? Is she a guy in drag?

She paced up to them in silence. In a heated discussion, they slapped the water in intense gestures.

She cleared her throat loudly enough for them to hear her over the motor's hum and whatever other noises might start coming from there.

They both looked up. His jaw dropped. The blonde's lips curved into a smirk Mona wanted to strip off with hot wax.

"You mind telling me what's going on here, Fausto?" Every muscle rigid, Mona waited for one of the lame excuses men stammer when all the blood leaves their brains. "Let's hear your old-fashioned Italian excuse."

"I haven't seen her in over three hundred years." He slid away as the blonde goddess unwrapped her hand from around Fausto's gonads and unfolded herself to a standing position. Water dripped from her full breasts, which looked damn real, too.

Sweating in her slacks and cable knit sweater, Mona felt like a *mamadelle* next to this nude Playmate of the Millennia.

"That's right, Mona." Her accent was tinged with classic Italian, as sickly sweet as jelled spumoni.

"There's something you should know about your boy toy."

"Shut up, Lucrezia," Fausto commanded.

Lucrezia? Mona's eyes widened in surprise. He rose from the tub, water sloshing over the edges, and strode over to grab his clothes. "Mona, *bella*, this isn't what it looks like. I have no interest in this woman."

She cast an intense stare at his crotch area, then back up to his astonished face. "No? That's not what Pepino there is telling me."

He reached for her, but she pulled back.

"Forget it, Fausto. I've seen enough. Does that thing have batteries or what?"

"Mona, please," he begged, and from the corner of her eye she could see Lucrezia wrapping herself in one of the ship's robes. But she made no move to leave them in privacy.

"She's trying to con me," he stage-whispered. "This is part of my past. My distant past, way before you were born—centuries before."

"You'd better tell her, or I will," came the accented voice as Lucrezia dragged up a chair and eased herself into it.

His gaze swept past Mona and landed on Lucrezia. "I'm going to tell her right now, so you can *vatenne!* Even if I was born yesterday and had no past to talk about, I wouldn't want you in my life. So sod off, and don't ever come back. We'll work out those—details later." He turned his back on her.

"What details?" Mona's ire intensified. So they had details now?

He pulled his pants on with no trouble, his arousal all but shriveled. "Mona, when we got divorced in

England, I thought it was legal, but according to Lucrezia, it wasn't, because we weren't English citizens. So, until I verify that, I have to assume we're still married." He halted, and his voice faltered, breaking with emotion.

"You're still married?"

He nodded, licking his lips, twisting his shirt so tightly, she could see the sweat oozing out. "Mona, please, it was four hundred years ago."

"So, what are you going to do about it?" She tried to keep her voice from a desperate shriek.

"I'll find a way to get divorced. Or have it annulled."

Lucrezia gave a sarcastic laugh. "You can only annul a marriage that hasn't been consummated, silly boy. And, *si si*, did we consummate!"

"Please, Mona, just listen." He reached for her again and she backed away.

"Why didn't you tell me this before? Are there any more four-hundred-year-old wives I don't know about? Who look like they're five hundred?" She shot a glare at Fausto's sparkling spouse.

She sized Mona up like she was fifty pounds of bologna in a five-pound bag.

"No, of course not." He shuffled from one foot to the other. "I'll get a divorce. I'll get her to give in." His voice cracked like a little boy's.

"How? By the looks of her mouth, it knows when it's found something to suck on."

"She said either I return to her, or she'll expose me to the media." He turned to face his wife—or whatever she was. "You're right, maybe it's about time I do expose myself—I mean, as a vampire." He turned back to Mona. "I'll expose her, too. She's a vampire. And she's committed some heinous crimes she wouldn't want the world to hear about. I don't like playing dirty like this, but I need to get her off my back and prove I love you and want to marry you."

Mona's heart softened at those words as tears stung her eyes, but she couldn't stand here another minute. "I don't know what to believe, Fausto. I thought I knew everything about you—your past. But this?" She gestured to Lucrezia, the robe hugging her curvaceous body. And this woman was over four hundred? Damn, she wanted to look that good at forty. Envy nearly blinded her, adding to her rage. God, she felt ugly! And not just physically—emotionally, too.

"I don't want to hear from you until I see divorce papers. But that doesn't mean I'm going to take you back."

"But why not?" His eyes pleaded.

She turned to leave, but he blocked her way to the door. She elbowed him aside. "Because you just humiliated me more than any human being deserves to be. And right now I can't even think straight. So get out of my way!"

She would have hit him if he hadn't stepped aside to let her go. Without a backward glance, she walked out of his lounge and his life, leaving him with his lawfully bedded wife.

Not knowing where else to go, she headed to Tessie's cabin. "Tess, please open up, I need to talk to you!" she wailed as she banged on the door.

Tessie was wrapped in a towel, steam pouring from the bathroom. The sweet fragrance of lavender floated around her. "Sorry I took a while to answer, I was taking an herb bath to calm me down. I'm a bundle of nerves. Hey, what's the matter?" She pulled Mona inside and closed the door, leading her straight to a row of bottles on the vanity. She poured a shot of strega, and Mona downed it.

"Fausto and I are over."

"Why? What happened?"

"His wife happened, that's what."

Tessie stumbled backward, knocking a pile of eyeshadow compacts to the floor. "What? He's already married? To who? What the hell happened?"

Mona sat, taking a load off her wobbly knees. Emotions, all negative, logjammed in her chest, her throat, her mind, each fighting to overpower the other. "I found him and his wife in the hot tub. He claims he has no interest in her and he's divorcing her, but—well, you know how parts of guys' anatomies don't lie. One head was doing all the talking, while the other one stood at attention and watched."

Tessie spread her hands before her as if laying out a map. "All right, he's married. He insists he's getting divorced, and thought he was divorced. Until then, you're not gonna live like a nun, and you're especially not gonna spend New Year's Eve in a cabin watching reruns of *Shrek* on a twelve-inch TV. Go to the ball, have a good time, dance, drink, eat, flirt, find an orgy or start one. There are plenty of single hunks aboard, and that's just the busboys. You're Cleopatra. You think if Marc Antony screwed up, she'd sit home playing with her asp? No, ma'am, she'd go out and do the town! And Italy isn't any less debauched than it was in her time. So go out and shake it, Cleo!"

Mona's spirits began to lighten. A smile curled her

lips. Tessie's pep talk did have some oomph to it. "Yeah! Why should I sit around waiting for him to get his life in order? And if he does stay married and celebrate his golden—platinum—hell, what is a four hundredth anniversary anyway? Whatever it is, screw him!"

"You go, girl!" Tessie high-fived her.

"All right, I'll go. It beats sitting in the cabin and accosting the cabin boy. But I'll have a shitty time."

"No, you won't. He will." She pinched Mona's cheek. "Just think, you're still single and free, and he's stuck with his old lady!"

"I got news for you, kiddo." Mona poured another shot. "She doesn't look a day over ninety."

"Oh, she's one of them—I mean us—I mean—never mind, you know he'd rather be with you! Just keep that in mind. And it'll be easier to ring in the New Year knowing he's wild with desire over you."

She sighed. "Yeah, that's a consolation. That *puttana*, why did she have to show up now? It's all that damn *Cutting Edge*'s fault! I'm so sorry I invited them on this trip!"

"Never mind, they're still on our side." She put an arm around Mona and gave her a squeeze. "They've already made this writers' cruise of yours a household word. We can have these all year round, you can live on ships if you want to, and your books'll take up every slot on the best seller list. They'll have to expand it just to let some other authors in!"

"Oh, Tess." Mona gave her friend a forced smile. "You really know how to pull somebody out of a sewer, don't you?"

"Now that's one thing I've never done. A

Dumpster, but not a sewer. I'll get dressed, we'll go to your cabin and get you Cleo'd up and hit that ball like lightning. And you're still my maid of honor."

Yikes, she'd almost forgot Tessie was getting married tonight. She tried not to let that bother her. She was thrilled for her friend, but being alone watching her enter holy matrimony was going to hurt.

She bowed her head and begged, "Please, God, let this work out. I'm furious at him...but I just know I'll take him back the minute he's free again. Should I? Oh, give me some guidance. I love this man so much!"

****

Fausto pulled on his shirt, grimacing at his ex-wife's sickening fragrance. He couldn't stand the sight of her. His stomach churned, his blood seared his veins.

"Why don't you look at me, Fausto?" came her pathetic plea from the tub.

He clenched his tongue between his teeth. "Because if I face you, I'll kill you with my bare hands. You have nothing else to do with your empty life than make mine miserable, go ahead!" He turned halfway around, so he wouldn't have to look at her. "Expose me to the world. That threat is as sick as you are. Now, you divorce me, or I'll expose your dirty secrets to the world. And I'll start by telling them who you are, Lucrezia Borgia! You're one of the most dangerous people alive. I don't believe for a minute you've turned a new leaf in the last four hundred years and hung up your daggers, garrottes, and poison *or* quit your orgies of murders. Every time a guy dies a mysterious gruesome death, I suspect you're behind it. So don't think you can toss your empty threats out at me. Because once you expose me as a vampire, I have no reason to shut up about who you are."

Her gasp echoed and faded into the tile walls. "Why would you do that to me? We once loved each other! How can you be so cruel, Fausto?"

"Oh, get off it. You have some nerve calling me cruel, you *donnaccia*. You never spent a decent day in your life. By the time I met you, you were a vampire and still poisoning and stabbing and sucking dry every man who got in the way of your horrid schemes, just like you did in your wayward youth," he spat. "You don't deserve to be alive, and once I expose you, prosecutors will be falling over each other to take your case. Whoever puts you away will have his name in lights." He cut through the air with his hands. "There's no statute of limitations on murder. Yours will be the most infamous murder trial in the history of mankind. A vampire woman being prosecuted for centuries-old homicides. And there's still plenty of evidence on record. You've been well investigated since then."

He heard a sob escape her throat as he slipped into his shoes, still unable to bear looking at her. "No, Fausto, we can start another life together! I thought you were dead, it was just by luck that television show is aboard the ship and I found it—and you. I feel like a piece of my life's been missing all these years, and I found it again."

"It was over when we got divorced. It's too late now, I'm in love with someone else, and you can't have me back. Mona is the love of my life; I will never love anyone else."

"Fausto, you're my husband, and you are coming back with me!" She stepped around him to face him, and he grabbed her wrist. "What are you doing?"

"I don't take orders."

With a viselike grip on her wrist, he led her into the cabin he used. He got out the handcuffs he kept stashed in the drawer and snapped one end around Lucrezia's slender wrist. The other end he secured to the headboard rail. Not exactly his idea of what he'd wanted to do with these cuffs, but they were coming in handy.

"Ha, still using those, are you?" Her voice dripped with degradation. "Last time you did this to me, it was for fun."

He pulled the phone toward her until the cord was stretched taut. "Okay, you have such high-powered connections, you're going to call one or two of them. You're going to notify whoever you need to and get that divorce. And you're going to get documents e-mailed to this ship tonight. Or else I expose you and your crimes to the world. Now I have some breaking news to go and report."

As he headed for the door, he realized one thing: she had done him a favor. It was about time the world knew who he was. He was proud of it and damn sick of hiding, living a double life in a dark closet, worse than any coffin dreamed up by ghouls who wanted vampires to be monsters in the dark caverns of their own minds.

"No! Fausto!" Her shrill voice rattled his eardrums. He halted, his hand on the doorknob.

"Do you know what this will do to us?" she shouted. "We'll be hunted forever, we'll be social pariahs, we'll be stalked every minute. The government will send the army out after us. We'll be the enemy, one notch below terrorists!"

He turned his head halfway. "What planet have you

been on? There have been nuts after us for two thousand years! Once I let them know who we are, they'll realize we mean peace and leave us alone. Now get on that phone and get me my divorce, or I'm telling the world who you are, you're still alive, you're a homicidal maniac who belongs locked up. I'm going to the media right now and tell them who I am. And if you don't want me to tell them who you are, get on that blower and get papers sent here so I can sign them. Which will it be?"

She hesitated, and he knew damn well it was for dramatic effect. No way would she let him expose her identity to the world.

"All right!" she finally said, her voice hoarse and defeated. "I'll contact my lawyer."

He nodded, satisfied for the moment. "So shut up and start making calls. You're not getting out of here till you've produced papers."

****

"Hey, I am gorgeous, if I do say so myself." Mona lifted her chin and gave the mirror a dazzling smile as Tessie did a fabulous makeup job on her. Shimmering silver eye shadow from lid to brow dazzled. Coal black liner gave her sultry cat eyes. A set of spidery false eyelashes fluttered when she blinked. Her ruby lips glittered, looking eager to be kissed, but she wouldn't be in any lip locks tonight, even if Marc Anthony did show up.

She lifted her hand to touch the crown of delicate braids on her head, encircled with a faux diamond headdress. The gauzy halter top and skimpy bottoms clung to her curves. Gold bangles tinkled at her wrists. Her shapely legs looked fabulous in rhinestone-studded high-heeled sandals. No dancing tonight, either, unless she ditched the shoes.

She spritzed herself with a new Italian perfume, *Pulsare*, the word for throb. Would she love to get something throbbing tonight! But it just wasn't going to happen. *He's married*, she kept telling herself.

"*Bellissima!*" Tessie walked in a circle around her. "You'll knock 'em dead when you walk into that ballroom. You sure you don't want to make a grand entrance wrapped in a rug?"

"No, that's too predictable. Just sashaying in will be enough. Like I learned in Creative Writing 101, keep it simple, stupid."

"Yeah, you're right." Tessie waved her hand and flicked a lock of her five-foot-long hair behind her shoulder. Her fleshtoned body suit looked great on her, with appropriate body parts painted on in the right places.

"I hope Quintus realizes that's a body suit and doesn't try to—you know. Do the nasty to it," Mona said as they took one last glance in the full-length mirror and held up the hand mirror for rear views.

Tessie gave the wig a quick shift. "Oh, he knows I wouldn't prance around in the buff—even if the prize for best costume *is* a free cruise. Now if it included first class plane fare..."

Mona let that hang in the air as they headed for the Tango Ballroom. She threw back her shoulders, thrust her breasts out, held her head high, and tried to forget she'd just lost the love of her life. Over and over she reassured herself, "You're strong, capable and deserving of love. Wherever that leads me, I'm not hiding from it any more."

****

Fausto opened his closet, but he'd already decided he wasn't going as Richard III. Those damn tights always chafed him in the wrong places anyway. No, he was going to wear something appropriate to the occasion—not just New Year's Eve, or just the night he was going to beg Mona to forgive him. This was the night he was going to tell the entire world about him and his people—a heavily veiled secret whose time had finally come. He now knew the joy of liberty through history, how the slaves rejoiced when they were finally freed. The Pilgrims' joy of escaping tyrannical rule was his own joy.

And in a few moments, he would be forever free, never again forced to conceal his true feelings.

He knew he wouldn't win any prizes tonight. What he was now donning wasn't a costume. It was simply what he felt like wearing. It would shock a lot of people, get the media scrambling for his attention, cameras and mikes shoved in his face, and hot lights blaring at him, but what better way to reveal truth than to simply dress truth. No more disguises. Tonight, for the first time in five hundred years, he was going out as no one but himself, Dr. Fausto Silvius.

Chapter Seventeen:
Riding the Waves

Mona and Tessie weren't even fashionably late. They walked into the packed ballroom as the clock at the entrance bonged ten times. Costume-bedecked partygoers mingled, danced, and flitted by.

A glitter ball shot rays of colored light around the room and over the sweaty bodies gyrating on the crowded dance floor. The band was playing some hip-hop tune she couldn't make out because of the crowd's chatter. Cutting Edge reporters skulked around, cameramen on their heels. Mona glanced down over her costume. Clingy as it was, it looked white-bread compared to some of the others. Besides the Elvises and Marilyns and Chers—and that was just the guys—some of the couples popped: Prince Charming carting Cinderella around in a mini coach, Fred and Wilma Flintstone, Ricky and Lucy. She thought she'd seen it all when a six-foot papier mache penis with balloons for testicles came prancing in, squirting Silly string out of a hole in the top.

"Hey, where's *his* partner?" Tessie pointed to the erect phallus as they headed for the punch.

Mona answered, "Doesn't matter, it looks like he started *and* finished without her."

"At least we've gone five minutes without a report—" Tessie's words drowned fast when Babbling

Brooke sauntered up to them, mike in hand, cameraman on her butt. Angelo, in his cop uniform, swaggered alongside her. He embraced Mona, thanking her for bringing him and Brooke together.

Brooke wasn't in costume. Mona figured a getup was beneath the dignity of a reporter of *her* stature.

"Mona!" She swept her electric blue-contact lensed eyes over Mona's costume and gave a little chortle. "Cute."

Cute? Mona thought, her unimplanted thirty-eight C's spilling out of her halter. "You, too," she mouthed, her lips at the rim of her punch glass. She bit her tongue, so desperate to ask Brooke how it felt being a vampire. Had turning been painful? How did she take it emotionally? How was she getting along with Angelo? If there was any time to turn the tables and pump Brooke with questions, it was now.

But the reporter started right in with her inquisition. "So, where are your beaux, ladies? And where are you newlyweds going on your honeymoon?" She turned to Tessie.

Tessie said, "I asked Quintus not to come to the ball. It's bad luck for the groom to see the bride before the wedding, and I'm not taking any chances."

"And you?" She shoved the mike at Mona.

"I don't have any comments about this, Brooke. But the writers' convention is going so well, I'm planning another one for the spring—if I'm not too busy writing my next best seller." She turned and walked away, as Tessie started yakking with some editors.

She heard Brooke say something into the mike about Mona's uncooperative mood but didn't stick around to listen. She really didn't give a damn what was being beamed around the world about her right now.

She searched for Fausto but doubted he'd show up. No, he was with his wife, doing God knows what—and legally. Were they arguing? Reminiscing or catching up on four centuries of life apart? Would they rekindle their long-lost love and start over? The thought of him ravishing another woman hit her like a punch in the gut. She couldn't bear to think about it, but her mind was intent on torture. This was a bad idea of Tessie's after all. She wasn't having a good time here. She kept her eyes glued to the entrance, wishing he'd appear. Unable to purge him from her mind or her heart, she wondered: *What is he doing? Where is he? How is he feeling? Is he thinking about me?*

No, of course not. Not with his wife hanging all over him.

Damn him! Her disgust festered as she stood against the wall sipping punch, watching all the dancing, drinking, eating, flirting …the indulgences she was denying herself. But the mile-high buffet turned her stomach. More booze would give her a wicked hangover. There was nothing for her here. She'd be a lot more comfortable in her cabin, in her robe, in her bed. So what if Shrek II was on again? She liked it the first two times.

She turned to leave. There stood Zanna in the doorway peering in, looking very out of place in orange sweats.

"Zanna, what are you doing here?" She knew Zanna was hardly the partying type. Staying home and parsing Scripture was more her idea of a noble pastime.

"I'm getting ready to leave but just wanted to see what was going on in there." Zanna clutched her purple duffel bag. Her red nails clashed with everything. "Looks like they'll suffer the wrath of the grape tomorrow—massive hangovers, that is. Oh, well. See you around." She turned to leave.

"Zanna, wait."

She made an about-face, her expression telling Mona to make it fast.

"Why are you leaving?"

"I can't stand living with my husband, who is now a non-human. I can't live like this. I also can't forgive him. And worst of all, I can't forgive myself for feeling like this. I dedicated my life to capturing vampires, and now my husband is one of them. I need to work all this out. See you."

She clutched Zanna's sleeve. "Wait just a minute. Listen to me. Why don't you let Royal turn you? He needs you more than ever now. And don't forget, you exchanged marriage vows. For better for worse, in sickness and in health. Not that vampirism is a sickness, but it would be selfish and cruel to leave him now. Vampires are good people."

"If they're so good, let Fausto turn you."

Touché, Mona thought, and grimaced . "I—" She didn't want to get into all that. But who was she to preach when she was still so afraid of being turned? She gave the sincerest answer she had. "Fausto doesn't need me turned the way Royal needs you. Let Royal feed from you and enjoy your new life. Because if you don't, he'll have to find somebody else. Hunters are no match for vampires, you should know that. You're the underdog. If they wanted to, they could wipe all of you out with one stroke." Her hand sliced the air. "The young ones are clairvoyant. They'll track you down and stalk you until you crack under pressure. They suck the psychic energy from victims, if they need to. But over the centuries, they didn't, because they're peace-loving people, not warriors. They have first strike capability but would never use it. Fausto could've crushed you in the lounge when you attacked Royal." Her voice rose on that emotional note. "But he didn't, did he? So go to your husband and honor the vows you took with him. Meanwhile I'm going to work out a few issues of my own."

Zanna stood there, chewing her fake nails. Finally, she said, "When I see you turn, I'll turn." Hefting her bag onto her shoulder, she trudged away. "Until then, I'm single, once again."

Mona's heart went out to Zanna, the troubled, confused woman. Part of Mona's quest would be trying to straighten out people like her.

If she ever started her quest. If Fausto stayed with his wife, she'd have to restart her own life and put vampires out of her mind. If, if, if...

But a spark in Zanna's eye gave her hope. She knew Zanna wanted to help herself. She just needed a nudge in the right direction. That dash of hope gave her an invisible push back into the ballroom. Why retreat to the cabin and mope? It was New Year's Eve on a luxurious ship, on a cruise she'd organized, and dammit, she was thirsty again!

And not for soda pop. She downed another punch, danced with Napoleon and another guy who was either Mozart or Thomas Jefferson, and turned down an adoring proposition from Darth Vader. Now if he'd been the Incredible Hulk...

Just then, Tessie rushed up to her. "You ready to help me change into my bridal gear?"

"You're not getting hitched like that?" Mona gestured up and down Tessie's fleshtoned barely-there costume.

"No, I couldn't do that to Quintus. I'd embarrass him to death. Come on, my gown's in the back, where the band hangs out."

They went backstage, and she helped Tessie peel off her costume and into her bridal gown. It was a simple blue satin sheath with a lacy shawl. Her only jewelry was her St. Anthony medal. "Always the good Italian girl," Mona said as Tessie slipped into plain pumps. They probably weren't even a big designer name. Deep down, Tessie was a Marshall's junkie.

Just then, the band stopped, and the cruise director took the stage.

"Ladies and gentlemen, we have a wedding at midnight, and since that's ten minutes away, please clear a path for the bride, Teresa, as her groom Quintus and Father Dragonetti await her arrival."

Quintus and Father Dragonetti approached the microphone, the priest flipping through pages of his prayer book.

"Ready?" Mona asked her best friend.

"Yeah, but if we don't get this over with, I'm gonna faint!" Tessie trembled as Mona waved to Father Dragonetti. The band struck up the beautiful Italian love song "Innamorata." Mona led the way, and when she reached the groom, she stepped aside for the bride to join him.

Tessie pulled a crumpled paper out from her

cleavage and unfolded it. She and Quintus read the vows she'd helped Tessie write.

"Quintus, I've known you for many lives before this..."

When they finished exchanging their vows, Father Dragonetti continued with the traditional ceremony: "Quintus, do you take Teresa to be your lawfully wedded wife..."

Mona blinked back the sting of tears, a weepy mess by the time Quintus and Tessie became husband and wife. Oh, if only things had turned out differently for her and Fausto...

She gave Tessie and Quintus hugs and headed to the back for another glass of punch. Sudden shrieks sounded through the room. The music stopped, the chatter ceased, and the crowd parted like the Red Sea. A tall imposing figure swept across the floor, taking center stage in front of the silenced band.

He took command of a standing mike. When she heard him address the crowd with a simple "Good evening," she stumbled back in shock, almost landing ass first in the punchbowl.

It was Fausto, in the most stunning outfit he'd ever worn. A black velvet cape swirled like liquid onyx. A gold medallion rested on his chest. His black hair was slicked back, revealing a widow's peak. His look bordered on sinister. His dark eyes penetrated the room with a devilish twinkle. A smile revealed two gleaming white fangs. He projected a picture of menacing confidence.

But to the crowd who saw a familiar figure they all feared, he was simply, "Dracula! It's Dracula!"

"Hey, it's one of the real vampires!" Toi Brennan

dashed across the floor, dragging a cameraman behind her. "Zoom in! Get a tight shot of the fangs!"

"Ladies and gentlemen…" As Fausto began, a hush circled the room. "I'm here to explain a few facts that have been grossly misunderstood over the centuries. Many innocent people have been persecuted, and even killed over the ignorance, intolerance, and cruelty borne from these faults, and the victims do not deserve it."

An excited buzz filled the room.

"There has been speculation, brought about by news hungry reporters and other attention-starved people, that vampires are aboard this ship. As a result, the ship's become a three-ring media circus. Cameras and reporters have accosted many of us, rudely in the extreme, but it's been denied over and over. However, now I want to bring those rumors to an end, and tell you, attending this ball, the media broadcasting to the far-flung reaches of the world, and to the world itself, that yes, there are vampires aboard."

He paused as another gasp rose and died down. Mona's jaw almost dropped into her drink.

"But I've come here to dispel some myths, and once and for all, set the entire world straight!" His voice boomed as he raised his arms, and the batwing-shaped cape billowed. He stood still, arms extended, as if perched for flight. She was sure some of these people expected him to change into a bat and soar around the room, swooping over their heads, but he simply lowered his arms and continued speaking.

"Vampires are decent people. We love our families, we work hard at our careers, we're devout Christians. What we don't do is bite random necks, sleep in coffins, turn into bats, and crumble into baby powder in sunlight. Those are myths, perpetuated throughout the ages. These clothes do not make me a bloodsucking ghoul." With that, he shrugged out of the cape, and it spilled to his feet. Toi Brennan slid across the floor on her knees, grabbed it, and slithered away.

"They're simply garments, like you wear." He slid out of his blazer and tossed it aside. He pulled the medallion from around his neck and pitched it into the crowd. A woman caught it, shrieking with glee. He then unbuttoned his shirt, opening it to reveal his muscular chest. He cascaded a hand over the curly dark hair. Several women intoned their delight. A mix of pride and jealousy hit Mona.

"We come from a long line of vampires from the fourth century." He gestured around the room, but to no one specific.

As he spoke, he slipped off his cufflinks and dropped them into a glass, one at a time. Trembling, Mona turned to the door, mouthing "Please stay away" in a silent plea to the hunters. She dreaded they'd burst in and kill him any moment. She tore her gaze from the door and stared at him performing this outrageous act.

He let the shirt drop and now stood in bare-chested glory. He slid his thumbs into the waistband of his tight pants.

"Our critics and enemies call us vampires, but they're off the mark. We're people, just like you."

He unbuckled his belt and slid it through the loops. He cracked the leather strip through the air like a whip. Mona's blood surged, both with passion for the man she loved, and raw rage. He was going to get them all killed! Didn't he realize what he was doing?

"Over the centuries, we kept it a family secret.

During the days of early Christianity, the hunters found out who some of us are, so vampires rebelled against the Church. And the Church fought back. With all the righteous vengeance they could muster."

He stepped out of his shoes.

Several women held their breath. Fausto now brought intense eyes directly onto Mona, as if they were the only two people in the room. Her breath faltered. "But I'm not hiding any longer. I don't go around sucking every woman's blood. Just the blood of my soul mate."

As he spoke, he unzipped his pants, let them fall, and stepped out of them. He pulled off his socks and was now standing before the crowd in nothing but sheer, bulge-hugging Speedo briefs. Mona sucked in her breath. She blinked against angry tears stinging her eyes.

A few waiters gathered by the exit doors, shaking their heads and whispering to each other. One of them dashed out the door.

Ignoring their partners like they'd never existed, women inched their way up to him as he continued. "We're real people. We have a right to dress how we want, worship how we want, marry who we want. See how absurd it is to hate us because you think we're different? Look at me, ladies and gentlemen." He looked down at his Godlike physique, ran his hands over his washboard-flat abs, and said, "I'm just like any other guy." The women cheered. A pair of panties flew through the air and landed at his feet.

"But I'm in love with one lady, the love of my life. I made a mistake, which I'm afraid drove her away."

Mona's chest tightened. What a fool she'd been to

fall for him, when he was already married and now making his love for his wife public.

"And I want to beg her forgiveness."

Mona choked back a sob as a stab of pain went through her heart. Betrayed twice, first by Ted, and now by Fausto.

Just as he was about to speak again, two security guards rushed up to him, seized him by the arms, and escorted him out a side door. The crowd buzzed. Some women began sobbing, wiping at their tears.

Tessie rushed up to her, gave her a warm hug, and spoke soothing words she didn't even hear.

Quintus cupped her elbow. "Mona, I need to talk to you."

"No, just let me be alone a while."

She turned and fled up the stairs, another flight, and another flight, until she was on the sun deck, so exhausted from running, she collapsed on the floor in a heap of tears.

****

The ship's captain had relieved Fausto of his duties, blackballed him from Apollo Cruise Lines, and told him he'd be escorted off the *Romanza* when they located a replacement doctor. Now Fausto sat on his balcony, alone, letting the wind whip through his hair and chill him through the flimsy blanket he'd thrown over himself. His clothes were still in a heap on the ballroom floor, unless souvenir hunters had snatched them all up.

He shook his head and sighed, sipping his strega. All he'd wanted to do was show the world he was normal, and now he had nothing—no wedding, a centuries-old wife doing God knew what to destroy him, and he'd lost the job he was so devoted to. If only he hadn't let Mona talk him into taking this cruise, he'd be home—grieving, but in peace.

Damn, what a mess he'd made of everything! How could he possibly straighten this out and get Mona back?

He drained the drink. *You can't*, he told himself. *It's over.*

****

Mona's cell phone rang, and she checked caller I.D. She didn't recognize the number, but she knew it wasn't Fausto, so she answered.

"Oh, it's you, Quintus. Why aren't you honeymooning?"

He didn't answer her question. "Where are you?"

"On the sun deck, aft. I just want to be alone."

"Stay right where you are." The phone went dead and not a minute later, he was there. He knelt on the floor next to her and brought her to her feet.

"It's freezing out here. Let's get you inside." They took the stairs down one flight and stood in the doorway. "Look, Mona, this is all an absurd misunderstanding, and unless I explain a few things, you and Fausto will never see each other again."

She shook her head. "Forget it, Quintus. He's married. I don't fool around with married men. It looks like I'll never see him again anyway."

"For one thing, she's handcuffed to his bed in his spare cabin off the lounge, and he's not letting her go until she produces divorce papers."

She gasped. "What? Wh—"

"Just shut up and listen. For another thing, he was forced into that medieval marriage. She's a bloodthirsty

243

murderer, her father was a Pope, and her brothers were ruthless conniving social climbers, as well as cold-blooded killers. She threatened Fausto's family with death if he didn't marry her. Her family wanted that marriage to further their own agendas. Not to mention money. He doesn't love her. He never loved her."

"But why didn't he ever tell me?" she wailed through tears.

He uncuffed his sleeve and wiped her eyes. "He knew you wouldn't want a man who'd made such a terrible mistake, who was so easily duped. Hey, he was a young fool, but—" He shrugged.

She nodded, feeling a deep connection to the man she'd never stopped loving. "I know what it's like to be duped. Ted made a fool of me, too."

"Then go to Fausto and straighten things out."

"Where is he?"

"In his stateroom. The captain fired him, and he'll be off the ship when they get a doctor to replace him. Apparently the muckity mucks around here didn't think his stripping act was befitting the ship's doctor."

She gave Quintus a quick kiss. "You'd better get going. You have a very impatient bride waiting for you."

"Don't I know it. She's not the only one who's impatient." He walked her to the elevators and pushed the up button. "See you—whenever," he said as the doors opened and she stepped in.

She went to Fausto's stateroom on the Madrid Deck and knocked, her heart pounding. He answered, black smudges under his half closed eyes, shoulders slumped. The blanket slid away as they fell into each other's arms. He crushed her to him. She felt the coldness of his skin, the beating of his heart.

"Fausto, why didn't you ever tell me any of that? I would have understood. I've been through the same damn things, you know that!"

"I was naïve enough to think something that happened four hundred years ago wouldn't come back to haunt me. But when she showed up, threatening me, I needed to force her hand. So, I locked her in my spare cabin off the lounge until she produces divorce papers. I decided to call her bluff and tell the world about who we are anyway. Why keep it a secret at this point? All I was doing was trying to show, not tell, how human we are, but it looks like it backfired. I've lost everything now."

"No, you haven't, my love. I'm still yours. I'll never love anybody but you."

He took a good look at her. "You sure you mean that?"

"Of course." She broke into tears, and he held her, swaying gently.

"Let's go see if Lucrezia made any progress," he said. "But first I'd better get decent. I'm never showing so much as my ankles in public again." He went to his closet and pulled on some clothes.

****

He unlocked the door to the doctors' lounge. It was dark, quiet, and deserted. He rubbed his hands together and gave Mona a hug. "Now, let's hope this is the last time I have to lay eyes on her *faccia brutta*."

"What did she think she could accomplish by threatening you like that?" Mona asked as they walked toward his cabin, her heels echoing on the floor.

"Maybe she wants to blackmail me. She knows

I've done rather well in the last four hundred years. I don't care why she thought she could force my back against the wall, but she should've known better than to think she could outwit me."

"Maybe she wants to have your baby."

He shuddered. "No, she's past her childbearing years. Around the age of three hundred or so is when a vampire woman starts to dry up."

"Gee, thanks. I really wanted to know that," she mumbled.

"Well, it beats fifty, doesn't it? And I've never heard of a vampire woman having hot flashes."

"Why not?"

"Our blood's too cold."

He opened the cabin door and faced an empty room.

"Where is she?" Mona noticed the handcuffs hanging from the headboard.

"Damn, she got away!" He went to the bed, turned over the pillows, peeked under blankets as if she were hiding there.

"Maybe she's one vamp who *can* turn into a bat."

"She's up to something. I feel it in my blood." With narrowed eyes, he glanced around the room, hands on hips, shaking his head. Mona went into the bathroom, but that, too, was empty. When she came out, she saw him pick up a lipstick-smeared tissue from the floor and throw it in the wastebasket.

"If you'd only told me this before, Fausto, all of this would've been taken care of!"

"If it weren't for *The Cutting Edge*, she never would've come crawling out from under her rock, so don't blame me," he snapped.

"I'm not. Not for that. But you could've been honest with me and told me you had a wife, even if it was a few centuries ago. It makes me wonder what else you haven't told me." A sigh became a sob as tears choked her. "I don't know if we can work this out, if anything will ever be right between us. Maybe we're fighting fate, I don't know..." She caught her breath. "I'm a cluttered jumble of emotions again. I don't know how the hell I feel."

"Mona, I'm so sorry all this happened—"

"What good is sorry? The man I love is married. Holy crap, the media's gonna have a blast with this story!"

"Mona, listen..." He held his temples as if he had a pounding headache. "I'll track my wi—my ex down. But she's got a jet. She could be anywhere by now. In hell, for all I know."

"That would be a good place to start looking."

"I didn't tell you exactly who she is, either." He ran his fingers though his hair. "She's a historical figure who left a very black mark on Italian history."

"Who? Mussolini?"

"She's Lucrezia Borgia, the most bloodthirsty, power hungry woman in history. She became a vampire just before the most famous of her poisonings, her lover Ercole Strozzi. Some poor civil servant found him face down in the Tiber. After a maid found her second husband bludgeoned to death in his sickbed, she forced me into marriage under threat of killing my family. I was nineteen. Her old man and brothers were all for it, too. They were all gold diggers. They wanted to get their mitts on my family money and climb a few rungs on the social ladder. We separated when the power of vampirism went to her head, even worse than when she was human, and I div—thought I'd divorced her. But by that time she had most of the Silvius fortune. I'm just glad she never took my name when we married. She'd have permanently soiled and maligned the Silvius name. If the hunters should get anybody, it should be her."

Her heart lurched. "Then that's it, let's get Zanna to capture her. I talked to her tonight. She's torn in half over her husband being a vampire, and she hates him, hates herself, hates the world. She left Royal, and she's all alone, licking her wounds. Maybe we can straighten her out and get Lu out of the way at the same time. Zanna has all the hunter paraphernalia, the holy water, the crosses. I know that stuff doesn't really work, but the old sword can throw a scare into her. Lu can't be far."

"I'd deal with the witch myself, but I'm afraid I'd rip her apart with my bare hands." His fists clenched. "All right, let's go see the hunter woman. Without her husband to back her up as muscle, she wouldn't dare lay a crucifix or a knife on me, so I'm safe, at least for the time being." He winked. "All right, where is the hapless hunter?"

She shook her head. "I don't know where their cabin is located. Can you find out?"

"Yeah, I'll use my doctor's clout. I'm still employed here until they dig up another doctor. Let me get a prop first." He went into the bathroom and came out, sticking something into his pocket.

They reached the registration desk, and he convinced the attendant to give him the Jones's cabin number. "I have to deliver medicine to Mr. Jones," he added for effect, and got the cabin number by flashing the clerk a plastic container.

"What the hell's that thing?" Mona asked as they headed down the hall.

"If you must know, and since you want to know everything about me, I'll tell you. It's my retainer."

"You wear a retainer?"

"Yeah, I was one of the first people to wear braces. My front teeth were a little crooked, and my eyeteeth were kind of prominent, making them look—now don't laugh—"

"I'm hardly in a laughing mood."

"Kind of made them look like fangs," he said.

She turned away, pressing her hand to her quivering belly. "Now that's what I call irony Poe would've wished he'd written."

They reached the Jones's cabin door, and Mona knocked.

"Who is it?" a muffled voice sounded from inside.

"It's Mona. Open up, please. I need to talk to you."

"What for?" Zanna hemmed and hawed; then Mona cast the tempting bait.

"It's for a hunting quest. The worst vampire alive. We need you to track her down for us." Zanna opened the door in a flash, but when her gaze landed on Fausto, she froze, her face draining to a deathly pallor. "What's *he* doing here?"

"Truce," he offered, holding up his index and middle fingers in the peace sign the hippies and Nixon used in the 60s. "If I had a peace pipe, I'd be smoking it right now, trust me."

Her eyes wide with wariness, she stood aside to let them in.

"You're still separated from Royal?" Mona glanced at the nearly empty whiskey bottles and crumpled corn chip bag lying on the table.

"Yes. He left the ship and checked into a hotel."

"You didn't even consider letting him turn you?" Mona asked.

"Did you practice what you've been preaching?" was Zanna's answer.

"Never mind." Mona took a breath. "We need your help, Zanna. I know I told you most vampires are good, God-fearing people, like most people of all kinds. But there are some bad apples in the barrel, and we need you to go after one of the most rotten ones."

"Who?" She looked from Mona to Fausto, and back again. A glimmer of a spark lit up her eyes, like she was glad to get an assignment.

"My wife—ex-wife. Lucrezia," Fausto said. "She told me we're still married and won't get out of my life until I go back to her. So, I threw out a counter-threat. But she flew the coop, and I know she's got something up her sleeve. Can you help us, Zanna? Please?"

"Where do you think she is?" Zanna brushed orange crumbs off her shirt. What a lousy way to spend New Year's Eve, Mona thought, but hers was just as lousy. At least Zanna got to pig out on corn chips.

"Maybe still on the ship, but not far from here. Can you hook up with Royal and seize her?" Fausto asked.

"I don't think I need him." Her features took on a calculating look as she laid her briefcase on a chair and opened it. She took out a crucifix and vials of holy water. Mona noticed some bottles of motion lotion—for hunting vampires? Well, maybe she did meet one she liked once in a while.

"You have something of hers so I can perform psychometry?" Zanna asked.

"I didn't know you had that ability," Mona said. "Why don't you use your talents for the good of mankind instead of wasting time chasing vampires around?"

"Well...I was kinda born with some psychic powers," she replied, eyes downcast, her tone flat. "Before I became a hunter, I helped the police find murder victims and helped them solve a lot of cases. I was even on a show called Psychic Detectives, but I had to quit."

"Why?" Mona asked, stunned.

"I didn't want the publicity. My hatred of vampires was getting to me, festering since I was sixteen, when they abducted me. It came to a head when one of the victims I located for the cops had been murdered by vampires. That's when I joined the Fellowship of the Faithful and became an eradicator. I thought I'd put my talents to use in hunting them, and I couldn't do it all, so I gave up the police work for that."

"But if you just go after the bad ones, you'd be doing all right," Fausto said. "As it is, you capture the wrong ones. Doesn't your psychic talent tell you which ones are the bad ones?"

"No. To me they're all bad. I never met a 'good' one."

"Until now," Mona corrected her, taking Fausto's arm. Zanna clamped her lips into a thin line, her features turning contrite.

"Well, maybe I'm just not that psychic," she finally replied.

"Trust us, the one I'm asking you to find is the

worst of the worst," Fausto urged, stepping forward. She inched back like a frightened cat. "Capture her and bring her to me. But alive."

"Why don't you want me to eradicate her?"

He answered, "I'm not a killer. But capturing her can be your swan song before Royal turns you and you join our world."

"And what makes you think I'm going to let him?" She began putting the hunting objects into a duffel bag but didn't touch the motion lotion. That reminded Mona, she was running low.

"I know you will," Fausto assured her. "When you meet her and see just how evil she really is, you'll be proud to be one of us. You've heard of Lucrezia Borgia, I take it?"

After a sharp intake of breath, she said, "That licentious, manipulative monster who stabbed, garrotted, and poisoned husbands and lovers, and God knows who else?"

He nodded. "She's committed crimes that the history books will never know about. And I'm asking you and Royal to bring her to me, so she'll get what she deserves."

"I'm—I want to go to my husband and talk to him, try to understand what's happened to him," she spoke haltingly, having trouble expressing her emotions. "But I haven't been able to. It's a lifetime of conditioning. Like all of a sudden devouring turnips when all your life you've hated turnips. Of course turnips don't kill people, bad analogy, I know, but..."

"Lucrezia is no turnip. She's more like anthrax. She's poison. And you'll see how wrong your conditioning was when you get hold of her. So do this for us? Please?" he begged. "I'll pay whatever price you name."

"You've got it all wrong, Dr. Silvius," she retorted. "We don't work for pay. In fact, Roy gave up his job for this, and we've been living off his savings. Money means nothing to us."

He held up his hands. "Fine. Just find her and bring her to me, then. And I promise you'll be a hero among your esteemed colleagues—if you want to be."

She shook her head. "I'm not doing this to show off, or for you. I'm doing it for a greater cause."

"It'll be the greatest cause a hunter can wish for."

"You have something of hers?" Zanna asked.

He started to say no, but his eyes brightened. "She was in the cabin I sometimes use. She blotted her lipstick and left the print mark on a tissue. It's still there in the cabin! I'll be right back."

With that he left Mona and Zanna alone. Mona didn't know what else she could say to this woman, how to convince her to let Royal turn her. They shared an awkward silence until Zanna offered Mona a drink.

"No, thanks, but you go right ahead." *If there's anything left*, she thought.

Zanna shook her head. "I'm all imbibed out. I always stop before I get to the stage where I know I'll be nursing a hangover. That's usually at the twelve-ounce limit. And I need to be completely sober if I'm going to be hunting."

"Yes, especially this one. I daresay she's the only 'bad' vampire you've ever hunted. Now that she's located Fausto, she's determined to make his life hell, and I'm afraid they'll never get divorced."

Zanna sat still, hands clamped to the sides of her

head, concentrating intently. "They will. Something's going to force her hand. I don't see what just yet, but he'll get his divorce. And soon."

Mona's heart lurched. If this was really true, then Fausto would be free before long. "Oh, God, let her be right!" she prayed out loud. Never did she feel more at somebody's mercy than at the hands of this self-proclaimed psychic.

Fausto came back with the tissue, which he'd wrapped in a linen napkin. Looking the other way, as if physical contact with it sickened him, he held it out to Zanna.

Mona rushed up to him. "Fausto!" she blurted out breathlessly. "She said something will force Lu's hand, and you'll get your divor—"

"Shhh!" Zanna hissed. "Not another word. Let me concentrate!"

She unwrapped the napkin and spread the lipstick-kissed tissue, pressing it between her hands. She squeezed her eyes shut, in deep concentration. "Lucrezia is still here, in Sicily, on shore. I see her walking, the sea to her left."

"Can you hunt her down?"

Zanna nodded, the tissue crushed in her palms. "She's coming more clearly into focus. Blonde hair, dark sultry eyes, oversized bozooms. There's an aura of evil around her." She shuddered. "Her aura is—my God, it's almost black! Her soul is so tarnished, there's such a pall of evil over her, she draws it like a magnet!" She opened her eyes and released the tissue. It fluttered to the floor. "Oh, yes, I want to hunt down this savage creature, I must! I'm not your biggest fan, Dr. Silvius, but I abhor cold-blooded murderers like her. Not to mention conniving gold diggers who dupe simpleminded males into marriage for status and money."

Mona couldn't hide a snicker. Fausto shot her a sneer. She gave him an Italian shrug.

Chapter Eighteen:
You Can Run But You Can't Hide

"I need to rest up before a hunt. I'll get back to you before daybreak," Zanna promised Fausto and Mona. She arranged her hunting equipment—garlic, crucifix, vial of holy water—in her duffel bag.

"You don't need all that stuff. Don't you know by now it doesn't work?" Fausto shook his head.

"Let me ask you something, doctor." She glared daggers at him, fists on hips. "When you have a patient you know is having a psychosomatic illness, do you dispense placebos to make him think he's getting better?"

"Well, sometimes," he admitted.

"It's all mind over matter, isn't it? Our minds can control our bodies' functions, our immune systems, and even influence outside events." Her lips spread in a killer sneer. "Some of us are better at it than others. Well, just think of these things as the equivalent of your sugar pills. When the hunted, especially an evil vampire, sees a crucifix about to be shoved down their throat, or gets doused with holy water or gets the Lord's Prayer chanted at them, it makes them go ballistic. They think good might overpower their evil. And when they do believe that, they're scared shitless. That's also how exorcisms work. These victims think they're getting evil spirits purged from their bodies, when it's really free will at work. So don't knock the cross or the holy water. And here." She tossed a string of garlic to him, and he caught it. "I won't be needing this tonight. Thought you could use it more. But for God's sakes, get a bottle of mouthwash to go with it. *Ciao*, doc." With that she was gone.

Mona and Fausto stood facing each other in the empty cabin. "Let's get a jump start on our honeymoon," he said with a lusty growl as he reached for her hand.

"The honeymoon comes after the wedding. Which will come after you find out if you're still married."

"Oh, I'll find out, you can count on it. I'll hire a lawyer and an archivist and whoever else I have to. Right now, does it matter, Mona?" He clasped her hands. "No matter what happens, this is my solemn vow. From this moment on, I'm your husband, in the eyes of God and the Church and every country in the world, and you'll always be my wife, whether it's now or later."

A surge of love swelled her heart, and her eyes stung with tears. "Oh, Fausto, I'll be your wife forever."

"You mean that?" His smile lit up the windowless room.

"I don't make promises I don't mean."

He crushed her to him. "Oh, *cara mia*, I've been waiting so long to hear that." He reached into his pocket and took out that same velvet box he'd flipped open in the restaurant.

Once again, he opened it, and the ring winked up at her as if to say "What took you so long?"

"Fausto, do you carry this with you all the time?

What if you lost it or got pickpocketed? Shouldn't it be in your safe?"

"There is one in my safe, in my stateroom. There's also another one in my spare stateroom's safe."

"Three of them?" She stared at him open-mouthed. "Why?"

"I just wanted to make sure I had a ring with me when you said yes. So call me the cockeyed optimist. But I always like to play it safe and have backups." He took it from the box and held it up to her. "You want to hold out your hand for me to put it on?"

He slid the brilliant diamond solitaire onto her finger, brought it to his lips, and kissed it. "I love you with all my heart and want to spend the rest of my days with you. Whether or not you want to join my world." The ring was a perfect fit. "I know you have skinny fingers, *cara*," he said, as if reading her mind.

She nuzzled his neck. "We'll work through all my kinks, but it just may take forever."

"It won't. A few hundred years tops. And we can have the wedding anywhere you want. Naked in a hot tub, on Mount Etna...whatever you want, *bella*, is fine with me."

"Then we can have the church wedding I've always wanted?" Her heart leapt.

"As many as you want. In every church in the world, if that's what you want."

"Mona Silvius," she said. "It sounds like it was meant to be, doesn't it?"

Back in his stateroom, he guided her to his massive bed and climbed in next to her.

Knowing she would soon be his wife gave their lovemaking a special poignancy, but sadness weighed at her heart. She still couldn't let him turn her. Vampirism was so far out of her realm, a life she couldn't imagine...and he seemed to read her emotions, because he held her especially tight, and she heaved a heartfelt sigh.

"What is it, Mona? Something's bothering you."

"Being married to you will be magical, Fausto. But I can't bring myself to let you turn me. I'm afraid we'll only feel half joined together, and not fully."

She saw the pained look in his eyes that told her marrying him would be enough. "I can't promise anything, but maybe someday...just let me love you now." She kissed away the hurt on his face, in his eyes, and drew him to her, letting him know that no matter what vows they exchanged, she'd be his until the end of her days.

****

Zanna didn't need Royal for this mission, but she wanted him there. Her guilt ate away at her like a festering wound. After capturing Lucrezia, she and her husband would sit down and have a heart-to-heart talk about their future. No more living in limbo.

She pushed open the single glass door of his hotel and entered the small stuffy lobby. An attendant sat slumped over, hands on his bulging belly, snoring. "Ahem!" she cleared her throat to wake him.

"Ah, *si, signora, mi dispiace*." He yawned and scratched his bald head.

"Apology accepted. Royal Jones's room please. I'm his wife."

"Oh, I'm so sorry, ma'am," he replied, this time in halting English. "Mr. Jones is in hospital."

"What?" She took a stunned step back. "What

happened?"

"Apparent suicide. Sleeping pill overdose. The maid find him, he look dead, the ambulance come rushing here, take him away."

"Where?" Frantic, she dug out her cell phone.

"I call you taxi."

****

Royal was in the intensive care unit of a run-down hospital that looked like it was built in the Dark Ages. Peeling paint barely covered the walls. A roach scampered by. The pungent odor of sickness invaded Zanna.

A nurse led her to his bed in a small room, separated from another patient with a flimsy curtain. Zanna rushed up to him, vowing to keep vigil here until he recovered. "Roy, speak to me. What happened?"

An IV drip was in his arm. The steady beeps of the heart monitor told her his vital signs were good. *Hope.*

"I thought it better I sacrifice myself, for the good of the world, because it'd be hypocritical to stay alive," he rasped. "I hate myself, you hate me, and you know how much I loathe hypocrisy."

"No! I won't let you do that! Listen to me—"

He cut her off. "Teresa told me I won't grow fangs or want to bite strangers, but I still disgust you. You don't believe any of it. I only want to feed from you, and that's because I still love you, like the story goes."

"Listen, Roy." She slid onto the bed next to him. "I've done a lot of soul searching, and I've decided I want you to feed from me. I want to join the vampire world."

"Don't joke, Zanna. My sense of humor left me when they pumped my stomach." He placed his hand there.

"I'm dead serious," she whispered into his ear. "Feed from me. Now."

She lowered her head and placed her neck at his lips. At first he only nibbled weakly, but he applied more pressure. His lips clamped onto her flesh. She gasped when two pinpricks burned her skin. Warm blood spurted from her jugular as he drank her elixir of life. She closed her eyes. From this moment on, her fate changed forever.

****

"Fausto, it just dawned on me...I just made love with the man who will soon be my husband." Mona lay next to him, their arms and legs twined. "But I already feel married, bound to you emotionally like never before."

"And after exchanging those beautiful vows..." He stroked her hair. "...pledging our lives, you have one little hurdle to overcome. The decision to let me turn you."

"How can I forget?"

"But of course you don't have to enter my world until you're ready."

"Thank you." She let out a cleansing sigh. "I greatly respect you for not pressuring me."

But this was the first time he'd mentioned it. "Let's not talk about that now. All I want to do is make love with you again."

"Come here, you live David statue." She pulled him on top of her. His body covered hers, and she clamped her thighs around his back. They gasped together as their bodies united.

"I love you, I love you," he moaned, and how right

it sounded from him. No other woman, even a wife of four centuries, could alter their shared destiny.

****

The shrill ringing of the phone shattered their rapturous moment. With a quick glance at Mona, Fausto picked it up.

"Yeah, all right, do what you have to do...good, glad to hear that...call me when you get back."

"Was that Zanna?"

He nodded, lying on his side. "Good news and bad news. The bad news is her husband's in the hospital. He tried to commit suicide when he knew he'd die because she wouldn't let him feed. The good news is she finally let him turn her, and now she's one of us. And our hunt for Lucrezia is on hold until he's better, and she's gotten over her culture shock."

She nodded in daybreak's glow. "I'm sure he'll be okay. He shouldn't have done that, but I understand. I know what it's like to think you've lost the one you love."

"Well, you never will." As he hugged her, their still-moist bodies met and slid against each other.

"Let's go on the hunt with them," she said. "I'm thinking of Zanna's psychic findings about Lucrezia. I'd like to confront the witch face to face and see what she has to say for herself."

"You don't want to do that," he countered. "Let Zanna capture her. After I deal with her, I'll make sure we get that divorce."

"Deal with her how? You said you don't want her killed."

"I don't. I'm going to turn her into the authorities, with a thousand pages of documentation showing that she committed several gruesome murders. There's plenty of evidence on her, and murder has no statute of limitations. Even in Italy." He gave her an ironic grin.

Mona let a smile curl her lips. "Now that's revenge with a dose of Italian class!"

****

The hospital released Royal the next day. Zanna never left his bedside. She wasn't able to until she fed from him and became a true vampire. When she woke, she stared at her arms, her legs, pinched her tingling skin here and there. She cowered, overwhelmed, as if the walls were closing in. Did that really happen the night before? "Dear God," she whispered, "I'm now immortal, never to die." Her entire reason for being changed in a few short hours.

As she led him back into his hotel room and they lay on the bed together, she nestled into the crook of his arm, their synchronized breathing the only sound of the early morning.

"How do you feel, Roy?"

"A little weak, but I'll be okay. How about you?"

"I feel like somebody else." She pinched her arm again.

"Well, you are now. And it's an improvement."

"Thanks a lot." She poked him.

"You know what I mean."

"Are you up to a hunt?" she asked.

"I see turning hasn't changed your views on vampires."

"Just bad ones. I promised a certain party I'd hunt down a very evil vampiress—for my swan song. He doesn't want her killed, just brought to him. He has plans for her, but I want to go after her anyway. And after this deed, I'm turning in my materials and resigning from the Fellowship."

His nod tickled her side. "Not a bad idea, considering the circumstances."

"And you?"

"To tell you the truth, I kind of felt like I'd married into it," he said.

"Even after Devon's death?" She turned to face him and met his intense gaze.

"I wanted revenge, Zanna. And short of killing the bastards myself or hiring a hit man, which I couldn't afford anyway, this was the next best way."

"It's not about revenge. It's about cleansing the world of evil."

He *hmmf*'d. "Yeah, that's what Hitler thought. And terrorists who want to blow up all us infidels. Now you know evil isn't what it's cracked up to be."

"Not always. Only until you see true evil, you think it's relative, just like being rich, or big or small," she said. "You can't really judge unless you have a reference point."

"Right on. But you're convinced the one you're after is truly evil."

"She's Lucrezia Borgia, Roy. Need I say more?"

"Nope. Full steam ahead."

****

When Zanna called Fausto's stateroom, he told her his news: "We want to join you on the hunt."

"You sure?" she asked. "I've never seen a vamp hunt another vamp before."

"This means a lot to Mona," he replied. "Besides, I'm a little, heh, heh...how do I put this delicately...kind of wobbly."

"Yeah, I hear ya," she replied. "All right, meet me on the gangway in five minutes."

"Uh, wait a minute..." The sight of Mona emerging from the bathroom in a sheer teddy and nothing underneath made him rise to the occasion. "Make it twenty minutes. But call me first. I need to, er...eat something."

"Whatever. See ya."

Mona rolled on top of him before he hung up the phone. "Now, what did you tell Zanna you wanted to eat?"

****

"Why didn't you take the money Fausto offered you?" Royal and Zanna entered their cabin. "It could've helped pay the hospital bill."

"I'm above taking money for hunting, Roy, you know that. Now go lie down. You haven't gotten your strength back. It's obscene the way these hospitals kick patients out before they're fully recovered."

"You can care for me better than any old hospital can."

"I know." She stroked his cheek. "And there's no more till death do us part. You're stuck with me for better or worse forever."

"That's okay by me, toots." He proved it by heading straight for his Scotch to celebrate. He poured a shot and was about to down it when he put the glass down and pushed it away. "I don't need this poison any more. Can I have a glass of water, Zan?"

"Of course." She brought him his water and he said, "I think we should hold a press conference before we go hunt Lucrezia what's 'er name."

"Hmmm..." She tapped her finger on her chin. "It's

not a bad idea. Now that I'm a vampire, I feel just as strongly about setting the world straight as I did when I was an eradicator. But first things first. We have to capture her before she kills again. I can see where she is now." She got out the lipstick-printed tissue again and held it to her forehead. "Pizza."

"What?" Royal's glass stopped midway to his mouth as he watched her close her fist around the tissue.

"I smell pizza. She's having pizza at Casa Dante, that restaurant on the corner. We're going to wait outside for her, get her into our van, and take her somewhere far enough so zoom lenses can't get to us."

Royal checked his watch. "The ship is leaving port in two hours. Will that be enough time?"

"Maybe, maybe not. But what's more important, catching a ship or catching the most evil vampire alive? Now let's get those lovebirds out of their nest."

****

"That's her." Fausto peeked into the pizzeria. Lucrezia Borgia sat alone at a small table, sipping wine. He stepped back and saw Zanna shaking in mild convulsions.

"What's wrong with her?"

Royal led her away from the restaurant and to an alley where he sat her down on a stone step. Fausto and Mona followed. "Is she all right?" Mona asked Royal.

Zanna's body relaxed, her muscles no longer in spasm.

"This happens when she has an especially vivid vision. What was it, Zan?" Royal knelt before her and smoothed back her hair.

"It's her—" she gasped, panting as if she'd just run

a mile.

"Lucrezia? We know it's her."

"No, she's the one. She murdered Sabino Musciatello in Tuscany."

"Who is Sabino Musciatello?" Mona asked.

"Another rich, handsome man whose girlfriend allegedly murdered him and dumped his body in a shallow grave. One of a string of similar murders."

"Is it enough to go to the police with?"

Zanna replied, "My vision isn't hard evidence, but it can help them. Of course we'd need hard evidence for them to build a case against her—unless she confesses."

"So she murdered Sabino." Fausto shook his head sadly. "That was big news over here because he's from a prominent family, and he's been missing all this time. The parents went on television begging his captors to return him. It broke my heart to see his mother grieving. It looks like Lucrezia might be the serial killer the police have been after. Over a dozen rich young guys have been murdered over the last few years, their bodies buried in shallow graves. That's if they find the bodies at all."

"I can concentrate on that later," Zanna said. "But for now, let's get her. Now that we have more than one good reason."

Mona clutched Fausto's elbow. "Wait, I know what we can do. You'd rather see her confess and go to prison for a recent high-profile homicide than bring up centuries-old murders, wouldn't you?"

"Of course." His fists clenched. "She deserves to be locked up for eternity. I want to see that *cagna* behind bars once and for all."

"Then we can get her to confess," Mona said. "Let

her think Zanna's going to kill her if she doesn't confess. Zanna, you can get the knife out and hold it to her throat if you have to. That'll get the confession out of her."

"And maybe something else," Royal added.

Fausto nodded. "Oh, yeah, one thing she values is her eternal life. But living her eternal life in prison for killing Sabino is divine justice. Good thinking, *cara*." He gave her a quick brush of a kiss.

She let a smile play on her lips. "Maybe I'll just stick to writing suspense. I might not be selling as many, but they're a lotta fun to write."

"So that's the plan." Zanna stood and paced back and forth. "Get her into the interior of this island, threaten her with the ancient blade, and she'll spill it all about the murder. Maybe even all of 'em."

"Don't get your hopes up." Fausto shook his head.

"How do you want to do this, in broad daylight?" Mona asked her.

Zanna brushed off her bottom, her breathing back to normal. She gave her head a lofty toss. "Follow her at a safe distance. But I can tell you she won't be walking too fast. She just scarfed down all but a small piece of a giant pizza with pepperoni, mushrooms, olives, sausage, and extra cheese."

"Wow, your psychic powers are awesome." Mona freely paid her the compliment. "How can you articulate to that degree?"

"It's got nothing to do with powers. I can see what she left on the plate." She slid on a pair of dark shades. "Now, let's wait in the car. I envision her going to the airport to board her Cessna, but I'll make sure she doesn't get there."

"She doesn't drive, either," Fausto said. "It's beneath her. She'll take a taxi."

"All right, I'll take care of that. Roy, you want to be a taxi driver for a while?"

"Depends." He turned to Fausto. "Is she a good tipper?"

"She's tighter than a crab's ass," he replied.

"You'll be compensated later, better than any cab driver can dream about," Zanna said. "She'll be calling a cab on her cell phone, but Roy will show up to take her to the airport. We'll knock her out. When the real cab gets here, Mona and Fausto, you tell the cabbie you don't need him after all, throw him a few euros, and send him on his way. That'll get rid of the taxi. We'll come get you two, and when we're a safe distance from here, Ludicrous Lu will have her moment of truth. Once she confesses to Sabino Musciatello's murder, maybe she'll tell the police where she buried his body."

"What if she won't?" Mona asked.

"Then I'll get my third eye to help the police again. I haven't been able to envision a location, but in some cases I've assisted in, the killer fails to cover his—or in this case, her—ass in some way. They do something dumb, like leave tire tracks in the dirt, or shoe prints, strands of hair, or even fingerprints. One guy in Georgia insisted to the cops his dead wife had left her car at the roadside and disappeared, but when the cops checked the car out, the seat was all the way back. Obviously, someone tall had last driven it. The husband was six-two. The wife was barely five-two. That helped name him as prime suspect. Another wife murderer blew it when police found dirt on his boots in his garage. Not just any dirt, but dirt that matched the shallow grave where his wife's body was buried. They nabbed him, all right."

"Lucrezia's been honing her craft for centuries." Fausto's doubt soured his tone. "She doesn't blunder like an amateur would."

"We'll see. She's finishing up now, and the waiter's bringing the check. Now she's getting out her cell. All right, Roy. Put on your driver's cap, and I'll hop in the cargo hold. You two, wait for the real cab. See ya later."

They stood a safe distance away as they watched Lucrezia get into the backseat of Roy's rented minivan. They zoomed off, and Mona heaved a heavy sigh. "And I didn't bring armpit shields 'cause I didn't think this trip would be exciting."

The real taxi came a few minutes later. Mona told the driver they didn't need the ride and ignored his Italian grumblings until she tossed a wad of euros into his lap.

Royal's minivan pulled up a minute later. As they approached it, Zanna opened a door to let them in. "Buxom Borgia is KO'd in the back," she said as Fausto and Mona slipped in. "She put up a struggle when Roy pressed the rag over her face, so I had to help. He hasn't gotten all his strength back."

"You need to feed," Fausto said.

"Already?" he asked.

"When you feel weak, don't take it for granted it's because you didn't have your Wheaties or because you just got out of the hospital. After a while, you'll get to know your body's signals."

"Can it wait till after we do this? I'd kinda...like to be alone with my wife when we...do it."

Fausto nodded. "Sure. You can have your tryst when we get back. I don't want to hang out here too long, in *her* company." He jerked his thumb toward the back of the van.

"What if she wakes up and attacks one of us?" Mona asked, her voice a little shaky. She shuddered, dreading to look back there. She didn't want to see the comatose vampiress, her body hitting the van's side with a thump as Royal made a sharp turn.

"We tied her," Zanna replied. "And I almost didn't bring the silk bonds on this trip," she added with a proud air. "Glad we put them to some use at least."

"Dr. Silvius, I don't know my way around Sicily," Royal said. "Where's a deserted stretch of road?"

"The island is full of them. Get on the A18, south." Fausto leaned forward. "After about fifty-two kilometers, you'll hit Fiumefreddo, where route 120 will take you within the shadow of Mount Etna. There are some side roads we can pull onto."

Mona turned to Fausto. "Babe," she whispered, "we made a huge score, capturing Lucrezia, but I want this to end in peace, you to get your divorce and her behind bars. She killed too many people to stay in the vampire community. Now I know why the world fears vampires. Because of monsters like her."

"You got that right. That's why I hope she'll be an example to educate the world about the bad ones, and the rest of us as good ones. So we won't have to take any more crap about who we are."

As they whizzed past the quaint farmhouses, clothes hanging on lines fluttering in the breeze, cows and horses grazing in grassy pastures, Mona wondered when she and Fausto would enjoy true happiness, with no interference from hunters, nosy reporters, ex-spouses, or agonizing decisions. Lucrezia's invasion made her realize how much she loved Fausto and couldn't bear to lose him. She caressed his hand and leaned into him. "It's all right. Lucrezia's far outnumbered and outwitted here," he assured her, as if he read her mind.

Mona bit her tongue, but she had a few tactics in mind to choke a confession out of Lucrezia, turn her in to the *polizia* and watch justice bear its fangs—er, teeth. That was if Zanna's threats and sword-brandishing didn't work. Mona made a living getting her heroines in one mess after another, then bringing the story to a joyful ending. Now, in a real-life mess, she needed all her creative energy to get out of it. *Think, author, think!* she silently urged.

Mona spotted a good secluded side road and ordered Royal to turn onto it. The van bumped its way over a narrow dirt road, winding farther up into the mountains. "Here," she told Royal. "Stop here."

In the distance, the peak of Etna poked through misty clouds. Images ran through her mind—Etna smoldering, then violently erupting, just as Lucrezia was sure to erupt when she woke up.

When the van came to a stop, Mona raced around and hauled Lucrezia's body from the back. It was hard to believe that someone with such an innocent face could have such a villainous mind.

Zanna helped lay Lucrezia on the ground while Royal poured water from a thermos over her face. Lucrezia sputtered and gasped, her beady eyes surveying the scene around her, then focusing on Fausto.

"I knew it. I knew I hadn't seen the last of you."

"You made my life hell once before, and you're back for more, but I'm older and wiser than I was then," he said. "Now you're going to get what you deserve."

"Fausto—" Mona began, but Lucrezia cut her off.

"How do you know what I deserve?" she hissed. "Are you a messenger of God now?"

Zanna stepped forward. "No, but I am. I get information from the ether and relay it to those who need it—"

"Like the police for instance," Mona said.

"Your number's up," Zanna put in, "because as soon as I laid eyes on you through that restaurant window, I knew you murdered Sabino Musciatello in Tuscany. There's a hell of a lot more victims, but this was the latest. And one of the most brutal."

Mona knelt and faced Lucrezia. Her stomach turned as a multi-legged bug slithered across the vamp's cheek—but a closer look showed it was her false eyelashes that got loose! Mona bit back a smile and said, "If you confess, we'll take you to the police and Italian jurisprudence will decide your fate. If not, we have a more gruesome fate awaiting you." She hoped the ruse worked. "Not only does Zanna help police track down murder victims, she hunts vampires. The vile, evil ones. And you're the queen of 'em all. Capturing you would put a golden feather in her cap, wouldn't it, Zanna?"

"I waited all my life for a conquest like this." Zanna's voice was husky with conviction. "In my world, this is totally justified. It's not murder to kill a monster who will just kill again."

Lucrezia blanched. "A hunter? One of those *pazzo* holy rollers the Vatican doesn't even have time for? All right, douse me with garlic, get it over with."

"You think this is a joke, don't you? Well, nobody's laughing." Mona's fists clenched with rage. Sweat ran down her back. She pulled Lucrezia upright. *My God, the woman's wearing Taboo perfume! What a stench! No wonder Fausto divorced her!* "This is it, lady. Now you're going to see what we do to people who give good vampires a bad rap."

"You *stunati*, I wouldn't be so foolish as to confess to any murders! This is just Fausto playing games with me. It staggered him when I showed up and dropped the bomb that we're still married. But I know you wouldn't let these maniacs behead me, Fausto." Her voice dripped with saccharin. "You're a nobleman, not a killer." Lucrezia's rant knocked Mona off balance.

"Are those real tears, Lucrezia?" Mona blurted, unable to keep quiet. "Or fakes, like the boobs inside your pushup bra? How dare you try to manipulate Fausto."

But the woman ignored her, turning to Fausto. "You still love me, I know it. We have too long a history for you to shun me. We need to pick up where we left off, give our marriage another chance."

His eyes stabbed her, his face crimson with anger. "What history? What marriage? We were together for eight years out of four hundred. That's hardly a blip. Although at the time it felt like eight hundred."

Lucrezia shook her head, with another half-assed attempt at anguish. "How quickly they forget."

"Roy, get the blade and unsheath it," Mona ordered, hoping her ruse worked.

Royal dashed for the van. He came back, and within inches of Lucrezia, exposed Percival. He ran a finger over the sharpened blade, drawing a few drops of blood. "Ready to confess to that latest murder or meet your maker?"

Now Lucrezia began to look her age. Her face drained of blood. Her eyes widened at the sight of the knife. Worry lines creased her forehead, and Mona could see the lump she swallowed.

But she wasn't opening her mouth.

"Well? What will it be?" Mona moved closer, Zanna and Royal flanking her, Percival's blade against the vamp's throat. One move and she'd be sipping frozen yogurt from a straw instead of eating it from a spoon.

The vamp refused to budge. "You wouldn't dare."

Mona wouldn't put it past Zanna to grab the knife and finish her off. She'd done it before.

She watched Zanna chew her bottom lip and mumble, "What a decision…do I make this final conquest before quitting the Fellowship in a blaze of glory?"

Come on, Lucrezia, Mona silently urged. *Confess already!*

Mona's mind whirred at top speed. She had to act fast before Zanna did, or the entire thing could backfire. "Wait! I think I can make her confess. Then we'll take her to the police, and they can deal with her."

All eyes fixed on her.

Now Mona was center stage. "Lucrezia, you claim you love Fausto and had such a good marriage. Well, you can have Fausto back."

Fausto's eyes grew wide, and his jaw dropped.

"What!"

Forcing herself to ignore the shock and hurt in Fausto's eyes, she continued, "You must really want him. So, I'm giving him to you. Enjoy the rest of your lives together. I'm still mortal, so I'll die in four or five more decades, but you'll have eternity to spend together."

Fausto took a step toward Mona, nearly knocking Percival from Royal's grip. "Yo, don't I have a say in this? Mona, do you know what you're saying? Or is the air that thin up here?"

"I know exactly what I'm saying. I'm making the supreme sacrifice." But she knew damn well Lucrezia didn't want Fausto back for keeps, just until something better came along—another victim. "You and Fausto are still married. So, go in wedded bliss."

Fausto lunged forward. "Whoa—"

"Quiet, Fausto!" Mona had to shut him up before he gave away what they knew. She hoped her glare would show him she was bluffing. Her heart broke to see how devastated he was, but only a move this drastic could get this woman out of their lives. She turned to Lucrezia. "He's your true husband, and now that you found out he's alive, you can claim him. I'll step out of the way. But you should know Fausto doesn't love you and never will. To get back at you for forcing him into a loveless marriage, using him for money and status, he's going to neutralize you, by giving you a transfusion of human blood. At your age, as a human you won't be long for this world. You'll be so feeble, you won't have the strength to go on the prowl for a vampire to bite you. Now, would you rather have that, or come clean and confess to that last murder you committed, and spend life in prison? With victims to feed from to keep you alive? It's your choice."

The moment burst with tension, the silence painful.

"You win." Lucrezia spoke, barely above a whisper. "I murdered Sabino Musciatello and numerous others. Take me to the police."

With a relieved sigh, Royal helped her back into the van. "Do I have to chloroform you again?"

"I'll keep quiet. Now let's get this over with."

In the van on the way back, Fausto leaned close to Mona and whispered, "For Gesu's sake, don't ever offer me to another woman, even in jest. I don't give a damn if it's the goddess Minerva!" His eyes locked with hers.

"I knew what I was doing the whole time, Fausto." She smiled and let a hand dawdle on his thigh.

"Oh, you did, did you?" He spoke between feathery kisses. "How did you come up with the idea of neutralizing her?"

She shrugged. "I'm a novelist. Thinking up plots is what I do for a living."

"How'd you think of it so fast?"

"I work under deadlines. I learned how to do that the hard way." She gave him another squeeze. "But there's one deadline we missed. The ship. It left port about an hour ago."

"Damn! Now we'll have to catch it in Malta."

"Fine with me." She smiled. "I need a vacation from that cruise anyway."

Chapter Nineteen:
I'm Vampin' You

Mona and Fausto drove Lucrezia straight to the police precinct and brought her in. "*Ciao*, Captain Angelo," Mona said when she saw him.

He kissed her on both cheeks and thanked her once again for leading him to Brooke.

"We can talk about your new lives together after I tell you what we've brought you." She led Lucrezia, hands still bound, up to him. "This woman has a confession to make. Or several. Then you and Brooke can celebrate. This is a mega news story, even bigger than the ones she's covering now."

"Brooke and I are reuniting in Rhodes, three days from now," Angelo said. "I had to arrange for time off. She wants me to quit the force and go back to Hollywood with her, but—" He turned his hands through the air and shook his head. "I no go for that glamour. I'm a small town boy. Maybe I convince her to stay here."

Mona chuckled. "If it's in a fifty-room villa, I'm sure that won't take too much convincing."

They waited for Lucrezia to give her full confession. She spoke in rapid Italian, so Mona couldn't understand most of it. Angelo listened, arms crossed over his chest. Not a muscle on his face moved or twitched.

Man, he's poker-faced, Mona thought.

Once the killer was booked, Mona and Fausto bade *arrivederci* to Angelo for now and headed out.

They joined Royal and Zanna outside the precinct, the two of them bleary-eyed as they slogged down the steps. "Let's call it a night and see how to catch up with the ship tomorrow," Fausto suggested.

"Whatever you say, boss." Royal gave him a salute. "I'm glad to put this episode into the history books. I thought being a hunter was tough before, but after this whole mess, now I've seen everything!"

Royal and Zanna gave them a lift to the elegant Royal Palace Hotel. "Catch you on board," Mona said as they got out of the van, and Zanna leaned over to Mona.

"Remember you were trying to convince me to let Roy turn me?"

"Sure."

"Well, it's advice well taken, girlfriend." Zanna gave her a kiss. As the van zoomed away, Mona stood, nodding, but her heart was still pulling her in the other direction.

****

"As long as we missed the ship, we might as well eat something decent," Fausto suggested.

"All right, let's go. *Andiamo!*" They walked down the street to the Casa Dante Pizzeria. The cooking aromas and the heat comforted Mona as he held the door open for her and they stepped in. She took the table farthest from where Lucrezia had sat. Fausto held the chair out for her. But as she bent her knees to sit, reporters and cameras burst in.

"Get out of our faces, you vultures!" Mona held up

her hands and turned her back on them.

A woman with a Channel Four microphone and camera crew ignored her. They swarmed around the table. Before Mona could tell her it was none of her damn business if she was a vampire yet, Fausto grabbed the camera and wrestled it from the cameraman's hands. A stab of fear shot through Mona. She yanked him back. "For God's sake, Fausto, remember what happened to Quintus?"

His arms dropped to his sides, and she tugged him away. The cameraman propped the camcorder back on his shoulder and Fausto said, "Let's get the hell out of here." Just then another team stormed in: a male reporter with plastic hair, two cameramen, and a flunkie picking up cables strewn around like spaghetti.

"Miss Rossi! Dr. Silvius! Glad we caught you at last. I'm Brian Sanders from World News Network, and we're here in the Casa Dante Restaurant, where the vampire doctor and his lady love, popular author Mona Rossi, have just agreed to tell us—"

Paolo, the restaurant owner, started yelling and gesturing in frenzied Italian as he tried to push them out the door. But more crew members stomped in, shed their WNN jackets, and filled every table in the place. Waiters scrambled around to take orders and serve wine.

Obviously, with that kind of business, nobody was getting thrown out.

Fausto led her toward the exit, but the Channel Four reporter dashed ahead of them, flattened herself against the door, and signaled for the camera to get a closeup.

"Miss Rossi! Or will it be Mrs. Silvius soon? Why

aren't you on the ship? What do you make of the breaking news and the riots? Are you avoiding the press conference?"

This halted Mona, who was about to reach around the reporter and open the door to leave. "What breaking news? What riots? What press conference?"

"The one the Church is giving—the Fellowship of the Faithful, who plan to start a worldwide crusade against vampires. The Church is sending envoys to schools and churches all over the world, to inform the public that vampires are evil. They're lobbying to exclude them from schools. The Pope is going to the White House to tell the president they should take military action against vampires. Where have you been? Haven't you been watching the news?" She gave Mona a snort of superiority. "Several vampire groups have been arrested. A riot started in San Francisco and the National Guard was called in. The White House is going to issue a statement tomorrow about how they're handling the situation. One Vatican official leaked something about declaring war on vampires."

"War!" Fausto thundered, thrusting his hands up. "They're not terrorists, for Gesu's sake!"

The reporter gave a phony studio smile. "Turn on the news, and see for yourself. But before you do, can you please answer a few ques—"

"No, we can't!" With that, Fausto nudged her aside, grabbed Mona's hand, and sprinted out.

"But wait!" She clamored after them, teetering in her open-toed pumps. *Why don't these chicks wear sensible footwear when chasing subjects?* Mona wondered for the millionth time.

"Just keep going, we'll outdistance her in a

minute," Fausto instructed Mona. By the time they jogged back to the Royal Palace, empty silence lingered behind them.

"You think they'll find us here?" she asked him as they crossed the marble lobby to the registration desk. Without an overnight bag between them, and looking rumpled from the day's ordeal, they got a few less-than-welcoming looks from the hotel staff until Fausto told them who he was.

Then they fawned all over him, gave him cardkeys to the bridal suite, and asked for their sizes, so they could send up any clothes they wanted.

"Hey, not a bad idea." Mona pictured a phone-booth-sized box of designer clothes arriving at the suite. "Can you send up a masseuse, too?"

Fausto gave her a glassy-eyed look.

"Well, we're on vacation. Sort of," she said.

When they were safely secured in the suite, with an empty sidewalk below them, she browsed the room service menu.

"Hey, uh...Mona?" He tilted the menu away from her. "Just asking...do you want to go home?"

"You mean home, to New York? No, I want to go back to the ship." The choice between veal rollitini and four-cheese lasagna slipped out of her hands as she met his stare. "I'd board tonight if I could."

"Well, Malta's only ninety-three kilometers away. The ferries don't run this late, but we can charter a boat and meet it tonight. The waters are calm. We can taxi from here to Pozzallo and get to Valletta in a few hours."

"You can arrange for that?"

"Sure. I could've arranged to have the ship called

back here, if they hadn't canned me." He gave her one of his half-smiles, and for an instant she wondered if he was serious. Hell, why not? Before the infamous striptease act, he had Apollo Cruise Lines in his back pocket.

"That would be fantastic, Fausto. Get back to the ship tonight! We can be outta here in an hour."

"Why that long?"

"Because I'm ordering room service. And I was hoping for a quickie dessert."

After room service and the "quickie" with whipped cream substituting for body butter, he made a call to a charter company who knew his family, and by half past midnight, they were in the fishing village of Pozzallo boarding a forty-foot fishing boat to Malta. He couldn't get a yacht on this tight notice, but for such a short distance, she could rough it.

Nico, the boat's pilot, was a young Sicilian right out of the navy. Mona studied his looks with her author's eye, his fisherman's cap pulled down almost to his thick brows, his dark eyes sharpened with maturity but still holding that playful spark of youth, his squared-off chin giving him a bedroomy look. She thought he'd make a great vampire. Did this guy know who Fausto was? Better to shut up about it. She didn't need him freaking out and throwing them overboard or something equally horrendous.

A gentle breeze dusted the calm water. They stayed outside instead of going below. Stars sprinkled the inky sky, the Milky Way a glowing backdrop. Fausto wrapped his arm around her, and they enjoyed the calm ride as the boat glided through the waters, kicking up foamy white spray that gently misted her face.

"Shouldn't be long now." She snuggled against him. "Hey, look." She pointed upwards. "That plane's flying awfully low." The lights of a small prop plane winked and grew larger and brighter as the craft soared lower, approaching them fast. The engines' steady tapping drowned out the boat's motor as the plane cut through the sky, so close she could see the outline of the wings and tail. "That shouldn't fly so low, should it?" She had to shout over the increasing volume, now a roar as the plane dipped, almost directly over the boat.

Blinding flashes of light stung her eyes, and a machine-gun-like burst pierced her eardrums. An explosion knocked her over, and she banged her head on the floor. The impact sent a stab of pain through her head so sharp, it rattled her brain. Agony ripped through her shoulder like a knife impaled it. Her mind knew what horror happened before she blacked out from agony. As she slid away through a tunnel of pain and delirium, her lips formed the words but no sound emerged. "I'm shot. I'm dying."

Fausto knelt at her side, shouted for Nico, and tore her jacket off as the plane soared past them and vanished into the night. Nico slowed the boat's engine until it came to a stop. His footsteps thudded on the deck as he rushed up to Fausto.

Together they brought her to the galley below and laid her on the bed under the bow. "She's been shot." Fausto found the wound in her shoulder and checked her pulse. It was slow and thready, and she was losing blood fast.

Nico got a first aid kit and Fausto tightened bandages around the wound. "Why would anybody shoot her?" Nico cradled Mona's head, raised it a few inches, and placed a cup of water to her lips.

"They wouldn't," Fausto said. "They were after me, but missed."

"Oh, no. Gesu. They're determined, aren't they?"

"I can't let her die. Mona, *cara mia,* " he whispered soothingly, "I will save you. You're not going to die. Mona, can you hear me?"

She took a few sips of the water Nico held to her lips, but sputtered and spit it out.

"Fausto, I'm...so weak..."

"Mona, listen to me. I'm going to bite you, and you're going to feed from me. If not, you'll die. Just relax, everything is going to be just fine."

Her lids fluttered, and her eyes wandered before focusing on him. "Yes, Fausto—make me yours." Her voice came weak and strained, and she struggled to speak.

"All right, my darling. Don't talk. Save your energy. And remember how much I love you." He lowered his lips to her neck and began a slow gentle nibble, then intensified as she lay her head back. Nico let go of her and blessed himself.

When Fausto finished, she went limp in his arms. "Get the boat going again," he ordered. As the engine revved and they were once again in motion, Fausto brought Mona's lips to his neck and breathed, "Feed, *cara*. Feed from me. Become one with me, and you will live forever." Her lips closed on his neck, and her teeth pierced his flesh as she drank from him. He shuddered in pleasure and the powerful force of love. Finally, they became one.

****

The *Romanza* was in the port of Valletta, Malta.

The gangway descended as the fishing boat approached the cruise ship. Mona's shoulder throbbed, but her arm was secure in the sling Fausto had made. He helped her onto the pier, and they walked the short distance to the *Romanza*'s gangway. As they boarded, the security team at the entrance cheered Fausto like he'd just saved the ship from sinking. "Dr. Silvius! Welcome back aboard!" Crew members and passengers, mostly female, rushed the entrance, nearly knocking Mona and Fausto over.

"Hey, what's all th—"

Mike Manzo, the cruise director, made his way through the pressing crowd and grasped Fausto's hand, pumping it and slapping him on the back. "You're a hero, Dr. Silvius! They want you back on board, and the ship captain, Captain D'Amato, wants to issue a public apology!"

Mona's jaw dropped. "What?" She grabbed Manzo's arm. "Two goons escorted him out. He was fired and banished from the cruise line! What the hell happened?"

Manzo flashed his bleached-teeth smile. "We nearly had a mutiny when the Cruise News announced that Dr. Fausto had been fired. The passengers went on a rampage. He'd made such a hit at the ball, they want him to strip after every show! So many people are trying to book our cruises, we're turning them away in droves! And the other cruise lines are now having 'stripathons,' where male dancers come from upscale strip clubs all over the world to work the cruises." He turned back to Fausto and planted a kiss on each cheek. "You're a mega hit, Dr. Silvius! Oh, and Brooke from *The Cutting Edge* wants to interview you in the theater—when you're ready, of course. And Mona—the three major networks and five cable channels are sending their top brass over here."

Fausto waved him away and encircled Mona's waist with his other arm. "Later, Manzo, they can all wait. I don't care if the Pope wants to interview me, just get Mona a wheelchair!"

Manzo's smile vanished as he snapped his fingers and turned on a heel. "Wheelchair for Ms. Rossi!"

A crew member rushed a wheelchair up to Mona. She collapsed into it.

The adoring, squealing crowd parted for Fausto to wheel her to the doctor's office. In the blessed silence, he laid her down on one of the beds. "How do you feel?" He smoothed her hair back and kissed her forehead.

"Like somebody else. When it happened, it was in slow motion, but now, it seems like it all flew by in a blur. It's crazy out there. You were the ship's castaway less than a day ago, now they're acting like we're Brangelina!"

He nodded. "I know. But I don't care about all that. I just want you to get stronger. Today is the first day of the rest of your life, my darling."

She focused on the bite mark on his neck, red and inflamed. "I didn't think I had it in me," she said as he traced his fingertips over it.

"I'll wear it like a medal. Now, you get some rest, and I'll get us a dry change of clothes."

"Will you hurry back?" She struggled to sit up, but dizziness overtook her and she fell back onto the pillow.

"You'll never get rid of me."

"Never say never," she said. "A thousand years from now, I might replace you with a hot five-hundred-year-old boy toy. Or a couple of two-hundred-fifty-year-olds."

"You and your damn orgies." He gave her cheek a light pinch. "How about letting me stick around? You'll always need backup."

She held out her good arm, and he lowered himself to her, embracing her.

"Hey, I'm starved." She rubbed her empty tummy.

"Then I'm all yours, *cara*." He lowered his neck to her lips.

"That's not what I meant. I'm just dying for a sticky bun and a cup of java."

"One sticky bun comin' up." He went over to the phone to call room service.

Just then Dr. Lombard came in and went straight over to Mona. "Feeling all right?"

She nodded and smiled, able to prop herself up on one elbow.

"Good, cause you might want to turn on the television. The White House is about to issue a statement."

****

They gathered around the portable television in Dr. Lombard's office as the anchor announced, "Ladies and gentlemen, the President of the United States."

The president sat at his Oval Office desk and addressed the American people and the world. "As you know, several riots between vampires and hunters have broken out in San Francisco, Rome, and other major cities. The National Guard was called in to quell some of this violence, but let this be a warning to these predators hurting and killing innocent people: anyone hunting vampires will be prosecuted to the fullest extent of the law. These hunters are terrorists and will be treated as such. Peace loving Americans will not tolerate their outward ignorance and violence."

"Sweet! The government is on our side." Mona balled her fists with glee as the President's image faded and the newscast resumed. "They don't hate us! We're not evildoers!"

"Caving in to the blue states, I guess," Fausto quipped. "Hunters are fighting a losing battle. There are more of us than there are of them. And the way we multiply, there always will be."

"Hey, get a load of this." Dr. Lombard pointed to the set. "Look at all these members of Congress admitting they're vampires. They're all coming out of the closet and issuing statements. Hell, they'll all have book deals within twenty-four hours."

"Live forever, serve forever," Mona said. "There goes term limits."

****

Fausto let Tessie into Mona's cabin, and Tessie rushed over and gave Mona a big hug and a wet sloppy kiss on both cheeks. "Thank God you're all right! How's the shoulder?" She squeezed Mona's good arm. "How you feelin'? You want anything to eat? Or a shot of something sweet and syrupy? Or a massage? I can send somebody up here from the spa. Hey!" She leaned over and whispered, "Did he turn you?"

"Yes. I was at death's door."

Tessie squealed. "Oh, that's great—uh, not about death's door, I mean him turning you. You're a brave one, girl—I mean ballsy."

"There's nothing ballsy about it. I had no time to think."

"But you agreed to marry him and were going to let him turn you, right?"

"Eventually." She thought a minute, then nodded. "All right, maybe not so ballsy. I'm more like titsy."

"Either one, you won't regret it, I promise!" Tessie gushed. "We've been having such a blast! Making plans for the future, looking at real estate all over the world on the internet—we might have a castle built on Sardinia, with a moat—so what if it takes twenty years to build? We can spare the time. Oh, and never to get Botoxed or nipped or tucked or liposucked! I said goodbye to my last strand of gray hair when I plucked it yesterday! And I got rid of my Deep Collagen Anti-Wrinkle Serum and my microdermabrasion system!"

"You tossed them overboard?"

"No, I sent them to my ex-mother-in-law."

"Well, I haven't had time to feel as liberated. I don't know how I feel. Just weird. And somehow connected to the cosmos, for eternity."

"You are, girlfriend. The cosmos is your oyster. Now that Brooke's been turned, she's creating a line of vampire clothes and accessories, and shopping channels are jumping all over her to sell it. Jewelry designers even hopped the bandwagon. They're revamping—no pun intended—their jewelry lines to appeal to vampiresses."

"They're all going nuts." Mona reached over and took a sip of the orange juice room service brought her.

"Hey, you want to go to Zanna and Royal's press conference? Come on, it's starting in ten minutes. They're taping it live."

"You up to it, Fausto?" she called over to him.

"If you are. I'd like to see what they have to say."

"Let's go then." She felt almost like her old self as she slipped out of bed and into her roomy clogs. "Oh, my God, I look like hell." Glancing into her vanity mirror, she ran a hand through her tangled hair.

"You look great." Tessie ran a comb through Mona's hair, twisted it into a bun, and pinned it in place. "It's not like you're going to be on TV or anything."

****

Fidgeting viewers packed the theater, but Fausto and Mona slipped in through the stage door and watched from the wings. Zanna, Royal, Brooke, and Toi stood on stage, straight-faced. This probably had a bigger viewing audience than the Academy Awards. Where was the red carpet?

The panel fielded questions about life as a vampire, how it affected their religious beliefs and their sex lives. Zanna bragged it was waaaay hotter, and Royal even threw out his little blue pills and her vibrators!

"Too much information," Mona muttered as Brooke challenged hunters to a televised debate. A few members of the Church asked the new vampires if they felt guilty. "Not at all," Zanna answered. "You're the ones who should feel guilty, persecuting people just for being different. Where does the Bible say vampires are evil? Or mention them at all?"

"Why did it take her being turned to notice that?" Mona asked Fausto as the Church envoy sputtered and blubbered and stalked out of the theater, followed by several others.

Then Brooke glanced over her shoulder, glimpsed

Mona, and gave a hearty wave. Mona cringed when Brooke jumped out of her seat and headed for the wings, clutched Mona's good arm, and dragged her onto the stage.

"Here is Mona Rossi, the romance writer who started it all!" The audience cheered and applauded like she'd just won an Emmy for writing *Desperate Housewives*.

"No, I did nothing, really..." She shook her head and held out her hands, but Brooke wouldn't let up.

"I'd like to ask Mona, and Dr. Fausto, if you'll come out here—" She motioned for Fausto to take the stage, and now the crowd stood on its feet, cheering and clapping and stomping. The floor shook beneath Mona.

"I didn't want to steal Mona's spotlight." Fausto spoke into the mike with a confident air.

Several women shouted, "Do another strip! Take it all off!"

"I want to say I'm very proud of Mona. She was at the brink of death from the gunshot, and that crime, incidentally, is being investigated as we speak, but I know it was a hunter after me, who hit her instead. Let me say publicly, whoever you are, you're a coward, and you'll get yours."

The crowd went wild.

Brooke waited out the applause, then said, "Mona, Fausto, I'd like to invite you to star in your own weekly reality show, as a special segment of *The Cutting Edge*, so people the world over can see how a typical vampire couple lives. We'll call it *Hangin' with Fausto and Mona.* Will you do it?"

With the crowd clapping and cheering, Mona shook her head, backing away. "No, never! I hate those reality shows! Forget it!"

But Fausto was nodding. "Sounds like a good idea."

She wanted to drag him off the stage and bite some sense into him.

Chapter Twenty:
Vamps and Scamps

The *Romanza* was now the most famous cruise ship in the world. Bookings on Apollo Cruise Lines increased tenfold since *The Cutting Edge* began beaming their show live from the Theater L'Opera.

"Let's ditch any idea of a reality show, Fausto," Mona insisted after they signed yet another slew of autographs at their table in the dining room. "All I want at this point is to do a little sightseeing."

She gazed out the picture window over Malta, a little rock in the sea: the classic Italian architecture, houses with shutters and balconies climbing up hills, the Middle Eastern influence of the sprawling stucco houses and mosques, the bit of Brit thrown in with a red phone box here and there, fish 'n' chips shops nestled in with the pizzerias.

Quintus and Tessie sat at their table, and they planned to stick around for the Chocolaholics Extravaganza, which the crew would begin setting up right after dessert.

"Hey, it would be fun," Tessie urged. "It could lead to modeling jobs and acting gigs."

"I'm no actress, and I don't want that kind of publicity," Mona insisted. "Neither does Fausto." She glared at him.

"It'd give the world the chance to see the real me,"

he said. "I thought that was your whole point. Show how normal we are."

"I have an even better idea." Mona clasped her hands under her chin and adjusted the scarf that hid her bite mark, less of an exhibitionist than Fausto. "How about if you write your memoirs, and I'll ghost write it for you. Tess, you could publish it, and follow it up with those thriller novels he's working on."

"Yeah, and make a movie of his life!"

Mona thought Tessa's contacts would fall out of her bulging eyes. "Who do you want playing you, Tom or Brad?"

Just then Nick, the dancer Mona and Tessie saw the first night up on the deck, came prancing by, followed by an adoring gaggle of older women. He stopped at their table and shooed the groupies away with a brushing motion of his hand. "Later, ladies, no need to clamor. There's plenty of me to go around."

"Evening, folks." He pulled up one of the empty chairs. "How's your lives treating you?"

"Couldn't be better, Nick," Fausto said. "You got some fan club there."

"I'm in demand these days." He smoothed his silver hair back. "I've been turning vimin left and right. Every voman vants to become a vampire. They don't vant to valse, they just vant to be vamped!"

So, he really was a vamp! Mona smiled. From the moment she first glimpsed him on the sun deck, she *knew* it!

"And you're complaining?" Tessie nudged him. "Now you can quit your dancing job and spend your time turning beautiful babes."

He nodded, buffing his nails. "I vas just offered a

television show, as a vampire cop."

"Ah, television's just a fad." Fausto waved his hand. "I'll be surprised if it lasts another thousand years."

"Yeah, stick to print," Mona said. "People will always buy books. And vampire books are the hottest thing out there."

****

"*Cara bella*, it's me! Let me in, I have something to show you!" Fausto rapped on Mona's cabin door. Heart thumping in excitement, she let him in. He waved some papers over his head and let them flutter to the floor like confetti. "I'm a free man, *cara*. These are my divorce papers."

With a gasp of delight, she picked them up and skimmed them. They were all in Italian. She couldn't understand a word, but they looked official, stamped and notarized, signed with a flourish—and an old fashioned fountain pen. "Lucrezia got these for you? In prison?"

"No, I did. Remember I told you that some members of our family became members of the clergy to keep tabs on the Church's hunting methods?"

She nodded.

"Well, some of them stayed in. One of them is Cardinal Clemente, at the Vatican. But not only is he one of them, he's also one of us."

"A vampire cardinal? At the Vatican?" She had to laugh. "Well, if that ain't a bite on the neck!"

"So now we really have something to celebrate, and when a Fiorella Petrizzo comes to your door, let her in. She's the couturier I'm flying in from Rome with some formal wear. Because tonight we're going to

Saint Paul's Shipwrecked Church and have that white wedding you've always wanted."

Her heart stopped. She took a deep breath, wanting to hear that again. "Tonight? For real?"

"For real and forever."

She fell into his arms, trembling with anticipation. "Oh, my God, there's so much to do!" She scooted him out. "It's bad luck to see me before the wedding, so we'll talk on the phone later. Right now I have some vows to write!"

****

She sat at her laptop composing the most important thing she'd ever write in her life: her marriage vows. She hit the backspace key and deleted the last line she'd written. "No, too Browning. I don't want to get into metaphors here." Her first deletion was two lines ending in love and above. "No unintentional poetry!" she declared as her fingers tapped the keyboard in her eighth draft.

She wanted to keep some of the traditional lines in there, so the "I now pronounce you husband and wife" part stayed, but she didn't know how well "You may now ravish the bride" would go over with a Sicilian man of the cloth. Still, she let a satisfied smirk curl her lips, despite her ragged nerves. She'd made about twenty-five typos in the last paragraph. Her hands shook so much, she pressed her wrists against the desktop to keep them steady.

"Now I realize we were destined to be together, Fausto, and every moment we spent apart up to now was mere existence, for you are the biggest part of my present, my future, and my life. Our happiness, loyalty, and devotion will be a complete joy as from this moment on, our destinies become entwined forever."

She deleted "if only I'd known we were meant to be together, I never would have made the mistakes I'd made, which I truly regret." He knew all about her screwups.

A reread of the words touched her heart and stirred a fierce love within her that had been tapped only a few times in her life. A tear of joy slid down her cheek. She savored its warmth. How wonderful to be so much in love!

She printed out the vows and stood at the mirror to recite them. It was hard to speak the words without choking up. Her voice quivered as she reached the part where God, in His grace, had blessed them with the rare gift of love. "Oh, Fausto," she vowed, no longer needing the sheet to read from. She'd committed most of it to memory. "I give you my heart, my soul, my body, my possessions, and most of all—all the love in my heart. From this moment on, I am yours in flesh, in blood"—they both knew the double meaning of that—"and in spirit."

She wanted him to hear the vows before the ceremony, but she knew he'd love what she'd written and wouldn't want to change a thing.

Her cell phone rang, and she dug it out of her purse. "Finally, we're within range." She pushed the button. "Pronto!"

"Hey, Mona, it's Julianna, in New York."

"Julianna, how the hell are ya? Watching television?"

"Am I ever. You did good, girl. I'm happy for you, but I just wanted to tell you, Ted, your ex, is in jail."

Mona's pulse quickened. "You got a vision?"

"No, the *New York Tribune*. He got caught selling your piano to an undercover cop, but it looks like he wants to ride your coattails to fame. He wrote an open letter to you at the newspaper, telling you how sorry he is he stole your possessions and admits you're a great success. He'll pay you back every penny. I guess he figures it'll come out of the proceeds of a book deal. Check it out online. It's on the first page there."

"Thanks, I'll take your word for it, but I don't want anything from him. That sonofabitch told me I'd never amount to anything, and I believed him. Then my writing got sloppy. Next, my sales were in the sink."

"Shows how gullible we can sometimes be, girl."

"I hope I'm beginning to change all that. Thanks, Julianna." She disconnected her phone and answered the door. It was the tailor with the beautiful satin wedding dress she was going wear later that night.

As she tried it on, she now was getting her lifelong wish, to have the old fashioned Italian church wedding, with the man of her dreams. She couldn't see him before the wedding, it was bad luck, but tonight, she would be where she belonged, in his arms. Forever.

Epilogue:
And Then What Happened?

The sniper who shot at Mona was a vampire hunter—the one who'd killed Fausto's family. He got nabbed because the police found the same German army rifle he used to shoot at Fausto in a small apartment in Palermo, Sicily. They matched the bullet taken from Mona's shoulder to that rifle. He's now serving a life sentence.

The Fellowship of the Faithful disbanded, and the Church issued an apology to all vampires for their brutal treatment over the centuries. But they still frown upon them marrying.

Mona sat five-year-old Fausto Jr. down on his swing and gave him a gentle push. The balmy Mediterranean breeze rustled the flowers in her garden. "Mama, one of the girls in school wants me to turn her. Can I?"

"You're a bit young, honey. It's better to wait till you're older, when it's with the right person."

"What if I never meet the right person?" he persisted, never satisfied with one simple answer.

"Never say never, my dear. Eternity is a long time."

A word about the author...

Diana's passion for history and travel has taken her to every setting of her historicals and paranormals. She is studying for a Master's Degree in Archaeology, and owns an engineering business with her husband Chris. They make their home on Cape Cod.

A longtime member of Romance Writers of America and the Richard III Society, she has written articles for *Romantic Times* and appeared on *The Book Swap Cafe*, shown nationwide on Comcast channels.

Visit Diana at
www.dianarubino.com
www.DianaRubinoAuthor.blogspot.com
and contact her at
Diana@DianaRubino.com